MAGIC OPS

MAGIC OPS

FEDERAL AGENTS OF MAGIC™ BOOK ONE

TR CAMERON   MARTHA CARR   MICHAEL ANDERLE

DISRUPTIVE IMAGINATION™

MAGIC OPS TEAM

Thanks to our beta reading team

Nicole Emens, Mary Morris, Larry Omans, Crystal Wren, John Ashmore, James Caplan, Kelly O'Donnell

Thanks to the JIT Readers

Misty Roa
Diane L. Smith
Micky Cocker
Angel LaVey
Jeff Eaton

If we've missed anyone, please let us know!

Editor
The Skyhunter Editing Team

DEDICATIONS

From TR Cameron

For Laurel, my love, and Dylan, my life.

To those who have chosen to spend their precious time
reading this work – thank you so much for joining me on
this adventure! The stories we share fill in the spaces
between us, linking us together in shared dreams for a
short time, and connecting us as a community for all time.

Joys upon joys to you – *so may it be*.

From Martha

To everyone who still believes in magic
and all the possibilities that holds.
To all the readers who make this
entire ride so much fun.
And to my son, Louie and so many wonderful friends who
remind me all the time of what
really matters and how wonderful
life can be in any given moment.

From Michael

To Family, Friends and

Those Who Love
To Read.
May We All Enjoy Grace
To Live The Life We Are
Called.

CHAPTER ONE

F BI agent Diana Sheen ducked under the yellow tape that secured the perimeter of the incident scene. A bounce in her step betrayed her excitement for what lay ahead.

One thing I can always count on is that the job is never the same two days in a row.

She'd caught her share of strange cases in the past, but this promised to be something special.

Magic is the ultimate wild card.

When a blue-clad patrol officer maintaining the outer perimeter moved toward her, she held up her ID and kept walking. She was often mistaken for a civilian. Her youthful looks and only slightly below average height caused others to chronically underestimate her. The leather jacket and boots she wore instead of the customary uniform might have contributed to the problem. She would acknowledge this to herself on a regular basis but would usually shrug it off.

Hey, I've gotta be me.

Diana's target was about thirty feet ahead and near a V formed by two police cars. A gaggle of concerned people in suits peered at what looked like large sheets of paper spread out on the car hoods. Bystanders asked questions, and uniformed officers yelled answers in the crisp autumn breeze. Unfortunately, said breeze wouldn't stop blowing her long black hair into her face.

She'd been a mile away, finishing up a guest-speaking session with the local university's Intelligence and Security program, when the call came in. The darkly gorgeous gothic structure that loomed ahead was illuminated by replicas of nineteenth-century oil lamps that dotted its facade. A trip to the Antiquities Museum had been in her plans for months, but this wasn't quite how she'd pictured it.

An afternoon outing, maybe a nice dinner after with someone interesting, but definitely not this.

Diana veered over the grass to intercept a tall man in an off-the-rack suit. The twilight was still bright enough to show the wrinkles in its unremarkable gray fabric. His tie was purple and his shirt crisp and white. His whole ensemble screamed "official." So, naturally, she greeted him with a grin and a raised fist. "Rodriguez, fancy meeting you here."

He returned the smile and bumped her fist familiarly as he fell in beside her. "Sheen. What are the odds?"

"I was at the U. You?"

"Physical therapy at the University med center." He gestured vaguely over his shoulder toward the tall institutional office building that marked the corner of the campus.

The life of a Washington, DC, FBI agent was full of potential for injury. She grimaced and couldn't remember a single time when the whole office was simultaneously healthy. "Do you know anything more?"

Rodriquez shook his head and his almost regulation-length brown hair flopped to the side. "Only what they said over the radio—hostage situation, vicinity response, special circumstances."

She nodded. They both knew the code for magic. The two continued their trek toward the command post. They stopped and stared a woman down across a car hood. Her sharp suit and prominent gold rank badge confirmed that she outranked the other field officers. Diana tried to avoid inhaling the acrid fumes from the running motors as the agents reported in and asked the officer's name.

"Thompson," came the brusque reply. The woman's voice was husky and reminded Diana of Kathleen Taggart in *Body Heat*. "A professor and his class were inside examining the museum's special collection. At least two suspects entered, ejected the security guards, and locked the building down."

"Any demands?" Diana's flat tone betrayed none of the excitement her body had betrayed mere minutes before.

"None. Only crazy talk about how we've stolen things that don't belong to us, how they'll take them back, and how they'll kill the class if we mess with him."

She frowned. "'We?' Who is we?"

"I have no idea. Like I said. Crazy." She twirled a finger next to her ear and exhaled a foggy breath into the chill of the October evening.

Rodriguez bent to examine the papers that splayed

across the hood and finally recognized them as blueprints. "Are there any other people in the museum?"

The husky voice carried a note of tiredness. "No. It was closed due to the class' reservation. Only guards and custodial staff were on duty. The professor teaches here every Monday."

Diana put her hands on her hips and frowned. "It's unlikely to be a coincidence, then."

Thompson's ponytail bobbed as she nodded. "I thought so too."

"HRT?" Rodriguez asked. His finger pressed firmly on the front door access point on the blueprint while he fluttered his other hand over the rest of the schematics as though he could convince a better entry to materialize out of thin air.

The officer grunted. "More than thirty minutes away. Apparently, the backup team is training out of town and the primary was called to an incident on the other side of the city." She raised dark eyes to look at Diana. "Before you say it, no. That doesn't sound like a coincidence either."

The agent dropped her hands to the car hood with a muted *thump* and bent to peer at the paper. "SWAT?"

"Wouldn't you know it? Two separate calls. Our people at one, yours at the other."

Diana shook her head. "This is bad." She wasn't sure if the comment originated from the situation, the access points, or both.

It's all bad.

Rodriguez's voice matched her pre-action excitement as he pointed at the blueprint. "The back door looks like the best way in. You said there are two of them, so if they're smart, they'll have eyes on it."

"I said at *least* two," Thompson corrected him. "There could be more."

Diana had heard enough. "Can we borrow wind-breakers?"

The woman nodded and a young patrol officer at her side darted away. He returned shortly with a pair of black coats with **Police** written in large white letters on the back. An older man followed purposefully, his hands in his pockets.

Thompson looked inquiringly at the officer.

"This gentleman wanted a word. He says he works inside," he explained as he handed the jackets to the agents.

All the superior officers turned their gazes on the man. Diana slipped out of her leather jacket, set it carefully inside the patrol car through the open window, and pulled on the windbreaker. Rodriguez did the same.

Since neither agent seemed in a hurry to speak, Thompson took the initiative. "What do you know, Mister..."

His gruff voice matched his pocked complexion and stubbly face. "Beale. Stan Beale. I figured you might need to get inside and thought I should tell you 'bout the tunnel."

The agents spoke as one. "Tunnel?"

"This thing is ridiculous." Rodriguez held the ancient ring up. It was easily as big as his palm and supported a cornu-copia of metal keys that could have served as props in a gothic vampire film. His hands were barely large enough to hold the ring, his flashlight, and his pistol. Diana's smaller hands only had to deal with her light and weapon respectively.

"Tough break, Rodriguez," she sassed.

He rolled his eyes. "Come on. Let's keep going."

The brick tunnel was inky black, and the mini Maglites they carried sufficed to prevent tripping but didn't offer much in the way of distant vision. The structure was probably twelve feet wide and a similar height, a throwback to a time when exhibits and artifacts traveled through the passage on the way to the museum to avoid potential theft. Now, the maintenance crew used it to stay out of the weather when they crossed from the museum's warehouse to the main building. It bore a variety of earthy smells ranging from the dank of mold to the moist tang of clay and the less pleasant scent of rotting vegetation. All these mingled with the faint chemical odor of cleaning solutions.

They'd passed through two of the tunnel's three doors. If the staff member was to be believed, the final door separating them from the museum basement lay somewhere ahead. The blueprints had marked the door sealed, but Beale laughed when he informed them that part of the job had never been completed. "Money troubles like everywhere else." Given the man's low status on the totem pole as a staff member, Diana couldn't blame him for the amusement.

Being ticked at your employer is normal. Still, it's worth remembering the attitude.

Rodriguez grunted to break the silence of their trek. A

veritable beast grunted back as the echoes returned. "This tunnel is a lucky break."

"Do you think it might not be?"

"They knew the museum was closed, and probably about the class. Why go through all the drama if they could have simply waited down here and stolen in during the night?"

Diana kept her voice soft and calm. "They can't know everything. If they planned the robbery with the public schematics, they probably thought the tunnel wouldn't work, the same way we did." She pointed at the door ahead, then set her back against the wall outside the door's arc. The position afforded her a perfect line of sight on anything it revealed when it opened. "There's cautious and there's simply paranoid."

Rodriguez holstered his gun at the small of his back to free his hands for the mammoth key. He slipped it into the lock, grabbed the door handle, and nodded at Diana.

She tensed her finger to depress the trigger safety on her Glock 19M and whispered, "Three, two, one."

Rodriguez twisted the key and wrenched the door open. She traversed her light and pistol in a *Z* pattern but encountered only crates and boxes. Most were neatly stacked to each side. Rodriguez drew his gun with a faint rustle and lowered the giant key ring onto a crate with a muted clank.

They advanced, covering one another, and cleared the room. The blueprints claimed the room's other exit fronted a stairwell that rose to the main floor of the museum. Beale had given Rodriguez a much more reasonable keyring for the museum's doors, but the knob turned freely in her hand. The door opened on oiled hinges to reveal the promised stairs.

The other agent could have been ordering lunch for all the concern he showed. "What's the plan?"

Diana smiled. "Same as always. Go in and talk them down. If they won't be talked down, try to shoot them in the leg."

He chuckled. "What if they're wizards or something?"

She leaned into the doorway to peer up the staircase. "Even better. Then we get to punch them in the mouth before or after we shoot them in the leg so they can't do magic."

Rodriguez's shoulders shook with suppressed mirth. "Shoot them in the leg" had been a running joke since the academy. As a rule, they'd been trained never to aim anywhere other than center mass. Once he regained control of himself, he gestured for her to take point.

They crept up the stairs and emerged into a three-way intersection. A loud voice ranted nearby and filled the corridor ahead of them with echoes. Diana checked the crude map she'd drawn on the back of her hand. "It sounds like it's coming from the main exhibit hall. Go straight, then take a left." They stowed their lights. There was no need for them when the hallways were illuminated. When they reached the corner, a brighter patch of light stretched along the tiles to suggest the presence of a well-lit room beyond.

The insistent tone sounded male but was strangely high-pitched, more like an adolescent. Diana put her back against the wall and risked a quick look. Frightened students faced the rear of the building from where they sat in a line with black rope bound around their wrists.

She held her left hand to the side of her mouth and whispered as she turned to face her partner. "How many in the class again?"

Rodriguez held up five fingers, closed his fist, and raised four more.

"Okay. I saw five at the back of the room. The rest must be in front. Hopefully." She pointed one finger at herself, then directed it to the left, and pointed two fingers at him and swung them to the right. He nodded, confirming her instructions to veer right when they entered. "Let's listen in," she mouthed. Again, he nodded.

It wasn't that hard to focus on the ranting. Most people in charge of a hostage situation felt the need to monologue at one point or another. This perpetrator didn't disappoint, and his voice carried shrilly from the vaulted ceilings and along the tile floors to their ears.

"You gather these things as if they belong to you or are objects to be studied, locked away, and admired. You are nothing but thieves, stealing that which belongs to the Oricerans." His voice rose from an accusatory barb to a seething screech. "Worse, you don't have the slightest comprehension what the artifacts are, what their purpose is, or who they are *meant for!* You appropriate our culture but do not even so much as appreciate it!"

She exchanged a glance with Rodriguez, and his face registered the same bemusement.

What the hell?

Diana shook her head, counted down from three on her fingers, and moved.

She thrust into the exhibit room at a full run and immediately broke left along the wall. The space was wide and open, which meant she would have to move quickly to avoid any risk that she might be shot herself. Her training kicked in and her mind categorized the scene in flashes. There were nine students in total, exactly like Rodriguez had said. All were bound and one slumped forward, bleeding from his forehead. A wooden lectern stood on the opposite side, to which the professor was secured by black rope. The man looked half a decade older than his picture on the university website.

An elf lurked in the shadows at the corner of the room nearest to her. This was not the beautiful glowing, friendly elf of Middle Earth.

Tolkien would spin in his grave if he saw this.

Poorly healed gashes ran down the dark skin on the left side of his face. The right side was a mass of wrinkles and scars that could only have resulted from a terrible fire. He had no hair, and his one unburnt ear tapered to a graceful point. It was possibly the only attractive thing about him. He wore a black cloak or robe of some kind that covered him from the neck down and obscured his limbs.

Diana took advantage of the situation to try to intimidate the elf into submission as she leveled her gun. "Down on the floor, sleazebag. Now!"

He laughed at her. The bastard actually *laughed* at her. His voice dripped condescension. "Aren't you precious? It's about time you got here. We've been waiting."

Everything slipped into slow motion. She felt danger to her right and twisted to face it. Her gun tracked toward the opposite corner. A robed figure emerged from behind the professor and gestured with a hand. Anger shot through her and she extended her left hand and squeezed it into a fist. The wizard's arms snapped to his sides and effectively wrecked whatever spell he'd attempted to cast.

Diana smirked.

You didn't expect power from a "precious" human, did ya, asshole?

The pistol barked twice, and scarlet blossoms appeared on his leg and on one of his locked arms. Time returned to normal as he screamed and fell, dropping the wand he'd held in his other hand. Bound though the professor was, he had the presence of mind to kick the instrument away from the downed wizard. With the first target effectively neutralized, she jerked the gun back to face the scarred elf.

She vaguely hoped that Rodriguez had remained vigilant against the possibility of more enemies and thus hadn't seen her perform the magic, but she couldn't risk checking. Thrusting the thought aside, she raised her pistol to eye level, sighted down the barrel, and advanced one slow step at a time toward the dark figure. "Nice try, asshole. But I *said* get your face down on the floor." Her voice was reasonable, calm, and nonreactive.

If you can't avoid the conflict, attempt to defuse it.

Annoyance had replaced his condescension. "No. I shall not. And what will you do now, little avenger?"

On the one hand, she hated it when people mentioned her height. Yes, at five-three-and-three-quarters, she was on the short side of normal. That didn't make it right to judge her for it. On the other hand, he had more or less given her superhero status. She smiled.

"Okay, let's talk about this." Her gaze remained locked

on his as her arms relaxed slowly. The gun lowered. She fired two rounds at his thigh without even blinking.

The perpetrator's robe opened as a scarred left hand extended between the arcs. The bullets slammed into an invisible barrier and clattered to the floor.

Diana growled under her breath. "Damn shields." She fired twice more and lurched into a run. She registered gunfire behind her and figured the rest of "we" had joined the party. Another pair of bullets flew, this time leveled at the elf's chest. Once again, they were easily deflected but the tactic had worked. Now, she was only a handful of feet away. She threw the gun at his head and added a telekinetic burst to hurry it along. He flinched in mid-cast and flicked a hand up to deflect the weapon. It was enough to distract him from the left hook that closed at high speed with the force of her forward jump behind it.

His eyes widened as he registered the threat and his mouth formed a word that he failed to finish before her knuckles smashed it away. Blood flowed as his lips split and he stumbled back. His head struck the wall behind him with a resounding crack. Diana used her forward momentum to launch her right knee into his solar plexus. The elf dropped and gasped raggedly for breath. With the threat effectively neutralized, she turned to survey the room.

There were no civilian casualties. A third suspect lay on the ground in front of Rodriguez, bleeding from a hole in his thigh. The sight of her partner in this op reignited her fears.

Please don't have seen my magic.

She retrieved a set of zip ties from her back pocket and

trussed the elf's hands and feet, then hogtied him for good measure. She knelt and tapped him on his bald dome. "Hey there, dumbass. Just a warning. If I hear anything out of you, I'll assume you're casting and kick you in the head until you're unconscious. Nod if you understand."

He nodded.

There was a shift of energy in the room, and she looked up through the skylight to see twilight transform into night. The broken elf at her feet laughed in a way that sounded both happy and relieved. She thought about it for a second, then reluctantly decided to let him have the moment.

I probably can't kick him for laughing.

Rodriguez approached and returned her fallen weapon. She popped the magazine and ejected the chambered round in case the pistol's brief life as a missile had damaged it. The grin on his face said it all.

"Now, correct me if I'm wrong, but weren't you supposed to shoot him in the leg?"

Diana scowled.

I wonder what the penalty is for accidentally shooting a fellow officer in the leg.

CHAPTER TWO

The light turned green at the perfect moment, and the tires squealed as Diana flowed from the offramp onto Pennsylvania Avenue. The fastback's transmission was as smooth as new ice and she shifted gears easily. Everything faded away behind the wheel to leave only the currents of the road and the sensation of raw power at her fingertips.

Her eyes flicked to the glowing clock which matched the one in her head. 8:12 PM. Barely enough time to get to her date before the venue closed. She saw a ripple in the traffic ahead, courtesy of a meandering minivan, and switched lanes in a burst of speed. The defensive driving courses she'd taken at the academy had added a layer of polish to her natural ability, and the Fastback allowed her to use all of it.

Diana pulled into the parking lot five minutes later and bounded into the building. The worker at the desk waved her on, and she thrust open the door to the back at an excited jog. She spotted him immediately, and he was as handsome as ever. "Maxie!"

The young Borzoi barked and gave a doggy bow, his front paws on the ground, and his tail circled wildly. His long nose was almost comical in that position.

An amused Doug spoke from her left. "I thought you wouldn't make it today." The man was well past retirement age. He'd worked at the shelter forever and was an absolute treasure, or so the other members of the staff had confided.

She answered without so much as turning aside from ruffling the dog's ears through the bars of the gate. "It would take a lot to keep me away from visiting with my Max."

Doug moved into her line of sight and leaned his back against the wall that separated Max's living space from the rest. "You know, we appreciate your sponsorship, but wouldn't it be easier to adopt him?"

Diana shot him a grin and finished the ritual they enacted at least once a week during her many visits. "He'd be lonely. I'm never home. Here, he has you and the other dogs to play with."

The man held out the customary leash. Diana unlatched the gate and Max bounded out, put his paws on her shoulders, and licked her face once. That was their agreement. She couldn't break him of the habit, but it stopped at one.

The shelter sat on a commercial block that sometimes attracted folks looking for trouble, but no one ever bothered her when she had Max by her side or vice versa. They started with a slow jog and sped up with each circuit of the block to take the last in a full run that left both of them panting. She perched on the front steps of the facility, and the dog lay beside her, his chin on her thigh. Soulful eyes gazed up at her with that same question.

She sighed. "I'd love to take you home, Max. But you'd be alone for most of the day, every day, not counting the out-of-town trips." She rubbed his velvety ears and the smooth fur on his head, then traced her fingers down his nose. This garnered a sigh of pleasure from the canine. "It's simply not the right time."

He barked at her and wagged his tail, and she felt forgiven. Momentary sadness was replaced with joy, and they went inside for the second part of their playtime—an elaborate game of fetch and wrestle.

A half-hour later, Max lay resting in his den. With the stress of her day's work partly burned away, Diana waved at the night guard and departed the shelter. The year and a quarter of donations since she'd met Max had earned her a few privileges, one of which was the right to stay past closing time. When she asked why the dog hadn't been adopted after so long, Doug would only shrug and answer that he seemed uninterested when other people greeted him.

"The right person will come eventually," he'd say. Then he would add, "Then again, maybe he's already found the perfect one."

Diana sighed as she drove home and wished as she always did that her life would allow her to bring Max along.

The brownstone had been in her family for three generations. When they retired early to Florida, her grandparents had turned it over to her parents and their new baby. Halfway through her childhood, they'd moved to a research facility in Colorado, and the house became a rental. Her parents never returned to it and were comfortable in the centennial state, but she reclaimed the home when she joined the FBI. Restoring the damages inflicted by time and the occasional out-of-control tenant was a work in progress. Her mother and father had offered to pay, but she preferred doing it herself when time permitted.

Unfortunately, that wasn't very often. So far, she'd fixed only the kitchen, her bedroom, and the basement. She had the bathrooms redone by professionals, knowing her own limits, but there was still a long list left to repair.

She hung her keys on a hook near the door and threw the deadbolts. A quick code armed the security system again, which assured her that no one had been in her home while she was away. She reached for her gun to stow it in the hidden safe in her hall cupboard but remembered that she was weaponless until they verified that she hadn't damaged the gun in the fight earlier that evening. Diana sighed.

Stupid elf. I should have shot him in the mouth.

The wood floors made every sound echo but the creak that accompanied each step sounded like home. Her next stop was the traditional rotary thermostat, which she spun up a couple of degrees on her way to the basement.

Unlike the old-world allure of the rest of the house, the bottom floor was clean and modern. She pulled off her brown shin-high harness boots and set them carefully aside. They weren't her favorites but definitely fell in the top five. She peeled her shirt off, threw it in the laundry hamper, and followed it with her socks and pants. A pair of lime green shorts, a remnant of poor sartorial choices in days past, hung on a hook and she slipped them on. Even the fact that they didn't clash with her black sports bra couldn't save them. There was a reason they lived in her basement, where only those closest to her were ever allowed.

She lit a cone of vanilla incense and crossed to the ballet barre attached to one wall to stretch. A well-worn teal yoga mat and mounted television stood on the other side of the room. The screen was large enough to keep her focus when she attended yoga classes via YouTube. The back half of the area was her second favorite spot on Earth after the animal shelter. The Wing Chun dummy she used to preserve muscle memory for blocks and strikes stood in the far right corner. She'd bought it new and looked forward to the day when the wood would show some palpable sign of her labors. After two years, all she really managed was to trade a number of bruises for a little polish on the protruding arms.

A heavy bag hung from a frame on the other side. Unlike the dummy, this particular fitness device showed damage from countless punches and kicks. Silver duct tape covered the places where she had kicked it in a rage after she'd forgotten to remove her boots first and thus doomed the bag to rip open. After today's action, though, neither of those could meet her need for release. That required the best training tool in the room.

The combat mannequin stood in the center of an open area, which allowed her to attack from any side. It was little more than a human figure posed in a combative stance with its fists raised like a boxer. It had been mounted on a turntable that would randomly reposition it when activated.

She started slowly and threw jabs and the occasional reverse punch into its solar plexus. At first, she winced when she felt the fleshy resistance. Once she warmed up, she forgot the pain and added hooks to the head, knees to the midsection, and kicks to the legs. Fully engaged and breathing hard, she tromped on the pedal to activate the turntable and circled to launch kicks and punches at the resistant material of the dummy. After ten minutes, she added shouts to her hardest blows and practiced spinning moves. She finally gasped twenty minutes later, unable to keep her guard up, and called the exercise done. A brief yoga cooldown completed her workout.

Diana left the basement, grabbed a Cherry Coke from the fridge, and guzzled half the can. She trudged upstairs on legs of lead and started the shower. A short blast of music sounded as she was about to step in, and she flicked her sweaty hair out of the way to lift the phone to her ear. Her playful growl was all too appropriate for the caller. "What?"

Lisa's familiar and equally mischievous voice shouted to be heard over the radio and engine of her car. "I'll be at the Beagle in forty-five minutes. You know you don't want to leave me alone in such a dangerous place," her friend teased.

She smothered a yawn. "I think you'll be okay this once."

Lisa's voice was filled with theatrical sadness and regret. "How will you feel at my funeral? Is that really how you want things to end between us?"

I'm sure you'll be okay.

Still, despite the creeping exhaustion, she burst out laughing. "Okay, you win. Forty-five minutes."

The call dropped. Lisa never said goodbye on the phone.

Diana shook her head and stepped into the shower. Her usual soothing soak had to be abandoned for a speed prep to get to the Beagle.

I'm going to need way more Cherry Coke to get through this night.

CHAPTER THREE

The Legal Beagle bar was only dangerous from a relationship-mistake point of view. It was within walking distance of her house, which was a plus. It was also convenient to the houses of many low-level politicos. Unfortunately, despite its weathered exterior, simple signage, and lack of windows, they still flocked to it, which was a definite minus. She pushed through the ever-present crowd of smokers on the street and slipped through the dilapidated door.

The inside was warm and inviting as an upscale restaurant blended with the comfortable vibes of a neighborhood hangout. Tables to the right held couples and groups indulging in late-night snacks—some for business, some for pleasure. A long polished wooden bar sat to the left. Its many tall barstools had been claimed by men and women in cheap versions of power suits with accessories in red, white, and blue. On the far end, Lisa waved and pointed to the empty seat next to hers.

Diana shoved through the crowd standing around the

high tops that made up the middle area, dodged some, and gently repositioned others. The bar was always hopping into the early morning, having adapted to the extensive and strange working hours required of those on the bottom rung of the government and the professions that catered to it. She avoided a broad gesture from a blond man who looked like he was barely out of his teens and slipped onto the stool next to her best friend.

Lisa made a point of checking her smartwatch. "About time."

She awarded her a ferocious fake scowl. "I'll have you know that I beat the getting-ready-for-a-night-out speed record."

Her friend raised an eyebrow and scrutinized her carelessly. "You call *that* ready for a night out?"

Diana couldn't help laughing. "Wench."

"And proud of it."

One of the three regular bartenders came over. Jason was a hipster who had given in to the allure of capitalism. His earlobes featured large spacers and his eyebrow a small barbell. A nose ring complemented the trimmed hair on his face and the stylishly long beard below. He slid a Dogfish Ninety Minute IPA to her with barely a hint of foam at the top, and she traded him a ten with a nod of thanks. Among the best things about the Beagle was its unadvertised "regulars" discount, which took a couple of bucks off the price for constant customers.

She sipped, sighed in pleasure, and swiveled her body toward her companion. "You're suspiciously bubbly."

Lisa grinned. "Starting next week, guess who's not a junior associate anymore."

Diana made a show of thinking. "Your boss?"

The other woman smacked her on the arm with a strong backhand. "Witch. Me, stupid."

She took a long sip and beamed. "It's about time they recognized your value. It'll be no time at all before they add 'Crawford' to the end of the firm's name."

"That's doubtful. A few years, anyway. But it's good to be on the way up. So good that tonight, *I'll* buy the next round to celebrate."

Diana whistled. "That *is* a change of pace."

Any response was cut off when the man on her left leaned across her to talk to Lisa. This was not an uncommon event. Since they had met in the Beagle a week after Diana arrived in DC, Lisa had been the sun that shadowed her in social situations. The girl's straight black hair and slightly flattened eyes suggested her distant Asian heritage, but the rest was pure middle America—tall, fit, and attractively curved. Diana managed two out of those three but still generated far less notice.

During that first meeting, a stranger had gushed to Lisa that her proportions were perfect and followed it up with an offer to do a free photo shoot with her. Diana was disappointed when Lisa scrawled her number on a napkin and later, broke down laughing at the revelation that she'd given him the digits of an escort service. That was when she knew they would be long-term friends. Now, they spent as much time together as work schedules and independent romantic pursuits allowed, usually a couple of nights a week. Some of those were spent at Diana's for a late-night movie and others out and about.

The present bother slurred a little, which suggested

he'd been at the bar for a while. "Did I hear you say you were a lawyer? I'm a lawyer, too."

Diana rolled her eyes. Lisa merely smiled and egged him on. "I imagine that half the people here can claim to practice law of some sort." She laughed to soften the comment. "What's your specialty?"

He leaned in a little closer, and Diana caught a whiff of his spicy cologne.

Beckham's Instinct. At least he has some taste.

Still, it didn't compensate for almost spilling her beer. She pulled the glass and her body back to permit him better access to the other woman.

"Well, currently, I do basic research stuff for a lobbying firm. But I'm looking for the right town and the right prosecutor gig. Then I'm gonna make the jump to judge."

"So, your goal is the Supreme Court?"

He laughed deeply. "Well, I hope so. But I'll be happy with any judgeship in the next decade or so, somewhere I could make a difference."

Lisa nodded and smiled. "Good luck to you. I have a secret to tell my friend here, so you'll have to excuse us."

He raised his hands in surrender and turned to the man on his other side. They laughed about something, and Diana put him out of her mind. "What's the secret?"

"Don't look, but I think you have an admirer. There's a guy at one of the low tables who's stared at us since you got here."

She rolled her eyes. "Please. Men always stare at you. It's their natural state. They can't resist it."

The woman fluttered her eyelashes. "Can I help it if I'm beautiful?"

"No, it's true, you *are* beautiful. However, the fact that the neck of your blouse reaches down to your belly button probably helps."

"Witch," she said, distracted as she fiddled with the garment in question. "Don't look now, but the guy he's with is coming over."

Bryant watched Trent weave through the crowd toward the women. They'd followed the woman for the last few evenings, waiting for this meeting. Direct surveillance was too risky, given Diana's skills. The skin-colored earpiece hidden in his right ear picked up the feed from the tiny microphone taped to his partner's chest.

Trent was fantastic with people and had a knack for appearing unthreatening. His cover was a low-level functionary with the State Department, which fit his blond, clean-cut California-boy look well. When he reached them, he positioned himself between the two, his body slightly closer to Diana.

The earpiece carried his confident voice cleanly. "Ladies, I noticed you from afar." He gestured toward Lisa. "I think I recognize you from somewhere. Are you with a law firm that does government work, maybe?"

She nodded with a neutral expression. "I am. Where do you think our paths crossed?"

He shrugged. "I'm with State, and we contract a lot with local firms. So, really, whenever I see someone who looks smart and capable and even half-familiar, I figure they're a lawyer."

Lisa laughed. How she managed to sound so sincere, Diana would never know. "Fair enough. What can we do for you, Statie?"

"Nothing much. I wanted to see if you'd be interested in joining me for a drink." He gestured at an empty table far from where Bryant sat.

"Only me, or both of us?" she asked.

Diana chimed in, recognizing her cue and putting some sultry in her voice. "Because we're something of a package deal. We are *very* fond of one another." She put her palm on Lisa's thigh and received a grin in return.

Bryant smiled as well and smothered it behind his hand as he reached up to scratch his nose at the table. If he hadn't been fully briefed on the relationship between the two women, he might've bought the idea that they were romantic partners. Background checks revealed each had dated people of a different gender extensively but not seriously over the last couple of years. He had to admire the play, though. It would set many an admirer back on their heels.

Not Trent. The man gave his casual guy-friend grin. Bryant was sure he practiced those looks in the mirror daily. "All options are on the table, but I'd consider it a privilege to chat to both of you."

Lisa shifted her gaze to her companion. "What do you think?"

Diana leaned back and looked at him. "Well, he *is* attractive. He probably works out fairly often. I'd say something gentle based on his pretty hands."

Trent laughed. "Jujitsu, actually."

She nodded. "I can always recognize another practitioner."

"How long?"

"A couple of years as part of mixed martial arts training. I've ranked up once."

He shifted a few degrees toward her and his grin broadened. "I'm your superior, then. I'm purple."

The women both laughed at him, and Lisa shook her head. "Bold. But you're right. Cute."

Trent looked satisfied. "So, is that a yes?"

Bryant knew they'd toyed with Trent and was sure he was aware of it too. But just as the game was starting, Diana brought it to an end.

"Only you, or will your friend join us?"

He tried to bluff. "My friend?"

Lisa nodded. "The guy you were sitting with at the back table. He's kinda hunky, looks like he lifts more than you do, and is doing his best not to look over here right now." Bryant stilled his reaction so he wouldn't reveal he was listening, at least.

Trent sighed. "Well, you caught me. I met him for drinks, and he suggested that you might be my type." He paused, then rolled his eyes. "I'm an idiot. I don't even know your name. I'm Trent." He held out a hand to Lisa and she shook it. "Lisa." He repeated the process with Diana.

She kept him pinned with a challenging look. "There's still a question on the table, Trent. Only you, or you and your friend?"

"I had planned on only me, but if you'd prefer both of us, I'm sure he'd be willing."

Lisa shook her head sadly and adopted a hurt tone. "Now I feel plotted against, like some prey animal in the savanna. That's a hard pass for tonight, Trent. If you catch us here another time, though, without a chaperone, feel free to make the offer again."

He smiled. "Fair enough." He gestured to the bartender, pointed at their drinks, and waved his hand to show he'd buy the next round. As he walked toward the exit, Lisa called, "Thank you!"

When Bryant turned back from watching Trent leave, Diana's eyes were locked on him.

Damn, she's good, he thought.

CHAPTER FOUR

The DC FBI regional office in Manassas was sparkly and fresh, appropriate to its new-kid-on-the-block status. Warm lights filled the hallways, and the smooth floor clicked under the heels of her boots with each step. Ahead and on the right was her destination, the domain of her direct superior, Special Agent in Charge Tyson Samuels.

Samuels was a lifer, already near retirement age, but still plowed forward with the energy of a much younger person. He stood from behind his desk and held a hand out. "Diana, it's always good to see you. Thank you for coming." His crisp charcoal pinstripe suit would have looked appropriate on a Capitol Hill lawyer and was downright snazzy for an FBI officer. It put her own basic blue version to shame. His hair was mostly dark-brown with gray creeping in at the temples. A thin face and sharp nose naturally conveyed his authority.

She gave him a grin. "Ty, it's been a while." They both laughed. She'd been in this office only two days before to review her cases. He gestured her to the ergonomically appropriate chair across the desk from him and they both sat.

His first offhand question held an undertone of seriousness. "So, how are things?"

Diana frowned. "Fine. Things are fine."

"No fallout from the incident at the museum?"

"Nobody died, so I don't even have to see a brain doc. It's all good."

Tyson nodded. Then, his expression shifted from his normal pleasant demeanor to something she'd only seen on his face once or twice before—doubt. "Diana, an opportunity has come up. I've gone back and forth over whether I think it would be good for you, but ultimately, it's your call to make."

He pressed a button on the complicated phone that rested on his desk, and the door behind her opened. She twisted to see who it was.

Her eyes narrowed when she recognized the man from the bar the night before. As he stepped forward, a soft vanilla scent with a hint of spice filled the room. He wore the FBI standard uniform—heavy-duty khakis, light shirt, bold tie, sports jacket, and shoes that were okay for dress but made for action with their reinforced treads and steel caps. She had a similar set but rejected them as often as possible in favor of one of her favorite pairs of boots.

She looked him in the eyes. "Fancy seeing you twice in the same twelve hours."

He slid casually into the seat beside her. "Yeah. I'd like to claim coincidence, but not so much."

Tyson intervened. "I've invited Bryant here to discuss

the opportunity I mentioned. I wasn't told you were under surveillance, but it's not unexpected, given the issue at hand."

Diana looked from Bryant to Tyson and back again. "I haven't had nearly enough coffee for this level of mystery. So, either pretty boy here needs to grab me a cup of coffee, or we need to get to the point."

Her boss laughed and the newcomer smirked at her. "Do you really think I'm pretty?"

Diana shook her head. "I was trying to be polite."

"Trying and mostly failing, then."

"Do you have a purpose, other than being a stalker?"

He raised a hand and smiled. "Yes. Yes, I do. My agency is always on the lookout for people with extraordinary talents and the brains to put them to good use. You appear to have both, based on your personnel file and the other material we've been able to dig up."

She lifted an eyebrow. "You've researched me?"

"Yep."

"Is that strictly legal?"

"Probably." He shrugged as if the legality of it didn't matter. "In any case, it was a means to an end, and the end is this. We'd like to offer you the choice to join our agency —provisionally, at first, but with the expectation that you will move quickly into a primary role as the head of one of our new offices."

Diana sat back in her chair and crossed her legs.

Interesting.

She motioned for him to continue.

His voice lost its playfulness as he began his pitch. "ARES is our name—the Anti-magic Response and

Enforcement Service." He must've seen her lips twist because he quickly added, "Yes, it's a bit of a mouthful. Someone in government came up with it before we were involved. Also, it's not technically accurate. We are *not* anti-magic. What we *are* is specifically detailed to deal with threats to this country that involve the *use* of magic."

More interesting.

"Is this because of the museum?"

He shook his head. "No, we've had our eye on you for a while. The museum was merely the icing on the cake. You handled yourself well in a difficult situation."

She persisted. "The museum is part of something bigger, though, isn't it? That's why you're moving now."

"That statement is both true and false. Yes, it's part of something bigger, but as I said, you were in our plans already."

Okay, that's really *interesting. I wonder if Tyson spilled about my magic? I can't imagine how else they'd know.*

She decided to play along for now and leaned forward. "So what *specifically* do you get up to? And who do you answer to?"

Tyson's deep voice interjected. "I'll address the second question. ARES is a black op that grew out of a need identified within the FBI. It is not acknowledged in any budget requests, and its personnel do not appear on any government rosters. I've been told there was a great deal of accounting and legal wizardry at work to make it happen, but it's essentially an independent agency. There *is* oversight, but only through a select committee that has no formal meetings or roster. It is important to note that the committee includes the Vice President of the United States."

She turned back to Bryant, who nodded. "That's a very succinct description of ARES. What we really get up to on a daily basis is less succinct. To be honest, we do something of everything, which is why having adaptable and talented people is so vital. We investigate crimes and terrorist activities that involve magic. We act as a response unit—much like a souped-up SWAT—for incidents involving magic."

She interrupted. "So, like the hostage rescue team or AET?"

"But without the specialization. Our people are also investigators, researchers, negotiators, and whatever else the moment calls for. We don't have the personnel or the funds to specialize beyond that. Yet."

"So, more like the Paranormal Defense Agency."

"Except without such stringent government oversight. And since we come out of the FBI, we're a little more focused on investigation than they are."

She kept her face neutral but had to admit ARES sounded intriguing. A memory twisted uncomfortably in her stomach, and she pushed it down by automatic reflex.

"So, tell me what I'd be doing."

"For a time, you'll act as an auxiliary to the DC office. Eventually, we'll send you to one of our startup locations."

"And where are those?"

His smile was teasing. "That's classified."

She rolled her eyes. His shifts in tone were too mercurial to be anything other than deliberate. He was playing her, testing her. *Too bad I left my taser in the car.* "Okay, then,

I presume that salary and benefits are at least as good as what I have now?"

Bryant grinned sheepishly. "Cash flow is something of an issue because of the impending startups. The pay will be about the same, with the promise of more once we're fully launched."

"Do I have my choice of which regional office I would move to?"

"Within reason. You might take one off the list, for instance."

She nodded, thought quickly, and voiced the questions as they occurred to her. "How big are the teams?"

"Classified."

"Who's in charge?"

"Classified."

Diana sighed. "Is there anything else you can tell me that *isn't* classified?"

His mischievous grin showed off more teeth. "I'm a Scorpio, my favorite vegetable is steak, and I enjoy long walks on the beach."

She turned to Tyson and managed to hide her exasperation to deny Bryant the satisfaction. "Is everything the clown said true to your knowledge?"

"It is. And I think he's said about everything he needs to say." Tyson shifted his sharp gaze. "Take a hike, Bry. She'll be in touch, either way."

Bryant nodded and stood in one smooth motion. He held his hand out, and she rose to take it. "A pleasure meeting you, rather than admiring you from afar, Agent Sheen."

"The jury's still out on whether I can say the same, Agent Bryant Classified."

He gave her hand an extra squeeze to acknowledge the joke, then released it and left.

Diana fell back into her chair and exhaled sharply as the door closed. "Is that dude for real?"

Tyson laughed. "I've known Bryant for a long time. It's actually one of the reasons I'm in the loop on this agency. He's a good agent and a great teammate. He does have the occasional attitude problem—like *most* of the finest agents I know."

"You wound me, sir." She placed a hand gently over her heart, which prompted another laugh. "I do have a serious question, though."

Her boss nodded and sobered instantly. "Go ahead."

"Do you think I should do it?" The man had been her mentor throughout her time at the FBI. She'd consulted him on every major decision, knowing that having a champion was important and that having access to someone who knew the way things *really* worked was even more important.

He wore another rare look, this one of discomfort. "Before I answer that, I have to ask you a question."

The thing in her stomach squirmed again. "Shoot."

"After what happened in Atlanta, do you think you can handle it?"

She opened her mouth to respond, and he cut her off. "No platitudes, Diana. I need a real answer. Can you deal with reliving that kind of fight over and over again?"

Finally, the squirming thing broke free and muted fear

washed through her. The magic attack back then had claimed the prototype army anti-magic unit she was shadowing and left her injured and healing for months. She liked to keep it buried, but that didn't prevent it from scratching at the walls. It was exponentially closer when she encountered magic other than her own telekinesis. The expensive private therapists she saw in secret had diagnosed PTSD, which could only be managed, never cured. She'd added routines to her life to cope. They stretched from yoga and meditation to researching all things Oriceran in her rare uncommitted time. Taking the job would potentially require her to face the challenge of that specter every single day.

On the other hand, it was a serious opportunity. This ARES would give her a chance to push beyond the normal progression and take a vital role in something important. It would only grow more essential as the worlds continued to overlap. She was certain she had reached one of those moments that defined a person. In this moment, she could choose the road that would lead her to certain adventure or the safe route that would remain far more ordinary by comparison.

Diana blinked and realized that Tyson was staring at her. She wasn't sure how long she'd been silent. Then again, time didn't matter that much when it came to a decision like this. She still had to put a bold face on, though. This kind of answer would require confidence. And sometimes, the best medicine for a traumatic event was to confront the experience head-on. "I can. Hell, it might be the best thing for me."

Tyson didn't answer. He stared her down silently with a probing expression. Fortunately, Diana was wise to that particular technique. She met that gaze and remained silent. Finally, he broke into a grin. "Then you should absolutely do it. You'll be fantastic, and there's a lot of career upside. Plus, you have a safety net."

"I do?"

He nodded. "While you're on probation with the agency, you'll be on detached duty from the FBI. This gives you a slightly higher salary, so I'll expect a kickback." His warm smile and familiar chuckle filled her with affection. "After that, if you decide to leave us, I'll get temps, so you'll have a home to come to." His eyes twinkled mischievously. "Or, you know, if you wash out of the training."

Diana snorted and stood. "Please. Have you ever known me to fail at anything?" She had, many times, but was fairly sure he wasn't aware of it.

"Other than following orders?" He laughed. "That's the spirit." He stood and extended a white business card. "Bryant's number. Now go show them what the best agent ARES has ever seen can do."

She left the office with a bounce in her step.

*I **will** show them, especially Bryant, how much more there is to me than their research suggests.*

CHAPTER FIVE

The diner was classic DC, a lot of money spent to appear authentic and homey. It sported cracked vinyl booths, a long counter with spinning stools in front, and the inviting smells of waffles and bacon. It also featured Bryant Classified sitting at the far end with a tall mug of coffee in his hand.

He was dressed for action in beat-up tactical pants, a tucked-in crewneck shirt, thick belt, and heavy boots. Her outfit was the same, plus her favorite leather racing jacket. The coat was black with a double red stripe down the left side and covered with zippered pockets. He'd warned her to wear clothes she didn't mind getting dirty, so she'd chosen her oldest versions.

He'd better not mess up my jacket.

The smell of food and fresh coffee made her stomach rumble as she crossed the center of the diner. She slid onto the chair next to him. "Bryant."

"Diana, how lovely to see you." His teasing tone failed to hide the ring of truth in his words. She'd heard the tell-tale signs in his voice over the phone when she'd called to accept. His in-person demeanor simply confirmed his excitement over convincing her to join the team.

The waitress interrupted with a tired, "Whaddya want?"

Diana ordered a bacon omelet and a waffle with a side of coffee. Bryant raised an eyebrow at her. "Do you always eat like you're not sure when you'll get to eat again? I didn't see military in your background."

"A lot of the SWAT guys I worked with were military. Some things rubbed off." She shrugged uncomfortably.

He raised his cup in a toast. She mirrored him and took a sip. The coffee was acrid, bitter, and perfect.

She set her mug down and swiveled her stool to face Bryant. "So, what's on the agenda, BC?"

He looked confused for a second, then smiled. "Ah. I see what you did there. Very clever." He leaned forward before continuing. "Anyway, it's time for us to determine what you're made of. Today, you get to run the gauntlet."

"That sounds overly dramatic."

"It's fairly apt, actually. It's a training scenario, and we've drawn the short end of the stick."

Diana snorted. "It seems like a common state of affairs, these days. Or are you flirting with me?"

He barked a single laugh. "No flirting, Diana. I don't know you well enough yet." The humor drained from his face and voice as he stared her down. "It'll be the two of us against at least three times as many, maybe more."

"Laser tag?" Much of her SWAT training had involved a version of the Army's electronic combat gear.

He shook his head. "Lasers are for wimps. We train with paintballs."

She winced. "Ouch."

Bryant nodded and scrunched his face in a grimace. "Plus, no body armor for us, only goggles."

"So, it's trial by torture, then."

"Only if they shoot you first." He shrugged. "The rules are, anything that gets hit is no longer useful. If you take one to the torso, chest, or head, it's game over."

A hopeless chuckle escaped her. "And I'll go through with you on my six?"

He gave that teasing grin again. "Sorry, you gotta have a partner."

"How do I know you won't shoot me from behind?"

He looked at her through the steam of his refilled mug and stopped it on the way to his lips. "You don't. But at least, for as long as this exercise goes, you can trust me to watch your back instead of shooting it."

Her food arrived, and so did his. Interestingly enough, he'd ordered the same thing. The only difference was he'd chosen pancakes over waffles. He gestured at their meal. "Eat up. We're on the clock."

An hour later, they stood before a nondescript warehouse in an office park. The building was indistinguishable from the dozens that surrounded it. She swung her Fastback in beside Bryant's SUV and climbed out. He looked at her, then at the car. She recognized that lusty gaze all too well. The Mustang always drew it.

"I gotta say, I love your taste in cars," he complimented.

Diana smiled. "She's my favorite girl."

"I can see why." He gestured at his own ride, a standard government model. "I prefer the tall dominating type myself."

She joined him as he walked toward an unmarked entrance. "It's all about speed and flexibility, baby."

"We're still talking about cars, right?" Bryant teased.

She didn't deign to give him a reply as he opened the door for her and she strode in.

The entrance looked like every other training prep area she'd ever seen. Signs recommending caution were stuck on large stacks of boxes that blocked her view, except for a narrow entryway ahead. To the left was a surface outfitted with rifles, pistols, and holsters. Prominently positioned among them were two sets of goggles.

She stowed her jacket, phone, and keys in a small locker, and Bryant did the same. Together, they crossed to the table and checked their weapons.

The rifle was modeled after a Colt carbine and held an appropriately sized magazine of paintballs, although it extended from the top of the weapon instead of feeding from the bottom. It was angled enough to allow proper sighting, a sign that somebody with experience had customized it. The pistols were replicas of the Beretta M9, with the mag in its normal spot. "Someone at ARES knows weapons."

Bryant nodded. "It's a passion for a bunch of us. Also, if you're going to be a part of the team, you'll have to drop the government moniker except around the bigwigs." She frowned, confused, and he grinned. "We prefer Black-ops Agents of Magic."

Diana repeated the words in her mind and smiled. "BAM."

He grinned and started to don his gear.

"Much better than ARES," she agreed. "BAM it is." She strapped the custom holster for the handgun to the back of her pants and looped the strap for the rifle over her neck and under her right arm. When she released the weapon, it hung comfortably across her body and didn't interfere with her access to the pistol. She practiced the draw a couple of times and adjusted the holster's position until it was as good as it was would get. As she grabbed the goggles, she turned to find Bryant was already donning his own.

"Okay, BC, what do I need to know?"

He pointed at the entrance ahead. "Simple scenario. We go through that opening. We try to make it to the end. If we reach it, we win. If we don't, we lose."

She nodded. "And exactly what skills are we assessing here? How high my pain tolerance is? Because seriously, even surviving this much time with you proves I can endure anything."

"Ha. Haha." His sarcasm was appropriate to the moment. "We're trying to get a sense of how you work, how you move, and how you perform as part of a team. Your instincts, your skills."

"If we lose, I'm out?" Diana couldn't hide the momentary concern that laced through her.

"It's less about whether we win than about setting a baseline to know where to start your training."

She blew out a breath and shook her head once to clear it. "That seems fair. Do you want to lead, or should I?"

Instead of answering, he gestured her forward. She nodded and took position on the right of the opening with her back to the wall. Bryant mirrored her on the left. Diana held up three fingers, then two, then one, and moved as she dropped the last. She swept her rifle over the hallway in search of targets as she pushed forward. There were none, only high boxes to each side and a left-hand turn ten feet ahead.

Her rapid advance put her back to the wall on the near side of an angle, and he slid quickly in on her right. A brief glance around the corner revealed a large open space that extended beyond her line of sight to the left and right, with an exit hallway across the chamber from their position.

Diana leaned closer to Bryant. "When we enter that room, you go right, and I'll go left." He nodded. She found the selector lever on her rifle and flicked it to burst, which gave her ten triple-bursts before she'd have to reload. Spare mags were stashed in her back pockets, and a cartridge for the pistol pressed against her thigh in her left front pocket. It was less than ideal and not how she would've equipped for a real mission, but limited options necessitated suboptimal choices.

After another rapid countdown, she turned the corner and burst into the open space, where she crouched and scuttled left as soon as she cleared the entrance. A single enemy waited in the room, outfitted like Bryant, and his weapon swung from the room's centerline to follow her. He must have assumed she'd go straight.

What am I to them, an amateur?

Diana shifted her sights and fired and the paintballs crossed the distance in an instant. The first missed as he turned, but the second two caught him, one in the stomach and the other in the chest. His own shot went wide and splashed on the wall to her right. She continued to move and twisted to provide backup to Bryant's side of the room, but her target was alone.

It'd been a while since she'd heard a southern accent as thick as the enemy's drawled, "Dammit." He sat cross-legged to confirm he was out of the game.

Bryant stepped beside her and grinned down at him. "I told you she had a hot hand."

She gave the defeated enemy a smile, then led the way from the room.

They navigated two more turns before they encoun-tered another opening with opposition, this time on Bryant's side. He disabled the foe with a tight trio of paint-balls but took a round to his right arm in return. She enjoyed how he hopped around in pain after the shot, and the man who'd fired the shot laughed hard. Diana had nailed the defender in the chest with one of the three she'd sent at him, and she frowned. *Either I'm slipping or the aim on these things is garbage.*

Her partner laid his rifle on the floor and handed her his spare magazine. She popped the one in her carbine and replaced it. The next obstacle was a metal staircase that stretched upward, likely an actual part of the warehouse that had been repurposed into the gauntlet. Diana disliked open staircases. They left a person exposed, even straight ones like this. It was wide enough for them to move side-by-side, so she waved Bryant forward. "You go up on the left facing ahead, I'll go up on the right facing back. If they're waiting in ambush, I'll get them first." He nodded and winced as his arm jostled against hers.

She stared at him. "Are you really that big a baby?"

He shook the damaged limb. "We'll see how you do when they tag you. Those little bastards hurt."

They positioned themselves and she breathed a low, "Go."

Their steps synchronized easily. Bryant held his pistol in his left hand pointing up and forward, and her rifle tracked their advance. Each step ratcheted the tension a notch higher.

The enemy had planned the ambush well. There was an overhead shooter exactly where she'd predicted. Diana shot first to fulfill her promise and found her target with a shot to his chest. His return fire wasn't even close. Her partner's pistol triple-popped as he presumably dealt with another opponent ahead.

The sniper was a total surprise. He lay in position atop raised boxes on one side, blocked from view until they got high enough. Diana saw him a split second before the gun barked and she yelled a warning. "Down." She followed her own command and fell hard onto her backside.

Bryant wasn't as fast, and the shot that should've caught her in the chest instead slammed into the center of his back. He yelped, dropped his pistol, and slumped with a moan. "What a world. What a world."

His antics were all background as she scrambled to locate and shoot the sniper. But the assailant was nowhere to be seen. Her weapon remained trained on the spot he'd last occupied as she stood and put her back against the left railing. She stepped over Bryant's prone and still-moaning form, finally reached the top, and turned the corner out of the sniper's firing arc.

There's no way they have only one location for him. It's too good a play. He'll be back.

Despite the seriousness of the moment, her mind added Schwarzenegger's accent, and she laughed. Diana crept forward and slid against the wall for cover until she arrived at another wide opening. She took a quick look and groaned internally.

The room ahead was a disaster. Catwalks snaked around the perimeter, and one crossed at the midpoint directly in front of her to an exit on the far side of the space. There were a hundred potential hiding places among the stacked boxes below for ambushers to lie in wait. She paused and studied the scene for any hint of movement. There was none to be seen.

Either there's no one there, or they're really good at what they do.

She discarded the first option. They *had* to be there. It was the perfect territory for an ambush. One, for sure, and probably at least two. She would have detailed three at a minimum if it had been her plan. One left, one right, and one ready to break around the corner that lay a short distance beyond the end of the central catwalk. Plus, the damn sniper.

If I were him, I'd be in position someplace high. Like right above me, maybe. She cursed inwardly and surrendered to the notion that, as usual, the only way out was through.

Diana set the rifle down and retrieved its spare mags, which she placed beside it. Her right hand drew her pistol while the left located its extra magazine in her pocket. She took several deep breaths in preparation before she broke into a run. Others usually underestimated her speed, and she counted on that to cause the first shots to miss. Everything shifted into slow motion as her danger sense screamed a warning. An image of the sniper entered her mind as if she was behind him and saw her own body on a direct trajectory from his barrel. Diana dove forward into a shoulder roll, tucked her limbs in tight, and a paintball whizzed past her.

She came up into a sprint after a full revolution and time moved normally again. The expected opponent broke around the corner ahead, and she smothered the instinctual reaction to trip him with a telekinetic blast.

I don't want to show all my cards this early in the game.

Instead, she pulled the trigger as fast as she could until the weapon clicked empty. Paint blossomed on him in five spots, and he stumbled backward. She ejected the magazine and slapped the other one in as she pounded toward safety. Everything slowed again and she slid like she was stealing home plate and smacked to an undignified halt against the wall. A paintball splatted on the wall in front of her, about four feet up.

Another roll took her out of the line of sight, and she swiveled on her stomach, her arms extended and her pistol aimed forward down the length of a short hallway with a bend to the right. Nothing awaited her there. Diana pushed carefully to her feet and approached the corner on soft footsteps with her weapon extended. A quick look revealed an empty corridor with another angle ten feet ahead. She exhaled in relief and stepped into it.

She never saw the laser tripwire she triggered, so when

the walls on each side exploded with a deluge of paintballs from their camouflaged packs, there was nothing she could do except scream in pain and fall to the floor.

Bryant had changed out of his paint-covered gear but still winced with each step on the way to meet the head of ARES' DC office. He had parted ways with a very angry but quite colorful Diana an hour before. The drive through DC's traffic always took much longer than it should, and the lurching walk through the halls had hurt both his back and his dignity. The man on the other side of the desk was in his mid-thirties and wore the buzz-cut he had sported as an Army Ranger. He rose to shake Bryant's hand and laughed when he flinched from the force of it.

Carson Taggart's voice was filled with amusement and good humor. "Handshakes never used to hurt you that much, Bryant."

He lowered himself carefully into the guest chair. "Well, sir, it's not every day I get nailed in the back with a sniper-velocity paintball."

The grin at his expense didn't vanish. "So, how'd our candidate do?"

"Aside from getting me killed, you mean?"

Taggart waved a hand negligently in the air as if his pain and anguish mattered not at all. "Sure, aside from that."

Bryant leaned forward, momentarily serious. "Diana's exactly what we're looking for. A natural leader with good skills and the aptitude to improve with training. Plus, she shows signs of magic other than the telekinesis we were told about."

That wiped the smirk away. A satisfied look of confirmed expectations appeared. "What type?"

"Johnson, playing sniper, said she knew when he was about to take the shot and dodged it."

Taggart raised an eyebrow. "Impressive. Did she sense all threats?"

"She didn't seem to. It was good instincts that predicted the ambush, but she didn't anticipate the sniper before she spotted him. And she didn't notice the claymores." He laughed at the memory of Diana's face after she'd "died."

Carson tapped a finger on the desk, his expression thoughtful. "What do you think the difference was?"

Bryant forced casualness into his voice to hide his own excitement. "Johnson says the second and third time, he kicked up his perceptions to make her easier to target."

The man's eyes widened. "You're saying she sensed he was using magic?"

"That's how I read it but there's no way to tell for sure." He shrugged.

"Does she know?"

He moved to shift the position of his sore back. "There's no way to tell that either, really. Diana didn't bring it up, and it's not in any of the research."

"You were there with her. What's your judgment?"

"I'd say no. She didn't seem to rely on it. It's probably something new to her."

Taggart reclined with a satisfied sigh. "If it is new magic, it'll be interesting to see what it can become."

Bryant nodded. "Right. My thoughts exactly."

"Okay. I'll take your word for it. Let's give her a day and see if she does anything stupid. Then you can tell her she's on for the run Friday night."

"Good deal, boss." He stood, leaning heavily on the arm of the chair for support, and generated another laugh from the other man.

"Get out of here, old man, and hit the whirlpool."

"Respectfully, sir? Bite me, sir." The door closed on the sound of his superior's laughter.

CHAPTER SIX

Diana shifted into neutral, let the car coast, and applied the brakes to stop an inch from the curb and five feet behind a large pickup. She'd not been to this part of town before, but it was similar to any number of other older neighborhoods that dotted the city's periphery. Her phone's GPS confirmed arrival at the correct spot, and Bryant was recognizable in the dim illumination from the streetlights as he exited the cab. She met him at the left side of his truck.

He twirled his keyring. "You made good time."

"I always make good time."

The quip drew a grin but it was tempered with something that looked like concern. His voice also lacked the familiar teasing tone he'd used with her. He put a key into the secure chest attached to the truck's bed nestled against the cab.

She stepped beside him. "So what's the score?"

He flipped the container open. "We have a lead on a terrorist cell the FBI has tracked." He handed her a standard issue SWAT vest but with the letters covered by a black patch. "Normally, we wouldn't intervene since the Bureau needs to put their information sources together to identify the group. But this one has some interesting wrinkles, so we're on it." He pulled out his own Kevlar and draped it over his head.

Diana peeled off her racing jacket and handed it to him with a stern look. He returned a small smile as he folded it carefully and deposited it in the cab. She nodded her acknowledgment.

At least he knows leather deserves respect.

Bryant flipped the container closed and locked it.

"You're spying on the FBI?"

"Technically, *we're* spying on the FBI." He walked around to the far side of the vehicle and unlocked the other half of the chest. "We monitor everyone, but with primary attention to things that might be magic-related."

Her discomfort probably showed on her face. "CIA?"

He nodded.

"NSA?"

"Yep."

"PDA?"

"Of course."

"Homeland?"

He grimaced. "That's a touchy one. They are very much on guard against data intrusions. We're doing old school human intelligence there."

"Like cloak-and-dagger spy stuff?"

His hand disappeared into the container and several clicks sounded from inside. He withdrew a Colt M4 carbine and handed it to her. "Kind of. One of our people works for them as an analyst and has climbed the ladder to some significant access."

Diana took the weapon and examined it once she'd ensured that the trigger switch was set to safe. A *click* released the magazine, and she verified it was full before she reinserted it and accepted a pair of extras from Bryant. "ARES' super-secret shadowy oversight group doesn't have a problem with this?" she asked as she stashed them in the thigh pouches of her tactical pants.

He shrugged. "That's above my pay grade to know." He turned back to the container to retrieve his own rifle. "But we're very sensitive to their operations and stay in our own playground whenever we can. We have enough to do. When we discover things that aren't in our purview, we help them connect the dots with a quiet word sent through various channels."

"All-righty then." The movie quote inspired another thin smile and a barked laugh. She could tell it was forced. The look on his face told the story. "You're worried. Why are you worried?"

He locked the cabinet with his left hand and held the rifle in his right, aimed at the ground. "The thing at the museum was one piece of a puzzle. This might be another piece of the same puzzle. If so, it's more dangerous than a standard break and bust."

She rewarded his honesty with a smile. "I didn't picture you as the timid type. Then again, you *did* send someone else over to chat us up at the bar."

That earned another heartier laugh. "When you really get to know me, you'll see I'm anything but timid. But there's a random variable in this one." He pulled the door of the cab open, retrieved a headset, and extended it to her. Both set their weapons down to don the equipment, then did a quick comm check. He removed a pair of sleek glasses from a pouch and put them on.

"If it's so dangerous, why are only the two of us going in?"

He pointed at an alley that ran south about a half-block away and walked in that direction. The system rendered his words as perfectly as if his lips were next to her ear. "The cell contracted with a magic-capable mercenary who goes by the name Guerre. He's been on our radar a few times but stays extremely well hidden. We think he has a cyber wizard covering his movements."

"You mean a data geek, right?"

"Yes. But cyber wizard sounds so much fancier, and it's what our data geeks like to be called. You do *not* want to tick them off. Trust me on this."

She nodded. It always paid to be friends with those who knew things you didn't, especially when those things could alter real-world reality with a quick adjustment to electronic reality.

"Got it. Dangerous dude, average terrorists."

"Check."

"No anti-magic tech?"

Bryant shook his head. "Supply problems. With all the high-tech gadgets those should have been top of the list."

"Yeah, there's rumors flying about someone trying to make sure we didn't get them. I hear the bounty hunters aren't having any problems getting their hands on them."

"We're working on it. I considered hijacking a shipment headed for the Brownstone Agency, but somehow, that seemed wrong. For now, we'll have to rely on the basics, plus our own not-insubstantial skills."

She squinted into the distance, past the alley's end, and saw a shop window across a street. "So, where's the rest of the team?"

"They have a perimeter around the business the terrorists are using for a safe house. Snipers have cover on one side, with a pair to catch runners in the other direction. Another set is watching the back door."

The alley's exit revealed a row of storefronts on either boundary of a deserted two-lane street.

"Are you holding traffic?" Diana asked.

"Nope. It's not busy after around nine or so."

That explained the timing of the raid, which meant she'd had to cut her visit with Max short when the call to action came. She broke into a jog to keep up as Bryant strode across the road.

"A team will follow us in, but I'm the best sneak we've got, and you appear to have a few skills, so we're in the lead," he said.

Another small alley ran to the rear of the buildings a few stores down, and he led her into it. When they reached the back, she saw their target to the left. A pair of fully outfitted agents stood with their backs against the wall, and a knotted black rope descended from the roof to puddle on the ground between them.

"Tell me that's a grappling hook, like in an old Batman episode," Diana gushed.

Her partner chuckled again. "A little more advanced, but yeah. It's only two stories, so they probably threw it up there."

"Dibs. Next time, I get to throw it."

That finally drew a real laugh. "You've got it."

She scanned the area and saw some likely defensive measures. "Cameras and alarms?"

"Both. We've already hacked and looped the camera feeds, and we used the master alarm code to put the system on standby."

"So why the roof?"

"They may not be top shelf, but that doesn't make them stupid. Our surveillance team's watched them all day and identified bells on both the doors. We've assumed they have microphones on the main floor that feed into the basement. It's what I'd do, anyway."

Bells. She shook her head. *The classics never go out of style.*

"Clever."

They reached the rope, and Bryant gestured for her to lead. "If it were easy, they wouldn't need us."

"True that." She grabbed the rope and climbed, pulling herself up easily and bracing her feet on the knots every foot or so. She felt a shake as Bryant started up behind her. "Bryant, is this a private line?"

"Yep. I'll explain the comm gear another time, but if you want to access everyone, it's channel two."

"Gotcha. Also, I know you let me go first so you could stare at my ass, letch."

She scored the second real chuckle of the evening and smiled.

When they arrived at the roof, they moved in a crouch toward the door that sealed the stairwell. Bryant drew a tiny pistol-like object from a pouch on his vest and put it against the lock. After three rapid trigger pulls, the door swung open.

He raised a finger to his lips, and she nodded as he took point. When the staircase widened enough for him to do so, he peered over the banister to check the hall below and continued the descent. They reached a landing with doors to the left and right, with bronze numbers and letters reading **2A** and **2B**. She imagined that in better economic times, the owners of the store below would live in one and rent out the other. The dust on the floor suggested the apartments had been empty for some time. Particles spiraled up into her nose as her footsteps stirred them up, and she suppressed a sneeze as she followed Bryant along the hallway that curved toward the back of the building.

They found the second stairwell directly beneath the first and started down. Each held their carbine extended forward, ready to fire. She checked to ensure hers was on triple burst, since the mystery of what they might discover called for more munitions and less precision. They passed the midpoint, and her partner craned his head around again before he resumed his course.

He moved a little slower, and it took her a moment to realize that it was her perception that had changed, not reality. Diana squeezed his shoulder gently, and he froze. She scanned the stairwell ahead and the parts of the room she could see. A faint glow caught her attention. Things accelerated to normal speed as she pointed it out. Bryant lowered his chest to the stair and peered at it for several seconds before he stood and turned back to her. He held a finger up, pointed at himself, and made a curve over the railing. Then he held up two, pointed at her, and made the same gesture.

She nodded and kept her rifle trained forward as he climbed over the banister and lowered himself carefully to the floor, using the slats for support. He moved aside to cover her, and she did the same. They paused for a moment to breathe. Then, he gestured down the hall, which was symmetrically below the one on the second level. He took a few steps and stopped, pointed at the right wall at knee height and chest height, and again at the left. She saw the tiny flickers of glass and recognized the laser projectors.

Through a series of complex gestures, he conveyed a plan to simultaneously break the beams with adhesive reflectors that would make it seem that the real beam was still present. She nodded her understanding and took a pair from him. For a moment, it annoyed her that he doubted her ability to crawl through the middle with him, then realized it was probably for the duo who descended behind them. When she'd heard him whisper, he must have warned them about the first obstacle.

They made it to the door and disabled one more trap along the way. It had a handle lock and a deadbolt, and Bryant released his rifle to dangle on its sling as he drew heavy-duty picks from another pouch. It took him fifteen seconds to defeat the deadbolt and only ten to release the handle. He motioned for her to kill her mic and leaned close to speak to her, his lips at the ear that didn't have the earpiece in it. "It's sure to be alarmed." She nodded. "Are you ready to rock-and-roll?"

Nice of him to check in without everyone listening, but unnecessary.

"Born ready."

He straightened and gestured her back around the corner before he twisted the knob and pulled the door open.

CHAPTER SEVEN

Nothing happened. Diana had expected an explosion or at least some shouts of alarm. There was only silence.

Bryant crept around the corner and she followed as he descended in a crouch. They each found and disarmed another trap on the way down before they paused in a dimly lit basement that must have equaled the full size of the building. It was stacked high with crates, boxes, barrels, and other odds and ends.

But no terrorists, and no magical mercenary.

"What the hell?" Her brow furrowed in confusion.

Bryant's face mirrored hers. "Weirder and weirder. Check left. I'll check right."

They circled the room in opposite directions. She looked behind containers, down at the floor, and up at the ceiling. They met again in the center, having found nothing of interest.

Diana racked her brain for an explanation. "Are you sure they were here?"

"Of course." He gave her a withering look. "We've had eyes on the jerks for a while. They definitely went in and they didn't come out the front, back, or top."

She threw her hands up, annoyed. "And yet they're not here. Clearly, there's something we're not seeing."

Bryant snapped his fingers. "Or something we *are* seeing." He released his rifle to dangle on its strap and closed his eyes. "Okay, let me concentrate."

He looked like he was meditating, and she used the privacy to inspect him. His face was narrow and hand-some, even behind the ludicrously fashionable glasses he wore for the mission. The dark hair that was just long enough on top to sweep to the side was appealingly care-less and set off his tanned skin nicely. He displayed the balance and ease of a natural athlete—and the body as well, trim but muscular in all the right places. All in all, an impressive physical specimen.

Too bad he's a chucklehead.

His voice, low and serious, jerked her out of her thoughts. "What is hidden, let it be found." A shimmer on the basement's back wall quickly silenced the laugh that threatened to burst forth. When it dissipated, there was a hole in its place. The opening was ragged, oval, and about five-and-three-quarters feet high.

She turned to him with an accusing glare. "You didn't tell me you had magic."

He shrugged with a soft smile. "I doubt you've told me everything about yourself either."

Fair point.

"Besides, it's good to have people with magic on the team. It gives us an edge the other agencies don't have."

"That makes sense, I suppose." She peered into the hole. "It looks like they've been digging for a while, but only with hand tools or something. They probably couldn't risk the noise of explosives. I bet a bunch of these containers are filled with stone and dirt."

Bryant nodded. "Sounds logical. Do you have your light?"

She glared again and rolled her eyes as she pulled the mini-Maglite out of her back pocket. They snapped the lights on and moved cautiously into the tunnel. Visibility was limited to a few feet at a time as the rough-hewn tube frequently struck what must've been areas of denser stone and took a turn. First right, then left, then right again.

They paused to catch their breath, and Diana gazed ahead with concern. "Where do you think it goes?"

"It's hard to tell. It feels like we're following the street roughly, though, so one of the other stores, maybe."

She hadn't noticed what other businesses were located nearby—a definite failure, so she let the subject drop. They continued to twist and turn, and she lost track of distance after a while. Bryant slowed, and she heard noises ahead. They advanced in a crouch and then in a crawl until he laid down on his side at a wider portion of the tunnel a few feet back from an opening. He wiggled against the left wall to make space for her to lie beside him. Their rifles aimed toward the room beyond.

An arrogant bass echoed in the silence. "You people have not gotten as far as you promised you would," it said with great disdain.

A higher, more resentful, and decidedly less confident voice answered in an accent that recalled an Afghan instructor at the Academy to Diana's memory. "Promises were made. We have stopped all work until you deliver on your end of the deal. When shall we receive the explosives we require?"

The great voice laughed. "Fools. That material is already secured. Half of it is on its way to the storage site you requested and the rest will be delivered here, should you ever complete your task."

The second man sounded skeptical. "You have proof of this?"

The bass descended into a rumble. "My word is enough for anyone with a modicum of sense. But perhaps you know of the various incidents this past Monday?" There was a pause. "All part of the plan to secure the explosives."

Diana gave Bryant a light punch, and he nodded.

"Very well." The Afghan sounded mollified. "We expect it will take another four days to reach the target." His tone turned hopeful. "Unless you would like to assist with your special abilities?"

The man laughed. "Such work is beneath me, which is why you are doing it. Even if it were not, I am not at your beck and call."

A third voice, also Afghan, joined the conversation with fiery indignation. "Who are you to say such things to him, to question us? We accomplished great deeds before coming to this country and will accomplish many more here as well." His tone rose a notch. "You could make this easier, benefiting all, but your own arrogance and blindness make a fool of you."

The first speaker's voice became eerily calm. "It appears a lesson is in order."

Bryant's eyes widened, and Diana felt him move. They burst from the tunnel together, hurtled forward, and raised their rifles. They emerged as a cone of flame erupted from the wand held by a black-clad man and crossed the short distance to another figure. The flames enveloped their target and consumed the defiant worker more rapidly than any natural fire could have managed. There was enough time for the beginnings of a scream before the spell burned the vocal cords and the remains of the worker crumpled into a charred heap.

They appeared to be in another basement, this one smaller than the one at the start of the tunnel. Bryant yelled, "Everybody down!" and veered left. She echoed his command and sidestepped right. Heads snapped toward them, and each of the five presumed terrorists reached for weapons. The agents' suppressed rifles generated tiny echoes in the small space as triple bursts stitched two of the enemies before they could bring their pistols to bear. The return fire from the remaining three resounded violently from every surface, and bullets lodged into the surrounding walls.

Bryant coughed as one caught him in the vest but continued to fire as he staggered back. Diana was in the middle of drawing a bead on her second target when things slowed down again. She dove forward while her instincts screamed at her to flee. The wash of fire sucked the oxygen out of the space she'd vacated and left her breathless as she lurched to her feet and scanned the area wildly.

The mage turned his wand toward her partner, and she screamed a warning. He dodged and darted behind the closest terrorist, and the flames washed over the enemy. She raised her rifle and fired a volley at the mage, who blocked them with a twitch of his wand—exactly like the bastard in the museum had.

But at least the fucker isn't doing his dragon impression anymore. That's something.

She flicked the selector to single shot and stalked toward him. The challenge forced him to maintain his defense while it preserved her ammunition. A cry indicated that Bryant had presumably dispatched the last terrorist. Additional rounds struck the mage's shield.

He smiled at them and bared pointed teeth.

Eww. Not a good look.

"So very talented, Earth people. You saved me the trouble of killing them myself since most of the work is already complete. When you are dead, it will be a simple matter to finish the task."

One hand dipped and gestured and a rock flew at Diana's head. She dodged and rolled, flicked her fingers to lend it an extra tiny push away from her for safety, and came up shooting again.

Bryant's yell added to the chaos. "Give it up, scumbag!"

The man merely laughed.

"Reloading," her partner called, and Diana pulled her trigger twice as fast until the rifle clicked empty.

She returned the call and triggered the magazine release. The mage flicked the wand and hurled large crates at each of them, forcing them to dance out of the way. She scrambled to the side, afraid fire would follow, but instead, he conjured an opening that showed a bare room of polished stone.

"Oh, hell no," Bryant said and broke into a run as their opponent stepped through. "Diana, go for reinforcements."

"Bite me." She was already in motion toward the portal. They made it through as the opening collapsed and she finished her dash with a diving somersault.

In the next second, she was on another planet.

The mage's boots pounded into the distance as Diana dragged herself to her feet. She finished loading her magazine into the carbine and looked at Bryant. "What are you waiting for?"

He shook his head. "Expecting you to stay behind wasn't realistic at all, was it?"

She grinned. "See, you're already starting to get to know the real me. Good job." She motioned with her rifle, and he led at a jog in the direction the wizard had gone.

It didn't take long to find him. When the hallway opened onto a small room, he was there, and he was ready. He held an ornate wand in his left hand, and the other hand toyed with a glowing whip that seemed alive as it twisted and writhed on the floor beside him. He bared his stupid pointy teeth again in a wide grin. "It's been some time since I've faced a real challenge. Usually, I must take on larger groups to find any satisfaction. But you are persistent. It will be a true pleasure to end your existence."

Bryant spat in disgust. "This is your last chance to give this up before you get hurt, asshole."

The mage laughed and flicked his wand at the man. A beam of light cut across the space between them and he was forced to dodge aside in a frantic roll. When it struck the wall, a small explosion threw shards of stone halfway into the room.

He has a blaster? Seriously?

She had no time to think as the whip snapped at her face. She raised her rifle to block it, and it wound eagerly around the weapon. The mage yanked hard, hauled the rifle from her hands, and twirled her as she slid out of the sling. She finished the spin with her pistol in hand and fired without aiming. He had already moved, and her bullets went wide. There was something weird about him, a shimmer that hurt the eyes, but she couldn't quite identify it. The whip flicked at her again and she gestured, summoned her telekinesis, and batted it aside past the edge of her face.

Bryant growled belligerently. "Enough of this." He charged the mage, weaving and shooting as he did so. The wand summoned the apparently standard-issue evil-mage shield to defeat the bullets, and the whip cracked toward the agent. He must have seen the attack on her because he sacrificed the rifle with the same dexterity Diana had summoned and landed easily. Without even the slightest pause, he hurtled at his adversary as he fired his pistol. When he was close enough, he flung himself forward in a flying tackle and missed entirely to impact into the wall behind and immediately slump, either dazed or unconscious.

There's no way he'd misjudge that.

With this crucial information, Diana put the final pieces together and recognized the shimmer she perceived for what it was—another illusion. The wizard wasn't where he appeared to be. She imagined he couldn't be too far and fired a horizontal group of three bullets to the left, center, and right of where she saw him. The one to the left was deflected while the other two missed.

She showed him her non-pointy and reportedly quite attractive teeth. "Got you, smeghead." He summoned his fire as she raced at him and he directed the wicked blast at her face. She slid beneath it, into where his legs appeared to be, and met no resistance. The left arm she threw out didn't miss, though. It hooked around his ankle, and she yanked to break his balance as she added a telekinetic shove against his support leg. He shouted in surprise and the illusion vanished as he fell and lost the wand. She wrapped her legs around him and gripped his foot to twist him into an Achilles lock. He screamed as she increased the pressure.

"It's hard to concentrate," she panted, "when your leg's on fire, isn't it, scumball?" He tried to speak, and she applied her weight with a small twist to draw another scream. Bryant stumbled over, looking dazed, and kicked the mage in the head with the point of his shoe. The man's struggles ceased. She released him and trussed his hands and feet with zip ties. She connected them with another tie and rose wearily to her feet. Bryant freed a piece of the enemy's robe with a small pocket knife and used it to gag him.

Diana smothered a yawn as the adrenaline that had kept her going began to fade. "Do you think that's safe?"

He shrugged. "It's safer than letting him talk."

She nodded and registered the sudden onset of dizziness in enough time to put her back against the wall and slide down it with a modicum of grace.

Bryant sat beside her. "So, that was fun."

Her laugh sounded weak and sickly. "You have an interesting definition of fun, Bryant. Remind me never to let you take me on a date."

He snorted. "Do you want to go back?"

Diana looked blankly at him.

"I can cast a portal to send you to my apartment. You can get help from there."

She thought about it. This had been a bad experience, and the memories it conjured up were worse. Screams of the dying echoed in her ears, and her guilt at surviving washed over her again.

Wearily, she closed her eyes and turned inward. Her therapists had taught her to observe her thoughts as an outsider and recognize that what she felt wasn't necessarily Truth with a capital T. It let her get a little distance until she could ask herself the question her brain tried to avoid.

Can I handle dealing with magic like this all the time?

She ran a replay of the mission from the moment she'd parked her car and nodded.

Adequate.

She hadn't been perfect, but she hadn't been overwhelmed either.

I can do this. Mind over memory.

She stood and forced herself not to wobble. "No thanks. There's still plenty to do here before we go home, don't you think?"

The wizard's bunker was small, only five rooms connected by short, narrow tunnels with no doors or windows. The room they'd appeared in was apparently kept vacant for arrivals and departures. They found his bedroom and another room filled with torture devices Diana preferred not to consider too closely. The fourth room held a large bathtub and related amenities.

The final room seemed to be a workspace—or maybe a playroom—and was triple the size of the next-largest. Tables were scattered in no apparent pattern and covered in unfamiliar tools and objects. They split up to search, and she discovered a dark wooden armoire with intricate carvings. She opened it and found a dozen black robes.

Of course.

As she pushed the door closed, her brain registered a strange hum that emanated from the bottom. She opened it again and dropped on one knee to push the robes aside. Her eyes widened in disbelief as she saw a troll, exactly like the ones she remembered from Saturday morning TV, staring at her with big eyes through the metal bars of a cage. He stood about five inches tall, had latte-colored fur, and his large pointed ears drew the eye away from his neon-purple shock of hair. A sad look covered his face, and he jerked back with a whine at irregular intervals, as if something was hurting him. She reached out and the air sparked, and she yanked her hand back with a curse.

Diana responded to his stress with the same tone she used with Max when he was anxious. "Okay, little guy, I'll figure this out." She lowered herself to her stomach and examined the cage and its surroundings. Finally, she found a small chip of stone that seemed out of place. The hand that extended before she'd thought about it was zapped.

She groaned.

Idiot.

"Okay, that one's on me. Stupid move. Don't judge." The troll was clearly watching her but offered no comment on her idiocy. "I'll be right back." She stood and rushed from table to table in search of something long that wasn't made of metal. A set of wooden tongs fit the bill. She returned and stretched them forward, fearing a snapping bite on her fingers, but it didn't come. Her forehead creased in concentration, she rubbed them over and over against the chip until it broke loose. The hum stopped. She tried to open the cage but found it locked.

"If I were a stupid ugly mage, where would I hide the key?" She found it in the pocket of one of the robes and bent to the small prison once again. The troll literally bounced now, a wide smile on his face. She opened the door, and he bolted free and dashed up her arm onto her shoulder. Then, he grabbed her earlobe and squeezed it.

Bryant picked that moment to arrive, and she pointed wordlessly at the tiny creature.

He shook his head with a laugh. "Sheen, there's only one thing I can say. Now, you've really done it."

CHAPTER EIGHT

Bryant winced as he sank into the well-worn institutional chair. Special Agent in Charge Carson Taggart laughed at him, retrieved a bottle of ibuprofen from his desk, and slid it across the polished wood. The agent caught it and returned it in one fluid motion.

"I already had my daily dose."

Taggart chuckled. "It's only noon."

"What's your point?"

Shaking his flattop-crowned head, the ex-Ranger dropped the container back in the drawer. His voice was rough but friendly. "Okay, Agent Bates, this is where you drop the whining and report on the last mission."

Bryant's exhaustion showed in his sarcastic "Sir, yes, sir." He realized he was slouching and pushed himself up with the chair arms. An aide arrived with two mugs of black coffee, and Bryant drank greedily. Thus fortified, he began his report.

"Penetration was by the book. They'd trapped the place

to hell and back, which makes sense given what they were up to. I might have missed one, but she saw it."

His superior raised an eyebrow. "Magic?"

"Yep." Bryant nodded. "She definitely has something going on where hostile magic is concerned."

Taggart leaned back in his chair and steepled his fingers. "It sure would be nice to know what it is."

"We could ask her."

The other man's headshake again failed to disturb a single black hair. It reminded Bryant of a perfectly mowed lawn. "It's too soon. Let's see what she reveals on her own. Continue."

"When we reached the basement, they weren't there. We figured out it was an illusion and dispelled it. That led to the tunnel, and the tunnel led to the basement of a building that must've been...what, halfway down the block?"

Taggart tapped a keyboard and squinted a little at the monitor on the corner of his desk. "That's what the techs say, based on your GPS."

"Anyhow, there were some unknown terrorists—"

"Known," his superior interrupted. "Al Qaeda."

Bryant's eyebrows shot up. "Seriously?"

"True as the sunrise."

"I thought they'd been folded into Al Arabiya?"

"It seems not. Or at least not all."

He shrugged. "Wow. Okay. Anyway, Guerre killed some, we nailed the rest, and he tried to escape through a portal."

"So naturally, you followed him. Why did you bring Sheen?"

A single laugh broke through Bryant's restraint. "I didn't *bring* Sheen. In fact, I told her to stay. She has chain of command issues."

Taggart grinned knowingly. "All the good ones do."

"Anyway, we brought him down as a team. She plays with others pretty well."

"Could you have taken him alone?"

The agent thought for a second. "Maybe, if I got lucky. Probably not without some grenades or something. He was fierce."

"Well, now he's fierce in the Cube." Taggart took an expensive bottle of bourbon and two etched tumblers from his desk. He poured a tiny draught into each and slid one across, then raised the glass in a toast. "To another successful mission."

Bryant leaned forward to clink glasses. "And to many more." Both men drank, then expelled an appreciative sigh in unison.

The boss knows his whiskey.

"So, anything else notable?"

Bryant thought about Diana's unique discovery and grinned viciously at the chaos the little guy would inject into her regimented lifestyle. "Not at this time."

"Will you *stop it?*" Diana hissed, her hand over the mic of her phone. The troll now used the side of the couch she wasn't occupying for gymnastics practice. He climbed onto the armrest to launch into a multi-flip floor routine, or up onto the back to do several tumbles in midair before he bounced into the cushions below. The finish of each invoked gales of laughter from the tiny being. Interspersed were shouts of joy and a constant undercurrent of chirpy babble she couldn't comprehend.

"What? No, I'm sorry, there was a noise." Her parents' amusement was audible over the line. Normally, they talked by video, but even though they were the most open-minded people she knew, Diana wasn't ready to reveal the presence of her new roommate.

Ha. More like life partner, it seems.

Several hours on Google researching trolls and human-troll pairings had not built her confidence. She found a decent amount of information on the former and very little on the latter, all of it connected to one specific pair. Leira Berens was a legend, as was her sometime-superhero companion. Diana realized she'd missed more of the conversation and tuned in barely in time to hear her mother say, "…about the new job." An educated guess suggested that the words before it were "tell us," and she launched into a quick, sanitized version of her adventures so far.

Her dad's unassuming voice registered concern. People sometimes underestimated him because of the way he sounded, but any lack of brawn was more than compensated for by dramatically impressive mental acuity. She liked to think she'd had some of that passed down to her. "Are you sure you're okay being around magic so often?"

She turned her head away from the phone and sighed before she returned to the call. "I'm paying attention to it. There's not much more I can do. What I absolutely won't do is hide from it."

"Exactly what I told him, her mother chimed in. "But you know he's a worrier." She'd been a rower in college and maintained her physique by continuing the practice every morning without fail, which made her an interesting complement to her thin, academic partner. Her IQ wasn't quite as high as her husband's, but she possessed a unique way of examining things that often resulted in innovative solutions. The two made an unbeatable research team.

"Thanks, Mom." At a knock on the door, her head jerked toward it. "Hold on," she told her parents, then swiped to access the camera on her landing. Bryant stared up with a small smile. She switched back to the call. "Bryant's here. Gotta go."

"Love you," her father said, his voice lost behind her mother's excited "That is definitely the name of a cute person. Is this business or social? Because—"

Diana closed her eyes and hung up. She pointed at the troll, who had just done a triple somersault and landed flat on his back and now rolled around in laughter. "You be careful, mister. There are no hospitals for magical creatures nearby." She unlocked the door, let Bryant in, and scanned the street for trouble before she closed and locked it again.

He spotted the hall coat rack and hung his black wool overcoat on it. Another acrobatic feat by the troll caught his attention and inspired laughter. "It seems like your new friend has fitted in very well."

She shook her head. "The bad news is he's a maniac. He's done this nonstop for hours. It's either sleep or freak out, apparently. The good news is, he's so small that a little fruit and cheese keeps him fed."

Bryant made a sour face. "Fruit and cheese?"

She folded her arms. "I don't know what to feed a troll. I put a bunch of stuff in front of him, and he seemed to like fruit and cheese. So that's what he gets."

He laughed. "Fair enough."

Diana took him on a quick tour of the first floor of the house, and they sat at the dining counter in the kitchen.

"So, you'll want this." Bryant slid an ID badge across to her. "It'll get you into the main headquarters."

"Which is where?"

The agent put two pieces of paper on the white surface, each with a string of numbers on it. The one for latitude had a small dot beside it.

His expression went blank. "Memorize those and then eat them."

"Seriously?"

He broke into a grin and laughed. "Nah. Just screwing with you."

She smacked him, not too hard but with some energy behind it, and he groaned in response. Then she pouted dramatically. "Aw, did the big bad magic mercenary hurt you?"

Bryant blinked and raised a single finger slowly in response. She stood, laughing at her victory. "I have water, coffee, and beer. Which do you want?"

"A beer would be good."

Diana took the few steps to the fridge and pulled out two Hellbender Ignite IPAs, popped the tops on an opener mounted on the wall, and handed him one. She crossed to the couch and sat on the side not currently occupied by a gymnast. For a moment, she stared at the troll with all the seriousness she could muster—which wasn't much in the face of his cuteness. "Okay, little guy, time to bring it down a bit. The middle section of the couch is yours." She turned to Bryant, who had followed her into the room. "You can have the far side."

Bryant sat cautiously. The troll still practiced flips between them but showed some signs of slowing.

The agent cleared his throat. "So, is everything okay after the last run?"

She nodded and took a long sip of her drink.

"Good deal. I did some research on trolls but didn't discover much. There are apparently some spells to help interact with them, but I couldn't find out what they are or if anyone can do them."

"Me neither."

He regarded the troll, who had now settled and lay on the couch, his back on the seat and his tiny legs on the backrest. "I know some people who know some people, and they're looking into it."

A smile crept onto her face. "Thanks.

The troll chirped, "Thanks." They both stared at him.

Diana shook her head. "Well, that's new. He must like you."

"Nobody likes me." He laughed.

The troll chirped, "Nobody," in a slightly lower voice, obviously trying to imitate the man.

She shook her head at the ludicrousness of the situation. "Life's an adventure, isn't it?" A sudden rush of nervousness cascaded through her, but she pushed it down and tried to sound casual. "I planned to watch a movie.

Since you're here, I might even make popcorn. Do you want to stay for a while?"

From between them, a tiny voice said, "Stay."

Both humans burst out laughing, and Bryant said, "It's got to be bad luck to argue with a troll. Sure."

She hit the required buttons on both her remotes and the opening scene of *Assassins* started to play.

Bryant leaned forward. "No way. I *love* this film. It's one of Banderas' best early ones."

Diana snorted. "Please. He was much better in *Desperado*. Anyway, Stallone's Robert Rath steals the show."

At a sleepy sigh, they looked down as the troll curled into a ball. A drawn out, "Rrrrrathhhh," preceded a snore far out of proportion to the creature's size.

She looked at Bryant. "Rath. I think he just named himself."

He rolled his eyes. "If you have to choose a Stallone character, why not Rambo?"

"I'm losing what little respect I have for you. If I were to choose just any Stallone role, it would have to be Rocky. Rambo? Please." She looked down and her face hurt from grinning. "But no, I can't argue with his choice. Tough, smart, canny, and always comes out on top."

"If those are the criteria, Rocky and Rambo are still on the table, not to mention Demolition Man."

"It's done. Discussion closed. His name is Rath." She pointed at the kitchen. "Popcorn and toppings are in the cabinet on the left. Bowls are in the one below it. Go make yourself useful." Bryant rose with a chuckle and moved in that direction. She called after him. "And stay out of the fridge! I'm the only one who goes in there."

He raised his hands facetiously. "Yes, boss."

She smiled, grabbed a bandana from the back of the couch, and draped it over the troll. He snuggled under it and displayed a sleepy smile.

"Nice to meet you, Rath." She spoke quietly so Bryant wouldn't hear.

Bryant banged around in the kitchen and she pushed to her feet with a sigh.

Idiot. He'd better not try to sneak into the fridge. I'd better hide my Cherry Coke if I have guests.

She looked back once more.

And maybe put a troll-proof lock on the fridge. I'd hate to see what caffeine would do to him.

She laughed at her suddenly bizarre life and headed for the kitchen.

CHAPTER NINE

Diana took the curves in the parking are much faster than necessary as excitement and uncertainty warred within her. A small voice cheered, "Whee!" from inside her large black leather purse, which was secured with the passenger seatbelt. She smiled, navigated another curve with a screech of tires, and mashed the brakes to stop perfectly between the lines of an empty space.

The building was in another industrial park but this one was older than the test facility with red brick, manicured lawns, and plentiful windows. The main ARES location in DC was innocuous among the many other identical constructions. She'd been told to use an employee-only entrance, as the other would take her into the cover business—a telemarketing company currently engaged by a lobbying firm of some kind. The workers had no idea what lay under their workspace.

She tapped her ID against a flat panel beside an otherwise unremarkable door and the locks clicked their release. Briskly, she stepped inside, only to find her way blocked several feet ahead by a thick curve of plexiglass. A matching piece rotated closed behind her to leave her encased in a translucent oval about as wide as her outstretched arms and twice as long.

She looked around, confused.

Bryant. That bastard. I bet he failed to mention this in the instructions on purpose.

A pleasant male voice emanated from hidden speakers. "Please place your palms on the handprints to your left and right." Sure enough, faint outlines of hands were marked on each wall. She shrugged her purse up to her shoulder and complied.

The panels lit beneath her palms and the space filled with a low buzzing.

I hope X-rays aren't harmful to trolls.

Apparently, everything was in order as the front barrier rotated aside to allow her to pass. She strode forward and turned a blind corner to discover a sleek lobby area with a curved glass-topped desk. A thin man with sandy hair, trendy glasses, and a dark suit rose behind it. He extended a long arm to shake her hand. "Agent Sheen, welcome. I'm Michael, and I will take care of your orientation today." He glanced at her bag, and she pulled it closer.

"Hello, Michael. Thanks."

He tapped the ID badge hanging from a lapel of his jacket. "You'll want to put yours somewhere it can be seen easily. The guards here tend to subdue first and ask questions later."

She nodded and clipped hers to her own jacket. Her suit was dark blue, with pants instead of a skirt. She wore mid-height brown moto boots in place of the standard issue footwear or something more attractive but impractical. While she was willing to meet expectations partway, she drew the line below the knee.

Okay, occasionally above the knee, but that's only the one pair. Well, two.

Michael gestured her forward and walked with her. "Do you have any questions before we get into the details?"

She pointed up. "The business above. Are they part of us?"

He had the enthusiasm and pride of a tour guide. "They are, although they aren't aware of it. Somewhere, way up the corporate chain, we own their parent company."

Diana nodded. "Security seems tight down here, given that you've chosen to put civilians a level away."

"It is a calculated risk, to be sure. There are safeguards in place for both them and us. For instance, the entry cylinder checked your fingerprints and examined you for metal, explosives, and every other kind of weapon material we can test for. It also matched your height, weight, and other distinguishing characteristics against the records in our database."

"Impressive."

He shrugged and gave a spokesmodel smile. "We can't be too careful these days, right?"

They had traveled along standard-issue corporate corridor with multiple turns. Everything was in an attractive and no-doubt calming shade of ivory. Her internal compass was fairly sure they were now somewhere on the far side of the facility from where she'd entered. "I presume this labyrinth is another defensive measure?"

"Got it in one, Agent Sheen. There are countermeasures

all along our route. If the facility were in intrusion mode, or if it didn't sense your badge, we would never have made it to the first turn." He tapped his ID against a thick door leading toward the inside of the building and typed a six-digit code on the keypad above the sensor. The barrier slid aside with a soft hydraulic hiss to permit access to the inner workings of ARES DC.

Ahead was a briefing space that featured a large table with a display surface. Seven feet or so away to either side, curved mounts turned it into an oval. The displays attached to them reached from two feet off the ground to about six feet high. They were arranged tall, rather than wide, and appeared to be blank. A dark-suited woman with a bright red blouse and glasses similar to Michael's moved from one darkened monitor to the next. She stared at what appeared to be nothing for a few moments before moving on.

Michael launched into his description with obvious pride. "We call this the core. It's where team briefings take place. The display mounts are on tracks." He pointed at the floor to indicate them. "That way, the space can expand or contract to fit the needs of the moment. To the left and right are extendable panels that make it possible to separate the core in its smallest version from the rest of the area, allowing our technicians and analysts to continue their work at the computers you see arranged around the periphery."

She studied a row of techs on each side who wore identical glasses and seemed laser-focused on their tasks. The monitors were blank, which meant they could be doing almost anything. She chose one at random and pointed.

"That man is playing *Galaga*. He thought we wouldn't notice, but we did."

Michael laughed. "You'll fit in very well here, Agent Sheen."

She returned a grin. "Diana."

He nodded.

"So the eyewear lets them see the displays, is that it?"

Her guide nodded again. "Standard AR glasses for everyone, although the ones you wear in the field are a little more resilient than these." He tapped his own. "We'll get to that soon." He pointed to the right. "That way is the administrative offices and such. You have a home there. It's rather small, but you won't spend much time in it anyway."

"It seems like space is at a premium."

Michael smirked. "That's because most of the place is reserved for the fun stuff. Let's go take a look."

He led Diana to the left and repeated the security procedure to leave the center section. The hall continued forward, and he pointed in that direction. "That way is medical and science. We have analysis and research labs that rival the best you can find anywhere."

"Better than the FBI?"

His grin was like that of a proud parent. "We used their top-line stuff as a starting point. But we've gone much farther in the process of creating our own."

She gestured around them. "Where does the money for all this come from?"

Michael shrugged. "That's beyond my knowledge, I'm afraid. I trust that someone has that figured out." He turned to the right and led her three-quarters of the way down. Before he opened the next door, he said, "You'll love this."

They entered, and Diana had to admit he was right. It was her kind of place. Technologies in various states of assembly lay on tables around the room, with happy-looking technicians at work on them. A firing range was set up on the rear wall, surrounded by thick glass. A door opened on the right side near the range, and an older man bustled forward.

His hair brought Einstein immediately to mind—or maybe Doc Brown from *Back to the Future*. It was unkempt and seemed impervious to gravity. His wide face held a warm smile and despite some extra padding around his midsection, he moved with grace. He wore a white lab coat over a black T-shirt and jeans. As he neared them, she could see his shirt read, **Ask me about my Erdos number** with a ridiculous-looking mathematical equation below it. As he reached them, she extended a hand. "Diana Sheen."

With a laugh, he raised his own hands, which were damp with liquid. Her nose told her it was gun oil, and he confirmed it. "I've been cleaning your new weapon, Diana. Come take a look." He bustled away.

Michael laughed fondly. "His name is Carl Emerson, but we call him Ems." He walked toward the open door and she followed. "He thinks it's short for Emerson, but the rest of us know that it's actually short for mad scientist."

"I heard that," Emerson called from the nearby room, seemingly unoffended by the moniker.

A little voice from her purse replied, "Heard that."

He chooses today to be chatty. Awesome.

The scientist sat behind one of the ubiquitous tables and locked the pieces of a Glock 19M into place. He pointed it away from everyone and pulled the trigger to receive a satisfying *click*. His expression a little smug, he handed it over for her inspection. It shone like it was fresh from the factory.

"It looks great," Diana complimented honestly.

Ems rolled his tall stool several feet left and motioned her forward. A plexiglass mold was mounted on the table with a seat in front of it. He pointed at the gun and the mold with two fingers, then at her and the chair. She sat and lowered the pistol into the cavity. He attached a cable running from a nearby laptop to a small port she hadn't noticed on the inside top of the grip.

With a few deft movements, he hit some buttons and gave her orders. "Hold the gun with your right hand." She wrapped her fingers around it. "Rotate a few degrees to the right." She did so and noted how weird it felt to hold it in that position. "Same distance to the left of center." She complied. "Now, let's repeat the process with your left hand."

When they were done, he motioned at the pistol. "It's now programmed to recognize your palm and finger-prints, no matter where they appear on the grip. This will prevent anyone but you from using the weapon. Before you go, you should take it to the range and get used to it." He slid a box of ammo to her. "Safety rounds. These are not to leave the building." She nodded, and he looked at her with an expectant smile.

Diana grinned at his enthusiasm. "Thank you, Ems."

He cackled and spun his seat a half turn to the right. "I see that your next meeting has arrived." She and Michael both turned together. A young woman with blonde curls that reached below her shoulders stood in the doorway.

She was thin and had a manic energy about her that was immediately noticeable.

The newcomer smiled at all of them. "I'm Kayleigh. Let's get you finished up, Agent Sheen."

She led them back into the main room to a table that was cleaner than the rest. Before Diana had a chance to examine it, Kayleigh said, "So, I hear that you made some terrorists upset with you on your first day."

From inside her purse, Rath spoke the clearest words he'd said so far. "That happens when you kill four of them."

The woman looked surprised. Michael clearly suppressed a laugh. Diana rolled her eyes with a sigh. "I absolutely should not have let him watch *Assassins*."

Kayleigh leaned in. "So it's true. You've been adopted by a troll."

Michael confirmed it. "He's in her purse."

Diana shot him a look and he gave an unapologetic smile. "I told you we scan for everything. Expectations of privacy were abandoned the moment you signed your nondisclosure agreement, Agent Sheen."

"It's the same for all of us." The other woman nodded. "Fortunately, the computers only display things out of the ordinary." Her voice took on a note of excitement. "Can I meet him?"

Diana set her purse on the table. "Come on out, Rath. The jig's up."

He emerged slowly—only his purple hair at first, then his ears, and finally, the rest of him. The tiny creature wore a mischievous grin.

"He's amazing," Kayleigh said and extended her index finger to him. "Pleased to meet you, Rath. I'm Kayleigh."

The troll blinked a few times before he took her finger in his hands and shook it. With great seriousness, he said, "Kayleigh, Rath." Michael repeated the process, and Rath said, "Michael, Rath." Diana simply shook her head. Once the greetings were complete, she put her palm down and the troll scampered up her arm to sit on her shoulder and lean against her neck.

Can this life get any weirder?

"Anyway…."

Kayleigh laughed. "Right, right. So, we have some stuff for you. First, your AR glasses. They're wireless and provide data here and in the field. The feeds only work in proximity to one of our encoders, so you'll get a repeater for your car and home before you leave."

Diana tried them on. Tags appeared briefly on people, then faded. Information scrolled on the left periphery of her vision, and an empty space remained on the right. "Can I customize the content?"

The woman nodded. "There's an app for that. We had the techs clone your phone when you entered, and we'll give you an identical secure one before you leave. Don't let it out of your sight, though, and don't let anyone play with it without disarming the security first."

"Or?"

Kayleigh smiled. "Or, it'll explode and take out the hand —or troll—playing with it." She stared at Rath, who echoed, "Explode."

She reviewed the rest of the gear, which included a device that could disarm most alarm systems and electronic locks, a nondescript set of earpieces that would work with her phone and the Agency's comm system, a smartwatch that acted as a panic button and locator, and the promise of an implantable tracker to be inserted between the bones in her arm before she left.

While Diana had acquainted herself with the gear, Emerson crept up on her undetected. She jumped when he spoke from a foot away. "Does the little guy ride around in your purse?"

Rath's voice was sad when he replied, "Purse."

"Well, my friend, that will never do. Diana, please bring your partner to my office."

The troll said, "Rath."

The scientist nodded. "I'm Carl Emerson. Everyone calls me Ems."

"Emerson." The troll sounded definitive that he would not use the nickname. Diana shrugged and followed the man back to his office. He rummaged in the boxes behind his desk and finally exclaimed, "Aha! There it is."

He drew out a cylinder roughly twice the size of the troll and turned toward his desk with it. "It's a gunpowder canister. If I move the latch and the hook from the outside to the inside, Rath should be able to pull it closed and hide if he needs to protect himself. I'll line it with foam and vinyl. It'll do as an emergency capsule, anyway." He located a soldering iron, a few pieces of metal, and a giant magnifying glass, then got to work.

Rath ran down Diana's arm to stand on the desk beside the man and watch his progress. At one point, he stuck his head under the magnifying glass and looked back at her, causing her to crack into laughter at the sight of his enormous eyes and smiling face.

"You're something else, Rath."

He gave a toothy grin and returned to watching.

Michael coughed softly. She had forgotten he was there. "I have to return to the main desk. My replacement has other tasks. Kayleigh, can you take Diana and Rath from here?"

The tech nodded. Michael gave Diana a parting handshake. "Good to have you here, Agent Sheen. And you, too, Rath."

Diana stepped closer to Kayleigh and lowered her voice. "Can I see you outside for a second?" The woman nodded, and they left the scientist to his task and the troll to his show.

The other woman led her to an empty space near the gun range out of earshot of the other techs in the room and handed her spare magazines for her weapon. "Go ahead and load them up. You can make sure it's sighted true before you go."

The agent nodded, and her hands worked at that familiar task without the need for conscious direction. "I came up against some harsh magic last time. Do we have anything that'll work against magical targets? They seem to have an answer to bullets."

The serious concern looked out of place on Kayleigh's face. "They do. Sometimes we use grenades when there's no fear of collateral damage, but we haven't found the right solution yet either, aside from countermagic."

Diana gave a rueful laugh. "Well, I'm a little short on that at the moment, I'm afraid."

Kayleigh nodded and looked in both directions like she was a confidential informant in a detective movie. "Okay, I *do* have something I've been working on, but it's not been fully tested."

"I'm happy to be your guinea pig if it'll ruin a bad guy's day."

The tech crossed to a tall locker set into the wall and unlocked it with her handprint and a code. She extracted a clear plastic box with several rounded rectangles inside, each about the length of her hand. "These are pepper gas grenades. I couldn't make them strong enough to be fully debilitating in case something goes wrong and our people are caught in the cloud, but it should at least distract them." She took three out, one smaller than the others. "The smallest is for a key chain or everyday carry. The larger ones aren't quite as concealable. They can fit in a magazine pouch."

That explains the shape.

"They sound perfect. How do I use them?"

Kayleigh pointed out the release catches and the plunger on top that would activate the grenades on a delay so Diana could throw them. The same button would spray a stream out of the smaller one.

"Perfect."

The woman's joy at someone appreciating her work was obvious. She stored the bigger ones in a small plastic container and handed them all over.

Diana had just tucked the grenades into a zippered pouch in the purse and the spray bottle in her front pocket when Emerson reappeared. He held the troll in one hand and the canister in the other and proffered both. "This should keep him safe."

"Safe," echoed Rath.

The agent set the two gently into her purse. "Honestly, I think I'm the one who'll need protection from his adventures." The troll gave a gleeful laugh that sounded like agreement, quickly punctuated by the *click* as the canister latched.

Awesome.

"So, how about we take care of the weapon test and the tracker? By my fancy new watch, I have twenty minutes before my meeting with the SAC."

CHAPTER TEN

Before she entered the SAC's office, Diana opened her bag and peered into it. Rath sat comfortably in a nest of her socks with his open canister beside him and stared at her. He smiled, and she grinned. "You be quiet, crazy man."

"Crazy," was the only response. A rush of fear washed over her at the responsibility she carried for his well-being, and she realized she couldn't keep him with her all the time. He certainly couldn't come on emergency responses or the more dangerous missions. It wouldn't be safe for him. She shook her head as the door opened and an aide ushered her into the room. It was smaller than she would have expected, but that fit the operations focus of the place. Her own area closely resembled a walk-in closet.

The Special Agent in Charge stood to shake her hand and introduced himself with a gruff "Carson Taggart," then motioned her to sit across from him.

She wasn't able to resist. "Finally, I get to meet the

person crazy enough to hire Bryant to their staff. Did you lose a bet or something?" With flawless timing, Bryant walked into the room. She turned to him with a raised eyebrow and said, "Again? Are you still stalking me?"

Taggart transitioned from chuckle to outright laugh and came to his defense. "No, I invited him to be here."

The agent gave her an aloof look and sat in the other chair. His smile looked goofy. She almost told him so but turned back to the SAC instead. "So, am I off probation?"

He nodded. "The paperwork is on its way. You'll work here with our team. Although, since we're fully operational, you get to be more or less a free agent."

"Nice."

A short silence ensued while he reached for a box of mints on his desk and offered them around. Diana took one and peppermint blasted through her nasal cavity as she put it in her mouth. She didn't quite choke, but she came close enough.

Bryant laughed. "He does that to everyone. It's a rite of passage."

When she could speak again, she asked, "When do I meet the rest of the team?"

Taggart clicked his own mint against his teeth with no apparent negative effects. "In due time. You'll train with them on a fairly regular basis."

She nodded. "I look forward to it. Do you give the orders in the field?"

He held up a hand and rocked it back and forth. "When it's an emergency response, I do. When it requires the coordination of multiple agencies, I do. And when we think there might be something exceptionally weird going on, I do. Otherwise, I leave it to the team lead."

"And who's that?"

Diana realized her instincts had failed her when Taggart pointed at the chair beside her. She put her face in her hand. "You're telling me Bryant is the best you have? I'm sorry. No wonder ARES is looking for new blood."

They both laughed at that. The agent shook his head. "Can I make her change the oil in the bus or something?"

"Denied."

"How about clean the locker rooms?"

"Denied."

"Strip the rifles and oil them."

"Denied."

Bryant sighed. "Damn it."

Taggart turned to face her squarely across his desk. "So, you'll be with us temporarily, until everything is in place to open the field office in Pittsburgh. Then we'll send you up there to get things running."

She frowned. "Not that I have anything against Pittsburgh, but I was promised I'd have some say in locations."

Taggart smiled. "Yeah, Bryant told me he said that. He likes to lie." There was a chuckle from her right, and she narrowly resisted the urge to slap the agent silent. "Seriously, though, you will have a choice eventually. The Pittsburgh office will be the first that's ready, so we'll start you there. After it's up and running, if you decide you want to transfer to another of our startups, we can put someone in to replace you."

"Why Pittsburgh first?"

"ARES has another Ultramax prison there, codenamed the Cube. It's different than the others and it's only for our use."

"That's ambitious. It seems like you're doing a lot at once."

The SAC nodded. "Definitely. Maybe too much. But we're in it now and there's no going back."

Diana grinned. "So, new unit, same as the old unit. Seems like the FBI was running at full speed to cope with the implications of magic, too."

There's no getting away from it. Everything is changing.

"What's the day-to-day going to be like?"

Bryant took over. "You'll work closely with me to learn the way we do things at the team level. It's a little different than what you're used to with the FBI. One day a week, you'll be with Lord Taggart over there, learning Special-Agent-in-Charge-stuff. Finally, one day a week, you'll be in school, refining your knowledge of magic. You'll learn how to use it, how to defend against it, that sort of thing."

Her eyes widened with each new task listed. "It sounds like a busy schedule."

They both nodded. Taggart added, "You'll work some long hours, and usually at least one weekend day."

She kept her face expressionless but inside, she scowled. The thought of Rath at home alone didn't sit well, and not only because he would destroy the place if left unsupervised. She was distracted from her thoughts when Bryant spoke again.

"And then, if you're good enough, you'll be off to Pittsburgh." He said it like it was a prize.

"Why do you say that with such glee? What are you not telling me?" She turned to Taggart as suspicion dawned. "Why isn't Bryant making the move from team leader to SAC Pittsburgh?"

Both men laughed and the agent said, "I told you she was smart."

"You certainly did. Well, Diana, that's the one negative to the job I haven't really mentioned yet. Bryant will take the position of regional SAC for the Northeast."

"So my direct report will be to him?"

"Yep."

Bryant clapped his hands together. "And since you've already signed the papers, if you decide to bail, it'll go down on your permanent record."

She scowled at him. "I will have my vengeance. In this life or the next."

His lips twitched. "Are you not entertained?"

Bastard. Yes, that was funny, but you'll still need to be taught a lesson.

She was distracted by a kick inside her bag and the low growl that emanated from it. Hastily, she coughed to cover it and changed the subject. "So, tell me about that stupid wizard we fought. Do we know what he and his pawns were up to?"

Taggart nodded. "It turns out they were tunneling toward the Starbucks at the end of the street. They planned to blow it up."

"That's an odd choice."

Bryant had adopted that oh-so-punchable smirk again. "Not really. Many good people who use magic tend to frequent Starbucks, just like everyone else." She buried the desire to slap him as her bag growled again.

"Okay, so why did international terrorists want to do that?"

The agent dropped the levity and took up the story at a gesture from his boss. "That wasn't their goal. That was whoever hired Guerre. The actual target was the magical rail system that runs below it. It turns out the terrorists had the experience to dig the tunnel and no pretensions about being too important for manual labor. They merely wanted enough explosives to ram a car bomb into the Saudi consulate. Fortunately, the survivor sang like a diva when we got him to the med folks."

The unsettling images her mind conjured must have registered on her face because Taggart spoke quickly into the silence. "We don't do torture. We do have an excellent knack for pharmaceutical manipulation, however. Plus, one of our medics is an Empath."

Concern transformed into curiosity. "A what?"

"She can sense emotions—much like a magical lie detector."

Diana was momentarily jealous. *I wish I had that talent.* "That *is* handy. How'd you find her?"

Taggart shrugged. "Dumb luck, really. She was a cadet at the FBI Academy, and one of her instructors noticed that she seemed adept at helping other cadets cope with the stress of the training. He kicked his observation up the ladder. When we took a closer look, we determined it wasn't merely skill but magical talent."

"How did he know to contact you?"

"He didn't," Bryant said. "We intercepted the message and deleted it from the FBI systems."

She frowned as she considered that, then let it go. "That makes sense. She'd be way more useful here. Okay, back to the important stuff. Who hired the magical merc?"

"The terrorist couldn't tell us. Guerre contacted them with the offer. But our prisoner heard enough boasting from the scumbag to judge that there was more than one person behind him. He's also sure they are people of magic and power. Or magical power. He was unclear on that."

Some sarcasm made it past her controls. "Well, that certainly narrows it down."

Bryant replied, "That's what I said."

The SAC sounded confident. "He has more. Our folks will get it out of him."

The troll in her purse shifted around, and she pictured him preparing to do another gymnastics routine. Diana wasn't sure she was comfortable revealing him or letting him reveal himself to Taggart just yet. She stood abruptly. "Okay, it sounds like everything is organized. Do I start tomorrow morning?"

Her boss nodded. "You'll be with me for the day."

She turned to Bryant. "Don't be too sad. I'm sure you'll have the chance to stalk me again soon. Or, as you no doubt consider it, 'dating.'"

He grinned and tapped his arm in the same spot where her own locator beacon had been implanted. "No need. We always know where you are now."

"Awesome." She rolled her eyes.

Taggart's smooth baritone advised "Go out, have a

meal, and celebrate a little. Tomorrow, the hard work begins."

———————

She wove the Mustang adroitly through traffic and considered taking some of her anger out on her heavy bag.

Maybe I'll put a picture of Bryant on it. It'd be more fun like that.

Rath sat in his canister, which was wedged into the center console cupholder with one of the booklets that came with the car. The cylinder wouldn't go anywhere for anything short of a crash, and she was confident he could yank the latch down in that unlikely circumstance. It was easier to keep an eye on him this way. She glanced down at him whenever it was safe to do so.

He seemed fascinated with the satellite radio. He pushed buttons and changed the stations. First new wave, then rock 'n' roll, then a quick tour from the seventies to the 2000s, and finally landing on the Beatles. When Yellow Submarine came on, he stopped tuning and bounced his head along with the music.

"Ha." She smiled at him. "So you're a Ringo man? I'm more a George Harrison fan, myself." They listened to the song as she navigated the DC traffic snarl, and the next tune began seamlessly over the finish of the first. The clanking sound of the silver hammer intruded upon her worries about the troll destroying her house in her absence.

Silver hammer.

Maxwell's silver hammer.

Max.

Excitement seared through her and electrified her brain. She wrenched the wheel to the right and calculated the quickest course to her destination. It took twenty-five minutes, and she counted every second of them until she finally pulled in. She shoved through the front door and didn't even notice if she was waved toward the back. Rath was secure in the purse that hung from her shoulder. People milled about and dogs barked, but she found Doug quickly and asked for a favor.

A minute later, she was in one of the adoption rooms. Two minutes after that, Max arrived, and Doug closed the door, leaving the two—no, three—of them alone.

The dog jumped up and gave her a lick, then stuck his long nose into her bag and sniffed madly.

"Okay, Max. Sit." He complied. "Actually, lie down." She sat on the floor beside him and kept the purse on her right side while she got a good grip on his collar with her left hand. She blew out a breath.

Please let this work.

"Okay, you guys. Here's the deal. I want you to be friends. I need you to be friends. You can keep each other company and look out for one another when I'm not around. It'll be perfect. We'll be a family. A very strange little family."

"Be family," said the small voice from her purse. She reached her hand in and Rath climbed up her arm and ran up across her shoulders to stop on the left side.

For his part, Max merely turned his long nose, looked at the troll, and barked happily, accompanied by a couple of thumps of his tail.

"Rath, meet Max. Max, meet Rath. He's not from around here."

The troll cried out in what sounded like manic joy. "Max. Rath." He hurtled down her sleeve and jumped onto the dog's back to nestle in his fur. Max twisted his head back as far as he could and flicked his tongue out to give the creature a lick that knocked him to the floor.

Rath popped up, brushed himself off, and launched himself at the dog's nose. She had a moment of panic that he might be upset, but Rath simply crawled up and gave the dog's long nose a big hug. "Max," he said again.

Diana couldn't stop smiling. She patted Max on the back. "Good boy, Max."

An hour later, the paperwork was done, pet supplies were purchased, and they were finally in the house. Rath jumped from her purse, scampered down her leg, and hurried over to Max, who she held by the collar. He grabbed handfuls of fur to pull himself up, then found a spot on the back of Max's neck.

Diana shook her head. When the idea had come to her, she hadn't imagined it going so well. Something about the relative ease so far made her sure it would turn to trouble of one kind or another eventually. She released the collar and Max immediately rocketed around to explore the house while Rath rode on his back and jabbered in a language she didn't understand. Both seemed ecstatic with the arrangement.

Later that night, her head bobbed from exhaustion as

she sat on the couch, as content as she could ever remember being. Max sprawled across the rest of it and his head rested on her leg. Judge Dredd dispatched justice on the TV, and Rath lay nestled on Max's back with a smile on his face.

As she drifted off, she could have sworn a tiny voice growled, "I am the law."

Surely not. I must be dreaming.

CHAPTER ELEVEN

Diana crawled into place beside Bryant and raised the monocular. She scanned the back windows of the lavish home, aimed it at the top left, and worked her way across the second floor, then reversed the pattern on the one beneath. "No sign of movement." The mic at her throat was sensitive enough that her low voice didn't carry.

"Acknowledged." Taggart was in the mobile command post for the op, several miles away. He'd explained that when the action kicked off, drones with cameras and data repeaters would sweep in and the small lenses on the teams' vests would feed video to him. During her first two weeks of training with BAM, she'd come to admire their professionalism and dedication. She hoped they felt the same way about her.

A sense of generalized unease centered like a knot in her upper back. All their information predicted some serious magic on-site. The movement to tap the pouches that held Kayleigh's special grenades was unconscious but delivered a little peace of mind. The anti-magic deflector around her throat delivered a little more.

Taggart's calm tone pulled her from her thoughts. "Teams, ready check."

A male voice spoke. "Team A, front, ready."

"Team two, left, ready," a woman responded.

A man with a New England accent spoke third. "Team three, right, ready."

Bryant's voice finished the sequence. "Team four, back, ready."

The next pair of callouts spoke slowly, any excitement they might have felt fully suppressed in the name of efficiency. The first was female, the second male.

"Overwatch one, front left, ready."

"Overwatch two, back right, ready."

The terrain hadn't been friendly to the snipers as the estate sat at the top of a steep hill. Their trek had begun immediately after darkness fell and they had made a slow way through the trees that bordered the property on three sides. Each had found an Atlantic White Cedar to apply their climbing spikes to and deployed a portable Kevlar and ceramic tree stand in its high branches.

Diana learned early on she didn't have the patience to be a long gunner. As a result, she considered them amazing, like some kind of aliens. There was a small note of excitement in Taggart's words. "Ready check confirmed. We are green. Weapons free, standard rules." Her first day of training had been a comprehensive review of the unit's procedures. Standard rules meant to rely on their own discretion but where possible, they should try to take prisoners. Her inner voice laughed.

Different unit, same stuff. Shoot 'em in the leg if you can.

She returned the monocular to Bryant, who slipped it into a pouch on his left arm. They were outfitted with rifles, pistols, and a pair of grenades each in case things got messy. Because they were in an evolving situation, they carried low-intensity flashbangs. The tech wizards had added an electronic component to the fuse that would send a pulse to the agents' AR glasses and dual earpieces to protect them from the light and sound if one went off. They couldn't do anything about the concussion, and the training sessions she'd undergone to learn to cope with that experience were ones she was happy to see in the rearview.

Team one called out, "Moving." When they reported, "In position at the front," teams two and three began their assaults. The comms were calmer than in any op she'd ever been on. What would've been an excited "breaching" when team one shattered the front windows was only a matter-of-fact status report. The others reported in one by one, and it was finally time for her and Bryant to move.

The plan was as tactically sound as the available information permitted. The terrorist was only able to give hints about the house but when they put it together with other data they had access to, the location became clear. They'd used satellite and long-range recon but couldn't get a drone close enough to see inside for fear of alerting the occupants. As such, Taggart had chosen a classic multi-point attack to inspire chaos in the defenders. As those within responded to each incursion, another would occur. And while they dealt with the ones from the front and sides, she and Bryant would strike from the back.

They ran together like shadows in the night and Diana took four strides for each of Bryant's three. Black balaclavas concealed their faces, dark body armor protected their vitals, and their matte-finish weapons would deal some serious damage to their enemies. She cradled a Colt M4 carbine, the handle mapped to the unique pattern on the tactical gloves she wore. An enemy would have to wear them to use her weapon. Bryant's rifle was strapped across his chest, the barrel down and to the left, facing away from her. He carried a short-barreled automatic shotgun filled with lock-busters, a special load of Emerson's design that traded range for extreme power.

When they reached the rear door, he moved to one side and fired at the visible locks to launch a pair of echoing explosions into the crisp November air. Diana imagined the place with snow all around and thought it would be beautiful. Bryant's boot struck the door and it swung open as she scattered her musings like so many flurries on the wind. She led the way while he stashed the shotgun on his back and extended his rifle.

The diversions seemed to be working as intended. She heard shouts of confusion from farther inside the large structure. They were in a mudroom, surrounded by shelves packed with an assortment of differently-sized containers. Another door led from the room into the main building. She gripped the handle and yanked it open, and Bryant hurried through.

Their comm carried his whispered, "Contact," and his suppressed carbine spat a triple burst of soft coughs. She followed him in and registered the presence of a commercial Wolf range along a wall.

Damn, I want one of those.

An enemy sprawled heavily. Another swung his rifle toward Bryant, and she delivered her own set of three rounds into his Kevlar vest, center mass. He staggered back and fell. Panic replaced surprise as he struggled to breathe. Diana kept her weapon trained on the kitchen's other access while Bryant zip-tied the fallen men at hands and ankles, dragged them together, and ran a line between them.

She snuck quick glances at their foes and noted areas protected by body armor—chest and thighs—and where she could deliver death if necessary. Their adversaries weren't terrorists this time, merely a mercenary company with notoriously low standards. Since ARES hadn't been able to determine if the mercs were aware of the evil nature of their employers, they would shoot to subdue rather than kill them whenever possible.

Too bad the mercs don't offer the same consideration.

Diana led the way from the kitchen into a formal dining room as large as her basement. Gorgeous cherry wood cabinets stood on the far wall, and a sleek wide table in the center was made of the same material. It could seat at least a dozen. A rifle barrel suddenly peeked over the top and she dove to the left. Bryant went to ground on the right. The enemy's bullets didn't come close, but the weapon was on full auto and sprayed lead at stomach height.

She smiled as she sighted through the chairs to where the merc's legs were visible and squeezed the trigger once. The first two rounds deflected from obstacles in the way but the third made it through. He yelled and collapsed with his hands clutched around his shattered shin. Bryant took a position to cover the far exit, and Diana yanked the fallen merc to the side so she could work on him while she kept an eye on the entrance to the kitchen. She zipped his wrists and ankles fast, then hogtied him and drew a scream as she wrenched his leg up. "Sorry, pal. It's nothing personal. Find a better employer next time."

When the man was secured, she retrieved a trauma patch from the pouch on her calf. This ARES innovation was an adhesive bandage with clotting agent smeared on one side. She wrapped it around the merc's leg and pulled the small handles to compress it. The ratcheted nylon clicked as it shrunk. She patted him on the shoulder. "You should make it if you don't do anything stupid. Try not to be an idiot."

Bryant had already cleared the merc's rifle, so she did the same to his pistol. She released the magazine and ejected the round in the chamber, then threw the pieces to different corners of the room. The time of the encounter took less than a minute. Training for trussing prisoners had been far more fun than the one for concussion grenades, except when it had been her turn to play the downed foe.

The exit led to a hallway with an open door across from them. Team three emerged from it, and they advanced in pairs to the building's center, which held the main staircases. The full group had reviewed the blueprints together in the ARES core and judged the main routes less likely to be trapped—or at least trapped less lethally. It would be far easier to position an automatic turret on a disused staircase. She was relieved to see that all eight of their team were present, although Gillians sported a trauma patch on her left upper arm. One of the others teased her, and she laughed with a shake of her head. "It's only a scratch."

The second part of the plan was markedly different than the initial assault. Teams two and three would cover the staircases, an agent facing in each direction. Bryant would ascend with a member of team one behind him. As Diana had quickly earned her bona fides as the backup ninja, she was assigned the down staircase, with the other half of team one trailing. Taggart's order propelled them into motion. "Phase two. Execute."

Bryant offered a fist. She bumped it and they went their separate ways.

CHAPTER TWELVE

Bryant used hand signals to instruct the agent following him to keep his distance.

It wouldn't be good to have him stumble into a trap I missed.

The main staircase was grand and narrowed from a flared base to a size that would still allow three people to walk comfortably abreast. It ended in a platform with additional staircases to both left and right to access the second floor. A heavy curved banister ran along each side.

Fancy.

The lead agent took the stairs one careful step at a time, set his foot down, and waited for a reaction before he lowered his weight in slow increments. He scanned in a pattern. First left to right on the base of each stair, then right to left on the piece perpendicular to it. He paid special attention to the sides as he sought out potential sensing devices. His AR glasses analyzed everything and displayed an overlay of things outside normal visible range. They'd allow him to discern laser or heat sensors with ease. Of course, they were only as good as the wearer.

In the first op with Diana, he'd not been as alert as he should have, and she'd had to step in. This time, he'd be more careful. The status section showed only routine check-ins from the other members, represented by dots corresponding to their team number.

Halfway up the staircase, he noticed something odd about the next step and froze with his foot in midair. He withdrew it and crawled backward until he was eye level with the stair. Instead of being of uniform height, this one had alternating panels that were about two millimeters lower than the rest. Pressure plates.

Clever idea but stupid execution. They should've made the whole stair a plate.

As he stepped over the trap, he froze again and grabbed the banister for balance as he stopped his foot from coming down on the next step.

Maybe not so stupid. I would've backed up the obvious one with a hidden one.

He shook his head. Facing off against smart enemies sucked. He turned, waved at the man who waited at the base of the stairs, and pointed the dangers out. Then, he stepped onto the banister, placed his feet in between the slats, and used it to ascend one sidestep at a time. He stuck his head around the corner when he reached the landing, aware of how exposed he was, and found no opposition in either direction.

Symmetrical short staircases led to a hallway on both sides, and he could barely see the edge of a door in the hall at the top. Bryant suppressed the desire to step onto the landing and continued to the end of the banister. He swung to avoid the obvious places a person would take their first stride into the hallway, pushed a hard nub on his left glove with his thumb, and pointed his index finger. A glowing dot appeared in his glasses. He used it to draw an oval around the area he thought might be dangerous and to put an X across it. The image was immediately uploaded to their local network to warn the other agents.

He unlimbered his carbine. Three doors were set into the wall at irregular intervals down the long hallway. The blueprints they'd uncovered showed the farthest left to be the smallest, probably a walk-in closet of some kind. The other two had originally been bedrooms. A mirrored version of the layout could be found on the opposite side of the structure. The closets also featured a narrow corridor that connected to another that traversed the back of the building, presumably so the wealthy owners could avoid seeing their servants at work. Bryant shook his head.

No matter what planet, no matter what people, it seems there are always some who think they're better than everyone else for one misguided reason or another. He smirked. *Well, it's time to lay down some education.*

The agent crossed softly to the nearest door and dropped to one knee. He extracted the fiber-optic camera cable secured in his left sleeve and pointed it through the gap between the door and the floor. After a short delay, the feed opened in a window on his glasses to reveal an elegant writing room as seen through the fisheye lens. There were bookcases in several places, and a beautiful desk faced the floor-to-ceiling windows. A puddle of light bathed a polished end-table beside a sumptuous leather armchair in one corner. Seated there was an androgynous woman in an elegant gray pinstripe suit over an expensive oxford and a crimson silk tie, presumably in her mid-forties. She had white skin, long platinum hair, and held a book that looked like it'd come from another age, oversized and luxuriously covered.

Or perhaps another world.

He let the camera retract as he stood and examined the door. It appeared to be a standard interior model that would be no match for him. He moved to the side with his back against the wall and pushed it open. Nothing happened, so he risked a quick glance and entered the room, his rifle trained on the woman in the chair.

She seemed amused, a small smile on her face as she put an opulent bookmark in place.

That is not good.

Bryant spoke in a calm tone but with the weight of iron behind it. "Hands on your head, get on your knees, and don't say a word." He motioned with the weapon to punctuate the command.

Her smile broadened as she snapped the book closed and Bryant's finger twitched on the trigger a split second before the pain erupted. The areas of the gun that his gloves touched suddenly felt like they'd been dipped in lava. He threw the carbine aside by reflex, and it skittered across the floor. Fortunately, he'd at least had the presence of mind to throw it away from the woman. He did the same with the spare magazines, which seared at his thigh. He wasn't sure whether it was an illusion or if they really had changed temperature, but it didn't matter.

"Okay, if you want to talk, let's talk." He held his hands up in a placating gesture.

While he had been in the room, the computer network

and techs at the bus had been hard at work. Data scrolled in the right-hand periphery of his glasses. The woman's name was Lienne, and she was on their radar as a person of interest, suspected of being part of a power-seeking group from Oriceran. She'd been mentioned by a couple of informants, but the team had never put eyes on her before. "Okay, Lienne, how about you come along quietly and we'll sort all this out down at the office?"

An even wider smile preceded a velvet voice. "After what you did to the fools we had in place to mess with your little train? It was only appropriate that we thank you properly." She waved a hand, and Bryant's data feed disappeared. "Ah. Now we have some privacy. As I was saying, after your actions, we felt an appropriate response was in order. So, I invited you to my home."

Shit. Here I worried about the small traps and missed the big one right in front of my face.

He lowered his hands and spread them in appeasement. "Well, I'm here. What do you want to discuss?"

The woman shrugged and the perfect shoulders of her suit bobbed once. She slipped her left hand casually into a pocket, which immediately triggered alarm bells in Bryant's mind. He stepped back carefully toward the opening and ran into what felt like a wall.

Uh-oh.

The Oriceran stood with liquid grace. "Your little organization has become a nuisance. It is time for you to be taken off the board."

Her hand emerged from her pocket, and she hurled a tiny pellet that burst into flame as it rocketed across the room. Bryant hissed, "*Scield,*" and a shield shimmered into place around him. He gritted his teeth against the pain of the charm that burned into his neck and dodged left. Tiny fireballs imploded in the space where he had been and spewed divots into the wall. He drew his pistol, flicked it to single shot, and fired. She conjured an invisible barrier between them with a flick of her fingers, and the bullets clattered harmlessly at her feet. He advanced with each round in the hope that he could get near enough to do some damage.

Her mouth moved, but his earpieces were dialed down to compensate for the blasts, and he couldn't hear the words. He felt the slightest warmth through the glove that gripped his pistol and grinned. "It's ceramic, asshole. That doesn't conduct heat nearly as well." He realized his error a second before it was too late and threw the weapon toward his opponent as the bullets cooked off and shrapneled metal and non-conductive shards in all directions.

"I hate this wench," he muttered. A yank freed the matte-black bowie knife from where it rode on the back of his vest. He held the dull edge of the blade along his forearm and extended his other hand toward her as if he held an invisible wand. She donned her arrogant smile again, and the shimmering field between them dropped. She spoke with a sibilant hiss that grated on Bryant's ears. "Really. Do you think you'll get close enough to use your little dagger on me?"

Bryant gritted his teeth and dug deep as he muttered, "Get over here." A line of force, invisible to everyone but him—as far as he knew—materialized and latched onto her foot. He yanked hard and she went down. The expected wave of weakness swept through him, but he had painstakingly trained himself to keep going despite it. He attacked the woman, who was already rolling away.

Heh. You got your suit dirty.

During one of the rolls, Lienne fired a blast of flame at ankle level, and he hurdled it. The one that followed struck him squarely, and his anti-magic deflector crystal shattered as it consumed the energy of the spell. She thumped into the wall and bounced to her feet. More fire pellets hurtled at Bryant, and his shield failed beneath the onslaught. One caught his shoulder and spun him violently across the room. Despite that pain, the pinprick burn left by the consumed charm was worse. It made the next thing he had to do suck all the more as he squeezed his eyes tightly closed.

"A light shines through the darkness," he intoned, and a blast of radiance filled the room, accompanied by another searing burn further up toward his left shoulder. The necklace held a number of single-use spells that had been exceedingly expensive to procure and both difficult and time-consuming to attune to. This one created a brightness that could be blinding. If it failed to destroy his opponent's sight, he'd been told there would at least be temporary damage that would make the user more difficult to hit. He took a deep breath and lurched to his feet to accelerate in a long curve toward his opponent.

She shouted, her perfect hair askew, and menace twisted her features. Her previous display of serene confidence was now thoroughly ruffled. The blasts of fire that punctuated her threats weren't quite on target. He closed the distance, jumped to slice at her neck, and his right hand flowed in a flawless arc. Somehow, Lienne blocked it when she fell backward and shoved a thin arm in the way of the blade. It cut a long gash in her flesh and she cried out in pain, then screamed in fury.

Bryant was hurled across the room by a ferocious explosion of heat and his back impacted into the far wall at high speed. Only the fact that he'd instinctively curled prevented him from cracking his head open. He landed with a *thump* and rolled to extinguish any flames, then pushed dazedly to his feet. His adversary staggered, her once perfect suit a mess, her shirt stained with her blood, and her tie askew. He summoned his magic line again and this time, wound it around her neck. When he pulled, Lienne stumbled forward, her balance lost. A twisting yank that added his body's torque to the line's power propelled the woman face-first into the wall beside him with a loud crack. She dropped bonelessly to the floor. Bryant checked her vitals, but she was gone.

Damn. Still, you earned it.

He made a quick circuit of the room in search of anything immediately useful before he finally turned toward the exit to assist in Diana's exploration. His face fell, and he sighed.

What he'd assumed was a magical barrier that would vanish when the woman was unconscious was actually a reinforced steel door that wouldn't. With a sense of foreboding, he drew the shotgun from behind his back and checked for visible damage. Finding none, he guessed at where a hinge might be and triggered the weapon. It blasted drywall away to reveal metal behind it and utterly failed to damage the heavy door.

He was trapped.

CHAPTER THIRTEEN

Diana crept carefully down the narrowing staircase. Her AR glasses showed no signs of traps ahead, and she didn't have any unexplained feelings of worry.

Only the normal ones you get when sneaking to confront a mage on his home turf.

The stairs ended at a pair of closed double doors. She arrived without incident and crouched before the one on the left. Tentatively, she turned the handle on the right door downward at an inch at a time. The door opened with a *click* and swung away. She looked back and nodded at the agent who followed her, then risked a quick look at what lay beyond. A ninety-degree angle turned left three feet ahead.

She stayed low as she traversed the doorway and flattened her spine against the wall to her left. A peek around the corner revealed a long hall with doors on either side that terminated in another ninety-degree angle to the left.

What is this, a bloody maze?

She stepped into the hallway, her rifle ready, and

jumped when the door slammed shut behind her. A spin to caution the agent about noise discipline was ineffective because he wasn't there. She looked around the corner, and he wasn't there either. Unless he was an enemy plant, the door must have closed of its own volition and locked him out.

A deep, amused voice echoed in the hallway. "Come into my parlor, said the spider to the fly."

Shit.

"Status report." There was no reply. She toggled her mic to make sure it was on. "Anyone there?"

Silence was the only response.

Awesome.

She turned, raised her rifle again, and paused for a centering breath. On the blueprints, the basement had been rendered as a single wide space. Clearly, it had been renovated without getting the proper permits.

We'll add that to the list of charges.

The first door she reached matched the double door she'd already used. She repeated the procedure from the staircase. A quick glance revealed an empty white leather loveseat, and elegant paintings covered most of the eggshell walls. She stepped inside, her footfalls silent on the luxurious midnight-blue carpet, and examined the rest of the living room. It was far more attractive and spacious than her own. The loveseat was one of a pair that faced each other, with a matching couch along the far side of the rectangle they created. A low silver and glass table filled the shape. One corner was home to a pellet stove that caused the air above it to shimmer with heat.

The living room was empty of other beings but showed

all the signs of an inhabited space. The remainder of the basement held a kitchen, a bedroom, an exercise area, and the room that held the water, electric, cooling, and heating systems. She returned to the doors that led upstairs and jiggled the handle, but they remained obdurately locked and allowed no passage through.

This doesn't make sense.

She returned to the living room and tried to look at it with fresh eyes. It seemed like the most comfortable space on the level, and she imagined she'd spend most of her time in there if hanging out in basements was her thing. And yet it was empty.

Diana searched thoroughly, even the furniture, in search of hidden switches or other secrets. At irregular intervals, the same echoing laughter made her whirl to check behind her as it had done since she entered the basement.

When I find that mocking bastard, I'll put an extra bullet in him for annoying me.

As she made a slow circuit of the space and ran her fingers over the parts of the painting frames she could reach, a prickling sensation intruded on the edge of her consciousness. It was subtle and easy to miss but returned whenever she neared a certain point in the room. Excitement tempered with worry blossomed in her chest as she traced her hands over the wall.

It felt exactly the same as the surfaces to either side of it.

Fuck. Okay. Think, Diana. What does this remind you of?

She wracked her memory for when she'd experienced this sensation before. It took a few minutes before she had it and she checked to be sure her microphone was off. *There's no point in making an idiot of myself for everyone to hear.* She stood in front of the wall, extended her arms, and closed her eyes as she reached for the prickly feeling. It was slippery and skittered away each time she tried to grasp it. After a minute of frustration, she chose a different tactic and allowed her intentions to fade as she emptied her mind. The sensation crept in at the sides, and after what seemed like forever, it was fully present. She whispered, "What is hidden, let it be found."

When she opened her eyes, an odd wavering effect hung before her—much like the air above the hot stove. She tried to peer through it but only saw the wall. The barrel of her rifle slid through and vanished, then reappeared when she pulled it back. Diana did the same thing much more slowly with her left pinky, and it too returned unharmed.

This is such a stupid idea.

Before she could think about it further, she leapt shoulder-first at the wavering wall. She plunged through an instant of blackness before she was back in the light. Diana landed awkwardly and stumbled, the floor not exactly where her brain thought it should be. She tracked her rifle around and took stock of her new location. It was an office, sized and furnished in a manner appropriate for the chief executive of a big corporation. Mahogany furniture filled the room, including an ornate desk with an almost spotless surface.

Behind it sat a man who clearly attempted to look like an elf. Long platinum hair cascaded over his shoulders. His perfect pale features were set off by a dark turtleneck.

Gems sparkled in his non-pointed ears, and he wore an ornate necklace with a heavy purple stone pendant. Its facets caught the light. He rose and gave a slow, entirely condescending series of claps.

"Agent Diana Sheen. Well done. I began to worry you wouldn't figure it out. Our children can sense and dispel an illusion before their second birthday."

She raised the rifle. "Less talk, more getting on the ground with your arms spread wide, Legolas."

Tolkien would've given this pseudo-elf his stamp of approval for sure.

The man rolled his eyes. "Next, you'll be reaching for pedantic comments about crackers. Such pettiness demeans you, not me." He snaked a hand out and made a yanking motion, and her rifle shuddered to break free. The strap kept it in place, however, and she recovered it and aimed again in one smooth motion. "Nice try. This is your last chance. Get on the ground or you're done."

He frowned, seemed to think about her request, and snapped his fingers. Another gesture was immediately followed by a *click* as the magazine fell from the bottom of her rifle. She watched it tumble and disbelief locked her gaze to it before she wrenched her eyes back to the mage. That superior smirk begged to be smashed off his face.

"Let's dispense with the petty threats and speak as polite people do, Agent Sheen."

She dropped the rifle and drew her pistol—her off hand clamped on the bottom of the magazine—but did not raise it. "Okay, say your piece."

He nodded and gestured at a pair of chairs set in the corner. She shook her head, and he shrugged. "Very well.

As you have realized by now, you are here at our invitation. It was a simple matter to feed you this location through sources you trusted. After you dispatched our pawns and the disappointing hireling Guerre, we felt a response was in order." He put his hands in his front pockets and her whole body tensed for action, but he didn't pull anything out of them.

"There are other disposable humans to be had, and there are many more locations than the coffee shop that allows access to the magical train. You have, at best, only cost us time. And unlike you humans, with your short lives filled with base obsessions, we have plenty to spare. You have accomplished nothing, and your efforts have resulted in the deaths of your comrades—and soon, of you."

Diana had heard enough. "We'll see, asshole." She yanked her pistol up and squeezed the trigger three times. In the instant it took the bullets to reach him, he gestured casually with his hand and conjured another of the damn shields to stop the rounds in mid-flight. She continued to fire as she charged and used her left palm to vault the desk. Still in motion, she aimed a two-footed kick at his chest with all her strength and momentum behind it. She registered his sidestep and prepared for a rough landing against the wall, but it never came.

Tentacles appeared from nowhere and encircled her, stood her upright, and held her suspended. The first to grab her vanished as her anti-magic deflector consumed them, but there were too many. Her pistol was trapped against her waist as the thick flesh of whatever had her bound pinned her arms. The loops were tight enough that it was a struggle to breathe. Fear washed through her.

The satisfaction on his face was revolting. He lowered the hand that had cast the shield, and she noticed the heavy bracelet he wore that seemed to be merged with his flesh. It pulsed, and the tentacles around her twitched in time with its changing glow. He flicked the other hand, and the nearby furniture slid away with a crash to make space for him to walk around her. She craned her neck to the left when he vanished from her vision for a few moments before he reappeared on the other side to complete his circle and stand less than a foot in front of her. "You're weaker than I expected." He reached a slender finger to touch her cheek. Pain crept outward from that point and ignited every nerve in its path. The invasion sickened her even as the spreading agony pulled a groan from her aching lungs.

He retracted his finger and laughed. Bereft of contact, the creeping tendrils under her skin vanished in a slow wave that matched the first. She panted and clenched her fists. The tentacles shifted. A small hope blossomed, and she struggled a little more while she allowed the real fear she felt to show fully on her face.

Enjoy, and don't pay attention to the man behind the curtain, you poser.

He nodded. "Now you see, human. Your species is as far beneath us as your Neanderthals were to you. Given enough time and the right circumstances, there is one chance in a billion that you might rise to our level. Sadly for you, however, you will not have even that most minute of opportunities."

Her groping fingers found the magazine holder on the back of her belt. She released another groan and panted to cover her actions. "You won't get away with this, scumbag. The agency knows where you are. After this, every SWAT and HRT team in the country will be after you. The bounty on every last one of you sleazeballs will be so high, you'll never have a moment's peace." The tentacles squeezed again, and she screamed to cover the sound of the Velcro as she pulled the flap open.

He laughed and touched her other cheek with agonizing slowness. This time, the pain was greater, and she devoted her concentration entirely to the need to endure it. Memories of the Atlanta battle washed over her and added to the terror of the moment. Angry tears leaked from the corners of her eyes. Despite all this, one part of her mind worked without conscious instruction, summoned the grenade to her fingers, and primed it. Now, all she had to do was get it free and toss it at him.

Nope, that's not going to happen, her inner voice said. A fresh wave of agony raged through her as he returned a second finger to her other cheek and she lost the ability to focus enough to summon her magic.

Okay, then. Let's do this. She released the switch. After four seconds of agonizing delay, the ordnance sprayed pepper gas in all directions. She had closed her eyes in readiness and held her breath, but the wicked vapors still burned the inside of her nose. Legolas coughed—a choked sound that made her smile through the pain—and the torture and tentacles fell away. As she dropped the half-foot to the floor, she snatched a handful of cloth with her left hand.

Diana twisted backward, then pivoted her body into a right elbow strike aimed at where she thought his head would be. It connected sooner than expected, which dissipated some of the blow's force, but he still cried out and stumbled. She vaulted into him and shoved him to the floor in such a way that she'd land on top of him. He struggled to escape from beneath her, but she levered herself up in a donkey kick and dropped a knee into his solar plexus.

His breath exploded from him, and she rained a series of punches to his face to ensure that he wouldn't mock anyone for a while. He must have turned his face away because she didn't feel the pleasant sensation of teeth cracking under her fists but was reasonably certain that she'd at least fractured his cheekbone. She found his throat with her left hand to use as a target reference and swung her arm far back to deliver the final punch and end the fight.

A blow to the back of her head was a total surprise and it shattered her senses.

Where did that come from?

She fell into darkness without an answer.

CHAPTER FOURTEEN

Diana awoke choking and gagging and panicked. She crawled instinctively as fast as she could until a hand grabbed her, and she fought to free herself. After a moment, she realized that it was attached to Bryant and looked around in confusion. "What happened? Where'd he go? Where were you?"

He exhaled in clear relief as he threw a smelling salts capsule aside. "You must have a seriously hard head, Sheen."

When she glared at him, he added quickly, "I had to shoot my way through a wall. They ran down that hallway. The rest of the team is about thirty seconds behind us."

She grabbed his arm and heaved herself upright. He was forced to balance himself to support her scramble to her feet. The room swayed and made her stomach lurch so she stood still, one hand on his shoulder, and focused on recovering her wits. "Where are my guns?" She looked around and located her rifle, but not its magazine. Her Glock was nowhere to be found.

After a minute, she was ready. "Give me your pistol. Shit. Never mind." Imprinted weapons would take some getting used to. Bryant drew a black bowie knife from behind his back and spun it to proffer the hilt. She noted that it had crusted blood on it.

Good. Let's find some more.

She nodded her thanks. "This'll do nicely. Which way did you say they went?"

He pointed at a hallway leading from the area that had been invisible during her battle with the mage. "I don't suppose you'd be willing to stay behind, given your—"

Diana raced toward the corridor. Bryant caught up to her in moments, and they pounded along a passage that turned consistently left and circled in toward a center room.

Or a different planet. Who the hell knows anymore?

Suddenly, the lights failed and plunged the hall into darkness. The night vision function of their AR glasses compensated immediately, and they didn't miss a step. "That's not good," Diana observed.

"Nope." They took another corner and paused to cover one another.

"They probably know we're coming."

"Yep." As they drew closer, the corners were spaced closer together. They lingered for a moment to enable the rest of the team to catch up. She stuck her head around for an instant and saw that light spilled into the corridor about halfway down. She leaned back. "I think we've found it—an opening on the left."

"I lead." Bryant pushed in front and stepped into the hallway. She followed with a growl of irritation. They made it halfway to the opening before her senses screamed a danger warning. It seemed to come from the end of the corridor, and given the agents behind them, there was only one option.

"Fall back," she shouted and shoved Bryant forward toward the gap in the wall. He lost his balance, but she kept him upright and both flailed into the room beyond scant seconds before the hall behind them filled with fire.

They both rolled cleanly to their feet to confront two mages in the chamber. Bryant dashed at the one she'd already wounded, so she focused on his assistant, who looked stunningly ordinary in comparison to the other. He was dressed in business-casual, a button-down and khakis. A translucent ball of force shimmered into being in his raised left hand, and he threw another with his right like a baseball. She dodged the first and the second, but the third struck home. It exploded into her like a giant's punch and hurled her back to career into the far wall. More were on the way before she recovered her wits. It took all her energy to avoid the missiles, which left her nothing to attack with. His delivery was fast enough to throw an occasional orb at Bryant, and she winced as one of them found its target and knocked him sideways.

It proved to be fortuitous timing, though, as he continued his momentum to evade a stabbing tentacle with sharp ridges down it. A whisper at the back of her brain became more insistent as her panic grew.

Let go, it said. *Let go.*

She remembered the feeling she'd had when she faced the illusion. This was the same. Diana took a deep breath, turned her mind inward, and relied on her body's reflexes to keep her safe from the blizzard of magical spheres. Time slowed as the prickling sensation swept over her and evasion became easy—like she knew exactly where the balls would strike before they left his hand. She advanced slowly, swaying and sidestepping as the orbs flew by, and the knife glinted as she pointed it at him in a clear threat. Her voice emerged in a taunting singsong. "I'm coming for you, little mage."

Her adversary growled a string of curses and pushed his hands together, then drew them apart to reveal a much larger ball. He propelled it like a basketball player making a chest pass, and there was no way to avoid it. She maintained her calm. Her arms moved without instruction to extend and create a scooping motion ahead of her, and the orb deflected up and over her head.

Huh. I've never tried telekinesis on a spell before. That's not supposed to work.

The mage's jaw dropped open, and she grinned. "You didn't see that coming, did you, jerk-face?"

When he opened his mouth to respond to her taunt, she threw the knife with all the strength left in her body.

Bryant wasn't a fan of this particular wizard and wished Diana had finished him off in the other room. He had abandoned the tentacle and summoned twin blades that appeared to be made of bound energy. Thus armed, he closed the distance between them despite the agent's best efforts to keep him at bay. He had already fired a full magazine at the bastard and almost had his head chopped off while reloading.

We need to get some anti-magic bullets. Someone wants us dead or at least wants to protect magicals, but who? This is ridiculous.

Another swipe cut at his right shoulder, and he twisted to let it pass in front of him. He felt the blow coming from behind and thrust himself forward into a roll. The sword swished malevolently above his back and he narrowly evaded it. He came up firing again, but the mage intercepted each round smoothly with the blades. The best Bryant could do was maintain the stalemate.

He ground his teeth and searched for options. There was no way to force his opponent into Diana's crossfire, and even if he could get him near, she had her own target to deal with. All he had was the pistol as he'd given his knife to her. He decided it was the perfect time for crazy ideas and lowered his barrel to fire at the mage's feet.

The round ricocheted strangely, and he barely picked it off. Bryant smiled and emptied most of the magazine into the floor directly ahead of his opponent. Platinum-head backpedaled frantically as he swiped at the rounds and lost his cool. When one shot remained, the agent yanked the pistol up and aimed at the enemy's left shoulder. The mage couldn't get the blade up fast enough and he screamed in pain and disbelief as the bullet pierced his flesh and spun him to the side. Bryant reached for his reload only to discover he was out.

He sighed at the injustice of the universe and charged.

Diana's brain couldn't process the image before her. The knife she'd thrown hung in midair, and the man's hands—extended protectively in front of his face—apparently held it in place. He wiggled his fingers, and the blade turned, then slid toward her and gathered speed. Her locked mind seemed entirely separate from the hand she extended as if to welcome the weapon home. Unbelievably, the knife froze in place.

Holy hell. This is more than telekinesis.

A strange rushing sensation in her veins felt like the throb of power.

Diana and her foe could have been statues with their extended arms and straining muscles. The weapon shuddered between them and a strange hum emanated from it. Like an automation, it jerked an inch at a time as it rotated slowly toward the man. His eyes widened and she doubled down to lock her entire will on the idea of pushing it as far away as possible. It completed the turn and crawled away from her.

"This can't be happening!" he cried scant seconds before the blade rocketed forward and pierced his right shoulder. His defenses dropped, and it rammed home to the hilt. He screamed and sprawled clumsily, a hand clutched over the wound.

Diana rushed in and delivered a kick to his head.

And stay down.

She anchored herself with a boot on his chest and yanked the knife free—possibly a little harder than absolutely required—then wiped the hair out of her eyes and looked for her partner. A dozen or so feet across the room, he charged the mage she'd used as a punching bag earlier.

The pseudo-elf settled his stance to intercept the man's attack with the strange glowing swords he wielded. Not even Bryant would be quick enough to avoid serious injury.

No way, not going to happen.

Her mind raced as she considered the options but came up with only a single viable one. With a blood-curdling battle cry, she hurtled at the mage, her knife held high and ready to strike. She reached for the power she'd had a moment before and extended her off hand to smash his blades aside, but nothing happened. No magic, no force, no effect, not even her telekinesis. He aimed a sword, and a blast of power raced toward her.

She had already begun an evasive maneuver, having seen the attack before it materialized.

At least that's working. Whatever the hell "that" is.

Diana wheeled to her left and continued her run at a less advantageous angle. The man backed into the corner and brandished a weapon at each of them.

"Stalemate, humans. If you take a step closer, you will be too close to avoid the blasts."

She skidded to a stop. "All we have to do is wait, scum-bag. Your wounds will catch up with you eventually. When you pass out, the game's over." The blood that dripped on the floor at his feet confirmed it.

He laughed but sounded a little desperate. "Right now, my minions are killing your people. Soon, they'll do the same to you."

She exchanged a glance with Bryant, but his face revealed nothing. Apparently, he didn't know what was going on outside the room either. The mage laughed again.

"Fortunately, though, I don't need to wait." He muttered an arcane phrase and vanished. Both agents scampered back, fearful of a force blade attack they couldn't see coming. She focused inward again and discerned a sense of motion near the center of the room.

Without conscious thought, she pivoted and hurled the knife. Their adversary became visible again when he collapsed, and blood flowed freely from the fatal wound the knife had sliced in his neck. He looked at them in disbelief and accusation before his expression turned to hopelessness. His last act was to launch a frenzy of tentacles that tore the other mage apart and forced the agents to dive beyond their reach. When they had recovered enough to stand again, the tentacles had vanished and both mages were dead.

Bryant turned to her and brushed debris from his palms. "Well, that was fun."

She bent to retrieve the knife and returned it to him. "Fantastic. Let's do it again sometime."

He pointed at the bracelet on the floor beside the wannabe elf. "Do *not* touch that. We don't know where it's been." His lips twitched. "I have a question."

"Of course you do."

Bryant paused, gave her a serious look, then broke into a grin. "Didn't Taggart ask for prisoners? Weren't you supposed to shoot him in the leg?"

Diana groaned and nodded at the running joke. "You'd be surprised how often I hear that."

CHAPTER FIFTEEN

A giant explosion filled the screen as the rocket impacted the building. Rath's eyes widened. "Boom." Max barked his agreement.

The troll cackled madly and bounced around the cushions as Rambo defeated anyone who dared oppose him. Rath echoed every one of Stallone's lines and sounded more authentic as the movie progressed. Occasionally, the dog would lift his head from the couch next to him, *thump* his tail, and give an approving growl or yip.

Rath had a bowl of grapes, each almost a third his size, and ate them carefully. Diana had a serious-face when she said he shouldn't share them with the dog because it wasn't healthy for him. Max made a couple of halfhearted forays, but the troll yanked them away and scolded him. "No. Bad."

When the movie finished, Rath was energized. He searched for another but the TV wasn't working right—something about parental controls, whatever those were. Mastering this new language was taking some time. His normally agile mind slowed to a chilly pace when words meant many things.

Max is a name, an amount, and a kind of machine. Oh, and a food with delicious cheese.

It made hardly any sense.

The TV displayed a frozen John Rambo in fighting mode. "Fighting mode," Rath whispered and nodded. He turned to Max and proclaimed, "We need fighting mode." The dog barked. The troll thought the dog probably had issues with the language too but managed to make himself understood reasonably well.

Rath lowered himself down the arm of the couch and gripped the fabric tightly to keep from himself from falling. He ran into the kitchen and climbed onto the counter by jumping from one cabinet handle to the next. Near the top, he missed one and fell with a tiny scream before he landed on the soft side of Max, who lay on the floor below. He laughed. "Fun. Good Max."

After three more climbs and tumbling leaps down to the furry landing pad, he remembered his original plan and proceeded all the way to the counter. He looked left, then right, and finally found it. A small statuette of a cat with one paw outstretched rested near the stove. It looked wise and serious and was painted in glossy red and gold. He ran over and pulled down on the paw. It *clicked* softly, and a tiny bit of wood, sharpened on both ends, slid to a stop on the cat's extended paws. He took it out and set it aside, then continued to pump the arm until he had a bunch of them.

Too many to carry. Rath peered over the counter and met Max's eyes. He had learned a new word from the movie that was perfect for the moment. "Incoming." He pushed the toothpicks off as the dog scrambled away, his claws clicking on the tile floor. Rath moved to the nearby junk drawer and wedged his back against the cabinet, put his feet on the inside of the drawer, and pushed. He found the spool of string he sought after a short rummage. The troll lost several minutes while he examined the other items in that mysterious container, most of which defied any clear use. Once, he had seen the long plastic and metal device shoot flame from the end when the trigger was pulled, and if he were only a little bigger, it would be perfectly sized for him. He made a note to return later for a closer inspection, then grabbed the string and whistled, and Max returned to the kitchen.

Rath jumped down onto the dog's back and used his fur to descend to the floor. He gathered as many toothpicks as he could carry and took them into the living room. This was his favorite time of day when the sun shined through the windows and cast a rectangle of warmth and joy across the carpet. He arranged his materials inside the lighted area and wound the string around his body to determine how much he needed and added a little extra. His teeth cut the string easily into four equal strands of that length that he arranged in pairs on the carpet.

A thought struck him. "Thirsty." He scuttled back into the kitchen, took hold of the long, knotted cloth that dangled from the refrigerator handle, and pulled. When it refused to budge, he growled and tugged harder, then made running yanks until the latch finally released. He dropped the cloth and panted for a moment. *When I'm bigger, this will be easier.*

With a grin at the thought, he climbed inside. On the bottom were cans of orange juice, his favorite drink. They were only a little taller than him and Diana had called them airplane-sized. Beside them rested a stack of thin straws. He took one of each, rolled the can out of the refrigerator, and jumped after it. Max, who watched with amused doggy eyes, sidestepped into the door to close it for him. Rath nodded. "Max. Good. Next, you learn to open."

The dog barked at him. Rath pushed the can into the living room, positioned it, popped the top, and took a long drink through the straw. He sighed happily. "Now, work."

He picked up several of the toothpicks and set them aside muttering, "Later." Max regarded him quizzically, his head cocked to the side, and the troll realized he'd spoken in his own language. He repeated it in English. The dog's tail thumped once, and he lowered his head to his paws to watch.

Rath broke each toothpick in half with wrenching snaps. When he had finished, there were enough to cover most of the strings. He set the first one across a pair of the tiny ropes a little down from the top and tied it in place with a knot on each string with the pointed end facing out. The next was reversed so the point faced inward. He tied that one immediately below the first. Rath sighed. "Will take long. Boring, but necessary." He snapped his fingers. "Rambo again."

The troll bounced up, found the remote, and started the movie once more. Before it was half over, he had finished his project. He arranged the two bandoliers across his chest and rotated them to tie the ends at the proper length. Finally, he looked down and admired his handiwork.

"Good. Is good." Max snored softly, and Rath smiled. "Max. Good. Rest between battles."

He took the remaining toothpicks and broke one in half. With a piece in each hand, he swung them in bold strikes from below and from the side, and then straight stabbing motions. The troll nodded and set them aside before he retrieved one of the unbroken ones. He wielded it two-handed, stabbed with it like a spear, and practiced the sort of blocks he'd seen on the kung fu channel. The tiny creature laughed with real delight.

No parental control of kung fu.

He couldn't figure out how to carry the knives, so he decided to be satisfied with the spear for the moment. Rath took a long drink of his juice, then ran back to the kitchen and experimented to find the right distance from which to look at his reflection in the oven glass. It would do, for now.

"Put down your weapons and prepare to be judged."

Would look better with armor. Maybe tomorrow.

He crossed to the other room and went to Max.

Time to train.

The dog woke up as the troll climbed up his fur. He raised his head and gave Rath the bounce he needed to vault onto his back. The troll found a comfortable position and grabbed Max's collar with his left hand, then made experimental stabs with the weapon in his right.

"Max. Kitchen. Go."

The dog gave a soft bark but didn't move. Rath sighed

and stood. He climbed up over the head and walked down the Borzoi's long nose to look him in the eye. He pointed at him, then at himself. "Max. Rath. Partners. Must train." The dog blinked, and Rath was satisfied with what he saw. He scrambled back to his previous position.

"Max. Kitchen. Go." The dog lurched to his feet and jogged to the kitchen. Rath had ridden on his back before but always lying down with both hands twined in his smooth coat. This was a different skill. He grinned.

Getting better.

"Too slow. Max. Bedroom. Go." They dashed out of the kitchen. When the dog reached the stairs, the troll added his second hand to the collar and barely managed to not fly off as they tromped excitedly to the second level.

Meant downstairs bedroom. Need to be more clear.

Max did not need to know about his mistake, though, so he simply said, "Max. Good."

He guided his mount to the edge of Diana's bed, which was large and comfy and covered with a thick blanket. His mind worked on strategies for attacking with a partner. "Max. Head up. Go." The dog raised his head and made a bridge to the bed with his pointed nose. Rath bounced a few times in thought. He smiled and clapped. He pointed at Max. "Rocket tube." He pointed at himself. "Rocket."

The dog's expression didn't change.

Yes. Language troubles.

The troll pantomimed what he wanted, and the dog's tail wagged. Rath climbed back onto his nose and crouched, and Max lowered his head gently.

"Max. Launch. Go." The Borzoi's neck snapped up, and his passenger was thrown in an arc toward the center of the bed. He tucked and rolled at the apex, held his weapon out to one side, and landed in perfect balance, the spear in guard position before him. He growled at the invisible enemies arrayed in a circle around him and leapt to the attack. Several minutes later, his foes had been vanquished and Rath was exhausted. He crawled to the edge of the bed, and the Borzoi stretched his neck out. Rath made it onto his nose and hugged it. "Max. Good. Living room. Slow. Go."

The little warrior was snoring softly by the time they arrived. Max rolled him gently into the corner of the couch and climbed up beside him, his head inches from the troll's sleeping form. Rath stirred in his sleep and yawned. "Partners. Good."

The dog's tail thumped once before he, too, succumbed to the wisdom of resting between battles.

CHAPTER SIXTEEN

The lead agent watched as his team underwent a close-combat training session. The morning had been spent on the rifle range, where everyone had performed with the same excellence they always did. Diana had proven to be a match for anyone other than Brenner and Johnson, the preternaturally skilled snipers. Bryant had cautioned the team against using magic, without providing an explanation. He wanted a clear assessment of Diana's mundane skills before moving on to the magical ones.

She sparred with Davis, the ninja she'd temporarily replaced, armed with stiff rubber Bowie knives. They each used classic positioning with the offhand blade forward and pointed at the opponent and the dominant hand knife reversed along the forearm to allow forehand slashes and backhand stabs. Davis made use of his longer arms to frustrate her attempts to get close. The rules prohibited anything other than knife fighting, or she'd doubtless use some of her MMA blocks and kicks to eliminate his advantage.

Diana attacked and had to duck as he swung at her head with his main blade, then stumbled back as the other stabbed at her. Her shout carried across the room and engendered a round of laughter from those not engaged in their own bouts. "Damn it to hell, man, what are you—part giraffe?"

She dashed in again and thrust with her off hand, but Davis delivered a brilliant one-two move. He slid to the outside of the strike to sweep his main blade in a block, then knelt to lunge up with the other. It looked awkward, but the blow would have cut deep into her triceps to disable her arm at a minimum and almost certainly cost her the fight.

The woman sighed and lowered her arms. Her expression was as upset as Bryant had ever seen it, but it had an edge of recrimination that told him it was self-directed. She pushed the frustration aside with a visible effort and turned to Davis. "Will you teach me?"

He nodded and started to do exactly that.

Taggart's voice sounded from behind his right shoulder. "She handles herself well."

Bryant swiveled to his superior who stood barely a step away. "You still have those ninja skills, boss." He turned back to face the fighters. "Yes, she does. I thought she would lose it there for a second, but we haven't managed to push her that far." He paused, then grinned. "Yet. I'm sure I can get there eventually."

Taggart laughed. "It's true, there are few people on Earth with the ability to be more annoying than you."

The agent waited, but his boss didn't continue. "So, did you come down only to watch?"

He grunted.

"Bad news then?"

The other man sighed. "It seems that's all we get these days, isn't it? Yes. The investigation team we sent in after you cleared the place found a number of artifacts in addition to the one the mage used. All but a few are powerful enough to be of concern on their own. That collection in one place is downright frightening." Taggart intruded into his peripheral vision, holding a phone. On it was a symbol that looked like it had been carved into metal. It was a pair of intersecting figure-eights arranged in an X shape. A glyph sat within each oval.

Bryant shrugged. "It's pretty, if a little simplistic. Where did you find it?"

"In the remains of the desk in the upstairs office. We would never have discovered it, the agent said, except that one of the blasts from your fight destroyed its hiding place."

He laughed. "Go me. That lady sucked."

"They all suck." He stowed the device in an inside jacket pocket. "The code breakers are working on it now, but there are no records in our history or in anything the Oricerans have provided that corresponds exactly to this image. Basically, we've never seen its like before."

"What are you not telling me?"

Taggart sighed. "It bears a resemblance to a...well, a cult might be the best word for it, from a while ago. The followers of Rhazdon."

Holy Hell. There's a name I haven't heard in a while.

"Which is definitely a worry, I guess. I'm unclear as to why, though. Is there something other than the image that's relevant?" He clapped his hands and barked support as one of his people made an impressive double stab.

The SAC's voice was more serious than Bryant would've liked and sucked all the fun out of the moment. "This was etched into a coin."

He sighed. "And there's never a reason to make only one coin."

"You have it in one."

"Dammit."

His boss clapped him on the shoulder. "That does about sum it up, doesn't it? Bring Sheen over once you're done." The agent turned and watched him enter the unmarked door that connected this boarded-up, soundproofed, and highly secure office park warehouse to their base through an underground tunnel.

Damn, damn, and double damn.

Diana had showered and dressed in what had become her usual training uniform—sneakers, jeans, and an FBI Academy t-shirt. Only the SAC felt obligated to dress up most days.

Taggart greeted her as she sank into the seat across from him. "So, you got stabbed."

She shook her head. "Seriously, he must've spent his formative years hanging on a rack or something." She grinned. "Knife fighting isn't my strong suit, but I'm getting better."

"That is why we train."

Bryant lowered himself into the chair beside hers. "You haven't made it to a session in a while, boss. Maybe you should go a few rounds with our newest recruit."

The SAC shook his head. "Those days are behind me. I'll stick with things that kill from long range, thanks." His chair squeaked as he rotated back to Diana. "How do you think the raid went?"

She took a second to order her thoughts. "The initial strategy was sound and worked well. They were reasonably easy to take down in the chaos. It helped that they weren't particularly good at their jobs."

"You get what you pay for," Bryant interjected, "and that group comes cheap."

Diana glared briefly at him and continued. "It might've been better to bring in a second team, so we would have had more support up and down." Taggart nodded. "But from what Bryant told me and from what I encountered, it probably wouldn't have mattered. The whole thing was a setup. We're merely lucky they underestimated us."

The SAC nodded again. "We are indeed."

She frowned. "How did we not know it was a trap?"

"The analysts are working that angle right now. Clearly, we were fed information, but we're still not exactly sure how. Our systems gather stuff from all over, and then they do the initial sifting and matching. There's too much data coming in for humans to take care of that part. Somewhere along the line, false intel got in and made it through the system. We will find the hole and either plug it or turn it to our advantage, rest assured."

Diana nodded, despite the unsatisfying answer. Taggart

stood and gestured for the other two to rise. "Let's relocate to the core. There are some things you should see."

A brown-haired, skinny tech awaited them in the core, which had privacy mode activated with the wall panels fully extended. They all donned their AR glasses, and he called up a display on the center table. On one side was a strange, etched coin with interlocking ovals and some symbols. On the right side, half the area was devoted to blown-up versions of the images, each in its own separate square. The other portion showed an analysis in progress, similar to facial recognition, which apparently tested the symbols against pictographic languages.

"What are we looking at?" Taggart asked the tech.

His voice made her subtract a few years from her guess at his age. "An ancient Dwarven language at the moment. The systems work from the most likely matches down to the more obscure ones. It's run for twelve hours and hasn't found one yet. We'll move on to records from Earth once the Oriceran languages are complete."

Bryant leaned forward to peer at the symbol. "What's it made of?"

The tech pressed some buttons and an analysis drew in on top of the coin's image. "Thirty percent gold, sixteen percent copper, and the rest are substances our computers don't recognize."

"So, Oriceran, then."

"We've reached out to an expert," the man confirmed. "We should have the data into the system soon."

Diana pointed at small raised bumps at the cardinal points of the coin. "Are those significant?"

Taggart and the tech both smiled, and the latter answered. "Good catch, Agent Sheen. Hidden under there are tiny chips of power stone."

She frowned. "So, the coin is an artifact?"

The tech shrugged. "We haven't definitively verified that. It could be simply a power source or even a trigger for a different artifact rather than one in itself—kind of like a portable battery."

Bryant's voice was dark. "Or a detonator." The tech assistant paled at the suggestion. Diana's stomach didn't like the idea either.

"What about the glyphs, other than pattern recognition?" She pointed again. "Do you have anything on them?"

"All we're sure of is that they're so smooth that the coin is most likely cast from a mold."

She looked at him, and he raised his hands placatingly.

"I know, that's not helpful. We will continue to work on the problem. Hopefully, we'll have something more soon."

Taggart thanked him and secured the room after his departure.

"Our working hypothesis is that these are membership tokens. It's essentially a covering all the bases perspective, as it assumes that this is not an isolated incident and there is a group of connected people at its core."

The two agents nodded simultaneously. She exhaled to discharge her frustration at the lack of clarity. "So, where do we go from here?"

Their boss smiled. "Same as always, Agent Sheen. We

let the techs do their work. We heal, we train, and we investigate every angle we can think of."

"We could case Brownstone and steal some anti-magic bullets," Bryant suggested.

"And get our asses kicked. His reputation is real." Diana rolled her eyes at him. "So, hurry up and wait."

Taggart laughed. "You're fitting right in." He withdrew a small case from under the table and pressed his hand against the sensor on the top before he dialed in a code. The latches released with a synchronized *clack*. The container held a pair of smaller boxes with their names on them.

Bryant received his with a smirk. "Presents, boss? You shouldn't have."

The other man's reply was good-natured. "Shut the hell up, Bry." He gestured at the packages. "It seems our enemies are fond of using illusions. These will help with that."

Diana opened her box to find a metallic broken-circle bracelet. It shone silver with balls on each end to help keep it secure on the wrist and was covered with engravings. She held it up to the light but couldn't make sense of them. "Is that a language?"

Taggart chuckled. "Probably. All I can say for sure is that we had to get them made on Oriceran, they were very expensive, and they're attuned to your auras, whatever that means."

She narrowed her eyes. "How did you manage that? Has Bryant been stalking me again?"

He gave her a thin smile. "Remember the VIP who visited a while back?"

Diana's brow wrinkled. She'd taken no particular notice of the person at the time since the woman had been escorted by Taggart.

"She took care of the attunement. These will give you a warning when an illusion is present by growing colder the nearer you get to it."

"How do they do that?"

He shrugged. "Something about different kinds of magic having unique signatures that can be detected. It's actually less complicated than being able to detect all types of magic. Or so they said."

Bryant laughed. "Having someone else make gear for our agents will piss Kayleigh right the hell off."

Taggart nodded and grinned. "Kayleigh is aware and is planning to collaborate with the creators on several projects. So is Emerson." An authoritative tone entered his voice. "Okay. Break time's over. Back to work."

***

Bryant slipped through the dilapidated entry to the Stagecoach Bar. It was a dive populated by middle-level disreputables from both Earth and Oriceran. He spotted two gangsters and a suspected arms dealer in a booth together and made a mental note. His contact waited at a table in the far corner, her back to the wall. She hid her pointed ears and long white hair under a watch cap, but there was no missing the peculiar darkness of her skin that marked her as a kind of Drow Elf.

Kienka had been one of the first to cross over, she'd explained, and had made a lucrative living ever since by trading on the margins of legality. She professed to be unconcerned with the nature or purposes of her clients, only in their ability to pay. Bryant slid a purple Crown Royal bag across the table as he sat in the booth opposite her. He had liberated all the power stones he could find at the raid scene, except for the ones obvious enough to be missed. The woman only accepted payment from him in magical items.

"Very nice, Bryant." She drew out the T, which made his name sound vaguely threatening. "What do you need?" On another woman, the voice would've been sultry. On her, it called to some instinct deep inside that made him want to run.

"Another shield and something to replace the light charm."

She chuckled darkly and hefted the bag. "This will cover the first but not the second. Are you sure you wish to be in debt to me?"

Bryant had little tolerance for her games tonight. "Whatever. You know I'm good for it. How long?"

"A week for the shield, another three for the offensive spell."

"Will it be as powerful as the light charm?"

She nodded. "At a minimum."

"See you in a week, then." He turned and strode toward the door. There was an argument at the arms dealer's table, and one of the gang members tried to draw a gun from his shoulder holster, only to be held back by the other. Bryant shook his head with a sickly smile.

There is more opportunity than ever before with the worlds coming together and these idiots are still obsessed with turf wars.

When he cleared the door, he sent a text through a series of ARES proxy servers that would hide the source to inform the FBI that two persons of interest were meeting with a person of much greater interest. He thought for a moment about warning Kienka that the authorities might show up but had little doubt she was already gone.

CHAPTER SEVENTEEN

Taggart stepped out of the Uber he'd caught halfway across town from the ARES base and stared at the Capitol Building with its instantly recognizable rotunda that reached for the sky.

Sometimes, all this need for secrecy is damn annoying.

He gathered with the crowd that prepared to take one of the regularly scheduled tours of the landmark and paid for his ticket. The drone of the tour guide faded into the background. He'd heard it all before. A search of his memory revealed that this was actually his third trip inside as a tourist. His clothes were a far cry from his daily uniform but blended well with the tourists in the group. Especially the Capitals baseball cap. He wore glasses with thick lenses and shuffled a little as he walked.

They entered the inner lobby and he stepped aside as if heading for the marked restroom. Once out of sight, he tapped his ID card on a dark panel beside an unmarked door and quickly slipped through when the lock released.

Several twists and turns followed along a hallway that he imagined most senators never saw but their aides and interns were very familiar with. Finally, he located the next unmarked door he sought.

Seventh on the left.

He tapped his ID again and the door opened to reveal a small conference room about twice the size of his office. Another entrance was visible on the far wall.

The space was sparse, merely a brown oval table and six chairs, a large display mounted on one wall, and a low credenza opposite it. Taggart crossed to it, placed his hand on the side of the carafe resting on the top, and smiled. The coffee on Capitol Hill was some of the best he'd ever had.

Gotta keep the elected representatives well caffeinated so they can dole out the tax dollars and fight over image rather than substance. He snorted. *Thank God ARES doesn't have to deal with any of that nonsense.*

A stack of heavy mugs was artfully arranged beside the carafe, and he took the top one, careful not to disturb the rest. He pressed the button to release the life-giving liquid and inhaled the scent as it filled his cup.

Amazing, as always.

He had barely settled into a seat along the side of the table when the door opened and Aaron Finley hustled in. The junior senator from Rhode Island was in the second year of his six-year term but had been in military intelligence during his twenty-year Army stint. ARES had done its due diligence and requested him when a rare opening on the oversight council had appeared.

Taggart rose and circled the table to shake the man's

hand and gripped his forearm gently. "Senator, always good to see you."

"Carson, good to see you too. How many times do I have to tell you to quit using my title? We're both soldiers, for fuck's sake."

He laughed. "At least one more time, I guess, Aaron. You know how it is. Memory fades as you get older."

The other man shook his head. "Sure, sure. Just so you're aware, I've already taken a vow never to play cards with you, you devious bastard."

Senator Finley still looked strong, although he'd clearly put on a few pounds since his active duty days. His hair was close-cropped in a military style and he walked with perfect posture and abundant energy. He drew his own cup of coffee and sat in the chair diagonal from the other man at the head of the table. "So, what's up?"

"Status report, mainly."

The man nodded and leaned back to go into what Taggart thought of as recording mode. His prodigious memory was one of the reasons he'd had such a successful military intelligence career. It was also why he now filled the role of go-between, as he could faithfully relate the concerns of ARES and the oversight council to one another. His integrity was such that neither party feared bias.

"You're aware of the recent encounters?"

Finley nodded.

"Good. That saves time. We found considerable information that appears to confirm our fear that an organized group is behind these, and several other, incidents."

Finley leaned forward again and seemed concerned. "Do you see this as an escalating threat?"

Taggart rocked his hand in a gesture of uncertainty. "It's hard to tell. From what the investigators have given me, I'd say they're still ramping up, gathering material and intel. Something is definitely on the rear burner, though, and getting ready to move to the front."

"Okay. Not great, but not critical. Gotcha."

The SAC retrieved his phone and pressed a few buttons to call up a silent edited montage of Diana's training sessions. He set it before Finley, pressed play, and spoke over the video. "Agent Diana Sheen is proving to be everything we hoped she'd be. She is strategically and tactically minded, unafraid to get into a scrap, and a natural leader." He paused for a moment's consideration, then decided he'd keep her magic abilities in-house.

And I definitely won't mention the troll.

"She'll do a great job setting up the Pittsburgh office."

The senator tapped the table with cupped fingers. "Now that's a project I'm excited to hear about. Tell me more." By all accounts, Finley was fully committed to ARES' mission and concurred that geographic expansion was vital to ensure quick responses to events. Office locations had been chosen for proximity to sites likely to have magical problems, either due to nearby Kemanas or based on a statistical distribution analysis of previous incidents. Pittsburgh was a particular hotspot that met both criteria.

"The Cube is up and running, right on schedule and accepting prison transfers. There is even a regular drill to make sure everything is functioning the way it's supposed to."

The senator grunted. "The Council will want to tour it."

Taggart laughed. "Of course, we can accommodate you and your august fellows, Senator Finley." He enjoyed jabbing the senator as much as the other man enjoyed poking him. "It's probably safest to do it singly, though."

He didn't respond, so the SAC plowed on. "We have the cover business up and running. It's a co-working space located in a building that used to house a newspaper."

Finley frowned. "Isn't that riskier than normal?"

"We think the trade-off is worth it." He shrugged. "It'll give some of our support staff and specialists better cover for entering and exiting the facility. Plus, we'll install wiring during the remodel to keep a close eye on the people in the spaces above. It's a new option, and we'll see how it goes. We bought the building, so if anything becomes problematic, we can simply make the necessary changes."

The senator sipped his coffee and Taggart took a larger pull of his own to soothe his dry throat and looked longingly at the carafe.

Too much talking, not enough shooting. I gotta get out more.

"Underground construction has proceeded for some time under the guise of river dredging and infrastructure improvements. We've tapped into the city's light rail system in order to travel undetected. Plus, we have direct access to the Kemana ready to finish once the politics are ironed out."

Finley looked pleased. "It sounds like that project is well in hand. You know how important it is to our future plans, obviously. If you can find a sustainable model to duplicate, it'll shorten the overall rollout schedule considerably.

Given the other stuff you've shared, it sounds like we need it."

Taggart drew a deep breath. What had come before was all within the normal bounds of their planning. Bryant's idea would be significantly far out on the proverbial limb. "On that topic, I have another new wrinkle to add."

His companion motioned for him to continue.

"Pittsburgh has been overrun by magical troublemakers for a while. It's become a little like the lawless days of the Wild West, with the best bounty hunters in the area focused on Philly and Boston and lower-level operatives unable to handle the load. Our team will have to do some cleanup work first—maybe even on an ongoing basis."

The senator frowned. "Isn't that sort of visibility a serious security concern?"

"We think we have a fix for that." Taggart smiled and unfastened the top of his shirt to reveal a necklace supporting a green pendant. "Try not to freak out." He pressed the stone and whispered, *"Procidat."* The tingle that spread through his face as his features changed felt like arachnid feet and made him shudder. He had practiced in a mirror and knew he now appeared stunningly average, another unremarkable person in the crowd.

Finley gasped. With a laugh, the SAC deactivated the illusion. "It's a little something our magic techs have worked on."

The senator was clearly impressed, and excitement radiated from him. "Can we use that to impersonate people?"

"That was the first question I asked, too. Not yet, they say, but they're working on it. No timeline, unfortunately."

He leaned back in his chair with a frown and folded his arms. "We can't have everything, I guess. I bet your non-magic techs are pissed."

And how.

"Let's say they consider it a personal challenge to create a hologram-based version. It's early days and they've failed more often than not but seem well motivated."

"A little competition is good for the soul. That's what my drill instructor always used to argue before he made us race back to camp at the end of a march."

"You got to march? We had to run the whole way. The military's gone soft since I got out." The two men shared a laugh.

Taggart drained the rest of his mug. "So what we're thinking is a second cover business—a bounty hunter agency. They'll wear masks or use the amulets, or both if the occasion demands. We can put some false pieces on the weapons, too. Basically, we do what is needed to make it look unrelated."

The senator nodded. "I'll kick it up the chain but I'm sure you'll get approval. Have you reached out to the leaders in the Kemana?"

The SAC shook his head. "I'll let Agent Sheen take care of that. Getting thrown into the fire is the best way to forge a weapon, right?"

"You're spending a lot of effort on her."

He nodded. "She's worth it. She'll be a star. And besides, Bryant will watch over her and set the stage for more new locations in the northeast and mid-Atlantic."

"How is that smarmy bastard?"

"He hasn't changed. He strikes sparks off Diana whenever they're together and keeps everyone around him sharp with his magic powers of annoyance."

Finley laughed. "I had doubts when you said he would be in charge, but he seems to have come into his own, too. You're a good judge of character."

Taggart smiled. "You're only saying that because I recommended you for the Council."

"It may be, may be." The man rose and looked at his watch, a duplicate of the one Taggart and his agents wore. "I have to be somewhere in five minutes, so I'd better get going."

"One last thing," the SAC said and slid a box across to him. "This is new tech—an anti-illusion bracelet. Yours is designed to look like a fitness tracker so it can't be connected to us. It'll grow cold if there are illusions around you."

There's no point in mentioning that we had someone spy on him to attune it.

The senator opened the box, admired the bracelet, and slipped it on. "Quick test?"

Taggart nodded, whispered the phrase to activate his amulet, and steeled himself against the crawling spiders. Finley shook his wrist. "Cold is right. Good work, as always, Special Agent."

"Enjoy your meeting, Senator." He smiled, checked his own watch, and made some quick calculations. There was more than enough time for another cup of coffee before he needed to rejoin the tour. He refilled his mug and retrieved his phone to access the secure apps and review the senator's calendar. Finley did indeed have a meeting...of a sort.

Lunch with the very attractive lobbyist representing one of the countries in the Middle East. Taggart shook his head.

It's fine to look, Senator, but don't touch. Your wife wouldn't like it. And in this world, there are eyes everywhere.

After a moment's reflection, he sent a text to his analysts requesting a human review of the data that would be collected by the senator's watch during his meeting.

Someone's always watching.

CHAPTER EIGHTEEN

I*diots. They're lucky they're dead.*

The elf was incensed but retained a calm exterior. Nehlan considered himself a master of control, which was one of the reasons he had risen to the position of authority he held as Second-in-command of the Remembrance. Still, if they had not already met their demise at the hands of the humans, he would have given Insela, Giandeh, and Lienne an experience of what true pain felt like. Insela had been Giandeh's underling, and Giandeh and Lienne his. The loss left him with only a single agent on Earth.

He shook his head and sighed. "Your deaths were too easy."

His expression grim, he stood and set his book on the table beside the wingback leather chair. The room was all wood, the natural growth of the tree that made up the structure of his home. It was small, which fitted the image he projected to his community, but richly appointed. He gestured at the scrying window that had replayed the last minutes of his minions' lives and the images vanished.

A second wave summoned a mirror, and he confirmed that his jade robes and black shirt and trousers were properly pressed. His feet were bare, as they always were in this place. He circled his arms and muttered an incantation, and a portal appeared, the connection to the place he truly considered home. He stepped through onto the receiving platform and the doorway slid closed behind him. Comfortable sandals awaited him, and he slipped into them and advanced through his domain.

The room he entered was formed completely out of dark wood and was hidden deep within an untamed forest. An errant portal had deposited him there many decades before, and he had chosen to take it as a sign. It had required countless trips to convince the obstinate forest to bend to his will, but he had finally done it. His base of operations now had several bedrooms, abundant training spaces, multiple kitchens, and all the other requirements of life. Only a trusted few knew of its existence. The wooden borders at the top and bottom of each wall were carved with intricate runes to conceal his home from the uninvited and prevent those few he permitted access from identifying its location. It was his refuge, his favorite retreat, and his ultimate defense.

He traced his fingers along the etched walls as he walked to verify the strength of the wards he had created.

I am safe. No one will find me here.

Nehlan sighed.

Unfortunately, if these fools continue to fail me, I will have to leave my protections behind and take care of these upstart humans myself.

His brow furrowed and his fine features twisted into a

snarl. Finally, he reached the room that only his closest lieutenants and superiors ever saw. It was triply warded, as it was the single area an outsider could enter without his participation so long as they held one of the coins and knew the proper invocations.

Those below him had no similar strongholds, and while his own superior likely did, he chose to travel rather than reveal it.

In time, I will be fully trusted. And if he will not do so of his own volition, perhaps an opportunity will need to be created.

He smiled thinly to himself. It would be unexpected indeed were he to rebel against his superior, the one who brought him into the Remembrance.

Which will work to my benefit should that moment arrive.

The elf invested an hour each day in intense training, varying weapons and tactics for the inevitable day when he would need to call upon them for advancement. Or survival.

One of the bracelets he wore on his right arm warmed and announced incoming magic. Nehlan stepped to the side of the room and stood against the wall. He positioned his left arm behind his back and touched the small container of deadly pellets that lay an instant away through a small slit in his robe. A portal formed, and his immediate subordinate, a dwarf with black hair and a close-trimmed beard, stepped through. Although smaller than he, Kergar's presence would be powerful for someone twice his size. He turned and made a small bow, and his arms swept to the side. "You asked for me, and I am here. At your service, master."

Nehlan's lips twitched. His subordinate believed that

such shows of obsequiousness would cause him to let down his guard.

Not in this lifetime.

"Thank you for responding so quickly to my summons. Please join me for some refreshment." Without waiting for a response, he turned and strode from the room. The house was kept by a pair of servants, a human husband and wife kidnapped from their world long ago. He had cast layers of spells to ensure their loyalty and servitude and to deny them even the thought of betrayal. They watched over his home while he was away and ensured that it would be ready for guests at a moment's notice.

He entered the dining room, an opulent space with tapestries on the walls and an elegant candelabra that illuminated the polished surface of a table that could comfortably seat ten. A light repast of fruits and vegetables from the surrounding forest was placed in front of two chairs set at a diagonal from each other. He chose the one facing the door, which forced his guest to sit with his back exposed. The slight nod he received told him Kergar was fully aware of the play.

"Please, eat while we converse." He took a small bite of a vegetable and waved the woman forward from where she stood in the corner. She poured a golden liquid into crystal glasses at each of their places, then retreated.

His guest sampled the wine and exhaled an appreciative sigh. "Excellent, as always. Your own?"

Nehlan nodded. "From the sterro fruit that grows nearby." In truth, it grew far away and was a nuisance to harvest and transport. However, keeping his friendly enemies in ignorance was well worth the effort.

His guest nodded and threw an arrogant look at the humans. "I don't know why you choose to have them in your home." His distaste was clear.

The elf laughed. "It amuses me to see my enemies become my servants." He let that thought hang for a moment before continuing. "To business, however. The soldiers you contracted to eliminate the humans failed. Miserably."

Kergar winced and patted his lips with a cloth before he responded. "The abilities of the humans were indeed unexpected. Our people were trapped between competing imperatives—effectiveness and secrecy."

"They chose poorly."

The dwarf shrugged. "A legitimate criticism, master. However, any might have done the same. There was nothing in our knowledge of the humans that suggested the magical abilities they demonstrated. I assumed Lienne, Insela, and Giandeh would be equal to the task."

Nehlan shook his head. "And there is your flaw. You underestimate them at every turn. In this, you are not unique." He stood and began to pace the room. "When we first started setting the stage for this undertaking, we sent scouts aplenty. They returned and told us we had nothing to fear. We took their words to heart and made plans based upon them—plans that took time to come to fruition. And what happened?" He raised a hand, the palm open toward the ceiling. "For the humans, the passing of time brought great change. The discovery of magic, the discovery of our artifacts, and the integration of those with power into the species. Some of our scouts started families with the humans they were supposed to watch to create hybrids with powers we recognize and some with powers we have never seen."

He turned back to the table and slid his hands into the waist pockets of his robes. "So, we are faced with the truth that reality is different than we anticipated, and yet we still assume humans are weak and powerless. You made this very assumption. I hope you will not make the same mistake again."

Kergar flinched at the threat in his tone. "You may be assured, master, that this lesson has been learned."

Nehlan stared at him for a long time, testing his resolve. His underling did not look away, and finally, the elf nodded. "Fine. We will relegate this failure to the past and speak of it no more." He took his seat again, lifted his wine to his lips, and gestured at the other man's plate. "Do eat some of the sterro. It is divine." He ate some of his own, and the dwarf did the same. "So, then, why were your plans inadequate to stop them before they could employ their magic?"

The lines on Kergar's face deepened as he frowned. "You will recall, master, that I did express concern about the humans we chose to hire as our pawns, both to destroy the transport and to protect the house."

The elf nodded.

"My fears were well-founded. We bought the best available, but those who are truly extraordinary have already been contracted by others seeking power and status on Earth."

Nehlan frowned, and rage stirred.

Others indeed.

They would see both worlds under their control,

reserving the choicest parts for themselves. He suppressed his anger with a thin smile.

Once the humans are dealt with, we will move into the end game, and then we will see who gets what.

He shook his annoyance off. "This does not make us look good in the eyes of those above. Not good at all." The dwarf finished his wine with a nod, and Nehlan waved the human servant forward to refill it. "I see only a single option at this moment. Have you seen it as well?"

Kergar gulped half the liquid and set his wineglass down carefully. His face twisted again "Yes, master. I will have to take care of this myself."

"Indeed, you shall. There's no moment like the present." He gestured again, and the human man came to escort his subordinate back to the portal room.

Nehlan drank his wine with a satisfied smirk. The sterro fruit was indeed the delicacy he had promised but was also a potent poison that built up in the body over time. The wines he served all contained an ingredient that delayed the onset of the poison, but when sufficient time passed, guests at his table would find their magic dwindling, consumed from within by the tiny seeds hidden in the fruit's flesh.

It had taken time and focus, but he'd finally found the right spells to render himself impervious to the poison—and better yet, to harness its magic to his purposes. Once the host died, the seeds would congeal and form a stone that carried the being's power. He thought of the jewelry in the locked and warded case in his bedroom—a matching set of bracelets, rings, and a necklace that were already one-third adorned with power taken from those he'd killed. Someday, events would see it completed, and then he would truly be a force to be reckoned with.

As he often told his lieutenants, deal with the now, but always, *always* keep one eye focused on the distant future.

Kergar stepped out of the portal with a curse. "The arrogant bastard thinks he can condescend to me? Well, after these humans are dead, we'll see what we'll see. Perhaps *his* boss finds him as annoying as I do." That idea brought a grin to his face as he opened the door from the barren back room that was his landing space and entered the main room of the bar.

The Twisted Lizard was a dingy place, one of many fronts he had set up at the outset of the operation. A human behind the bar nodded, and Kergar whispered a word under his breath that pierced the illusion to reveal Enthan's true features. He swept his gaze across the room, which was filled primarily with his lieutenants in disguise as well as some purely human retainers and hangers-on. He gestured at the front door and spoke a word, and the door slammed, startling those arranged at the square tables that occupied the majority of the space. The few at the bar did not react. They were his best and knew his mercurial moods well. He could still surprise them on occasion for a laugh, but more often than not, he enjoyed the fact that with them, he didn't have to pretend—unlike with the pretentious asshole who currently made his life difficult.

He raised his voice. "We're in operational mode as of now, people. Our first foray was a failure due to the weakness of those we sent. It's time for us to show these foolish governmental drones the truth of their inferiority." He gestured to two of his lieutenants at the bar and pointed at a side door. "A free round for everyone, Enthan."

The room cheered as his pair of underlings closed the door behind them and cut the small office off from the rest of the bar. Kergar trudged behind the old desk and sat in the worn chair behind it.

Worn. Everything about this place is worn. Everything about this planet is worn. It needs to be razed and created anew.

His lieutenants sat in the equally threadbare chairs across the desk. They operated exclusively as a pair and had been with him for some time. Drisnan was the leader of the two, by virtue of his quick intellect, and was an experienced wizard. Cresnan was the muscle, a rough-skinned Kilomea who towered over his partner. Their long experience together led to an unspoken understanding that made them formidable foes.

"It's like we told you, boss," the larger one said. "We need to take out the whole organization. Set up an incident —maybe blow up some buildings—and kill them when they respond." His partner nodded, a bloodthirsty grin on his face.

Kergar spread his hands. "I would like nothing better, believe me. But it is still too soon for the Remembrance to come to light. We must continue to move in the shadows. So, here's a different idea." He gestured and an image appeared in midair, a frozen moment from the battle that had claimed Insela and Giandeh. Two humans were present, a tall man and a shorter woman. Each had displayed power during the fight, and the man had also defeated Lienne on his own. They were, in their own way, almost as considerable a danger as the pair before him.

"Perhaps the thing to do is to attack the head and weaken the body. These two were the most effective in the battle at the house. Which should be dealt with first?"

The mind and the muscle looked at each other and grinned. "The woman, of course." A predatory gleam shone in their eyes.

Kergar clapped briskly. "It is decided, then. Find her, isolate her, and kill her."

CHAPTER NINETEEN

Diana was tying the final knot of her gi when Lisa finally arrived. "About time. I thought you would be lame and chicken out."

The woman dropped her gym bag on the bench next to Diana. "In your dreams. My chat with Steve ran long."

"I thought you looked a little breathless and excited."

Lisa laughed. "Shut up. Just because you can't get a date is no reason to make fun of me."

"Like I need a reason to make fun of you." She laughed as her friend stuck her tongue out. "So, is he proving to be everything you thought he'd be, based on his oh so used-car-salesman online profile?"

Diana took a pair of sweatpants to the face as her companion hurled them from inside her bag in a snappy motion. "Yes, he is, thank you very much. Better, even."

"Have you actually been on a date with him, or are you only cyber lovers?" She raised and lowered her eyebrows suggestively.

Lisa stopped pulling her exercise gear out and pointed a

finger at her. "One more wisecrack out of you, woman, and I'll throw something heavy at you." She sat and pulled off the thick-heeled trendy shoes she wore. "Like this. Although it would be a tragedy to get blood on something so beautiful."

Diana grinned. "I'll pretend you're talking about my face, rather than the shoe. When will I get to meet him, so I can tell him all your secrets?"

"That depends. Will you actually join me at the Beagle at some point or constantly turn me down? I'm sensitive, you know. I can only handle so much rejection." She sniffed, then pretended to sob.

"I know." She sighed. "The new gig has sucked up a lot of time. I'll do better."

Lisa donned a haughty expression. "See that you do, Agent Sheen." She broke into laughter.

Diana stood and slipped the blue belt around her waist, knotted it tightly, then rechecked to ensure all the other knots on her uniform were equally secure. *It wouldn't do to have a wardrobe malfunction while rolling.* "I'm heading out. Don't be long, or Jackson will make you do push-ups until your arms fall off."

Lisa nodded and moved notably faster.

Jackson was crazy tall, like six and a half feet. He was proportional and built like a rower or wrestler, more for speed than power. His dark skin set off the pure white of his uniform as he exchanged words with potential clients at the front of the room. The other students milled about the padded floor and bowed respectfully before they stepped into the training area. Jackson was a traditionalist, which was one of the things that drew her to him as an instructor. The fact that he was a bona fide ball-buster and national champion didn't hurt either.

Lisa joined her and executed the proper bow Diana had taught her. She had warned her friend about Jackson's sixth sense that ensured he was always aware of what went on in his school. Also, she'd cautioned that her behavior would reflect on them both and she thus needed to keep her head in the game.

"You weren't kidding. He is cute."

"He's married."

"Happily?"

Diana nodded. "And his wife's trained for more than a decade. She'd twist your slutty ass into a pretzel before you knew what was happening."

Lisa smacked her. "Having a healthy attitude toward sex is not being a slut, Diana. You should try it sometime."

"Wench."

"Prude. Oh, look, he's coming this way."

The students dashed to arrange themselves in rank order. Diana pushed Lisa into place and slipped into her own position farther up the line. Jackson paced in front of them, reviewed their arrangement, and nodded. He gave a slight bow, and the students returned much deeper ones.

His voice was deep and resonant. Diana imagined it was how a tiger might sound if speaking English. "Three phases. Drills, sparring, rolling." He gestured at several higher ranks. "Pairs will work with senior instructors. Get to it."

Diana grinned, shook her arms out, and stretched her neck. Her mixed martial arts sessions were one of her favorite activities. It struck her that relocation would mean she'd have to find a new instructor, but she shrugged the worry away. *Surely Jackson will have a recommendation, and it's not like DC is that far from Pittsburgh, anyway.* Lisa joined her, and they moved to a corner of the room where one of the senior instructors waited.

Her friend adopted her "serious and honest" tone. Diana had heard her use it to lie before, but not often. "I'll try not to embarrass you."

She grinned. "You could never embarrass me. But if you make me look stupid, I'll kick your ass."

They were still laughing together when the instructor threw pads at them. "Less talking, more punching."

Their mood sobered instantly, and they marched across the width of the dojo. One attacked while the other swung the target pad in position for different moves. When they reached the far side, they switched roles and traveled in the other direction. By the end of the ten-minute warm-up phase, they were both sweaty and energized and threw kicks and punches for all they were worth. Even though it was Lisa's first time at a mixed martial arts lesson, she had some basic karate in her past, plus kickboxing for exercise, so her moves were adequate for the warm-up. When a loud clap signaled the switch to sparring, a different instructor led her away to review fundamentals.

Diana crossed the room to where her gym bag sat against the wall and retrieved her gear. She slipped her shin and foot guards on, donned her fingerless gloves, and slid the bite guard into her mouth. There had been a time when she had been one of those who thought the mouthpiece wasn't important, that she wouldn't take *that* hard a hit. A thousand-dollar dental bill for three cracked teeth had quickly corrected her opinion on the matter. She returned to the instructor, who had found a size-appropriate opponent for her. She raised the glove and bumped fists with him. "Jonathan."

"Diana. What's shakin'?"

"Same old. You?"

"Promotion. Moving on up." He had been with the Secret Service for five years and wanted to be one of the goofballs who ran beside the president's limousine. Other than that, he seemed to have a good head on his shoulders, and Diana enjoyed their bouts. He had short, black military-cut hair, a clean-shaven face, and skin the color of a quality dark beer. He was more muscular than she was but only an inch or so taller. The instructor touched each of them on the shoulder and guided them into position for the start of the round. "Three minutes, full speed, twenty percent power."

They launched into motion and traded kicks and punches. Jackson believed control was everything and permitted his students to spar at full speed but pull back at the last instant to avoid damaging their partner. Of course, accidents happened, but the reality of fighting without a ton of stuff weighing her head and chest down met her needs far better than wearing protective gear and full boxing gloves.

Distracted for a moment, she caught a foot to the cheek, sidestepped to avoid most of its force, and shook her head.

Focus, Diana.

She tried to close with him, but Jonathan had a wicked low kick that forced her to block with every half step to avoid a painful blow to the shin.

And getting nailed in the shin hurts like hell. Even with the pads.

Diana growled in frustration and tried a new tactic. She timed his next kick and stepped in quickly to deliver a jab to his midsection.

He blocked it and kicked her in the shin. She hopped backward, angry at herself for not seeing the trap. If it were a real fight, she would attempt a jumping sidekick and then rely on her ground skills, but they had to stay on their feet until instructed otherwise. She threw her own low kick, and he raised his foot to block it, then pivoted to throw that foot in a weak sidekick. A sharp block and a hard push broke his balance. She managed a quick one-two-three jab to the midsection and threw a hook at his head. He ducked it and came up with a double punch to her chest that sent her staggering back.

She distantly heard the instructor shout, "rolling," through her battle haze. Her extreme focus on one opponent was a weakness, Jackson had told her, and inadequate should she ever find herself fighting multiple foes. She banished it with a shake of her head and saw Jonathan's legs tense as his body leaned toward her.

It wasn't time slowing down but rather long training that revealed what his next move would be. A smile spread over her face. He rushed forward and grabbed at the lapels of her uniform, his plan to overwhelm her with sheer force. She levered one leg between them, planted it on his midsection, and used his momentum to propel herself backward. Diana executed a flawless Tomoe-nage, used her foot to lever him up and over, and grabbed his forearms as he tumbled past. He landed on his back, head to head with her, with a loud *thump.*

Captain Kirk had the best moves.

She spun and latched her legs around him. The landing had blasted his breath away and his defense was sluggish. In an instant, she had locked one of his arms against his body with her legs and bent the other into an armbar. She gave it the slightest pressure and he tapped his hand against his leg.

With a small crow of victory, she released him, and they both bounced to their feet and exchanged fist bumps again.

Jonathan grinned. "Nice move. It won't work next time."

Diana returned the smile. "My bag of tricks goes way deeper than that."

"I'm looking forward to it."

"Me too."

They separated, and Lisa spoke behind her. "He's cute."

She turned and rolled her eyes. "Rule one. You don't date anyone from your dojo. That has the potential to mess things up for everyone."

"You have too many rules, Diana." Her friend paused, then said with forced casualness, "Will you spar with me?"

Diana shook her head. "While I have the skills to teach you the basics, I'm definitely not good enough to spar with you here." She grabbed Lisa by the arm and pulled her across the floor to where one of the most experienced brown belts stood. He was a giant bear of a man who wouldn't be out of place in a professional football locker room. "Benjamin, my friend is interested in a round of sparring. This is her first day."

He smiled and nodded. A deep rumble emanated from his chest as he replied. "Of course. I'd be glad to teach her a few things. She's not particularly breakable, is she?"

She grinned. Benjamin's humor was well camouflaged until you got to know him, and Lisa's eyes had already widened. "Less than most."

He nodded again and gestured the other woman toward the safety gear in the corner of the room. Diana suppressed a laugh as Lisa turned back momentarily and mouthed, "I will kill you for this."

CHAPTER TWENTY

Rath ensured that his bandoliers were properly crossed and secured. He had discovered a patterned shoelace in gray and black in the drawer of awesome random things and had fashioned it into a headband. It was pulled tight and knotted in the back. He looked at the Borzoi, whose nose was an inch away and sniffed at him with warm puffs.

"Max. Good boy." He climbed onto the dog's nose. "Door."

Max kept his head tilted so Rath wouldn't fall as he plodded softly to the front door. Rath crouched. "Launch." The dog's head snapped up, the troll jumped, and the combination hurled him in a shallow arc to land in perfect balance on top of the control pad for the alarm. He kicked at the cover until it flipped open, then dangled by an arm to punch the buttons in the order he had seen Diana press them. A soft beep sounded as the system disarmed.

Phase one complete.

Rath dropped down to the cover, which stuck out like a

platform, and stared at the door's top lock—something called a bolt. He backed up and began to run toward it, then skidded to a stop as common sense momentarily overrode adventurism. Cautiously, he peered over the edge. "Max. Safe." The dog moved obediently into the space. Now, if he fell, he'd land in Max's softer fur rather than on the threadbare carpet. He nodded and commenced his run again to vault himself at the lock across the way. He caught it, clutched the upper part, and used his weight to make it turn. When it clicked, he dropped to the next and repeated the procedure. Finally, he landed on the door handle and turned the small lever there.

"Good. Is good." He and Max had made it this far before, but no farther. Rath knew Diana would not want them to go out without her, but there was only so much you could learn by training inside.

Must train.

The dog moved position and Rath jumped to land on the back of his neck and slid to his collar. He settled into place and grasped it strongly with both hands. "Max. Knob. Turn."

The dog put his paws against the door, craned his neck to reach the knob, and locked his teeth around it. The troll held his breath. The grip was slippery, and so far, it had defeated them. But today would be different, he was sure of it. Teeth clinked on metal and Max growled softly, the door popped open with a quiet *snick*. Rath beamed. "Good Max. Teamwork."

The dog barked and the duo ventured outside, leaving the front door to swing not quite closed behind them. The neighborhood was filled with interesting features that Rath had seen through the windows. Trees, stone paths that people walked on, plus stone paths that people piloted what Diana called cars on. He liked cars. Riding with her was thrilling, and he loved the way the colors blurred and how he was thrown around.

Max navigated the steps down to the walking lane and Rath patted him on the left side of his neck. He turned left. "Good. Teamwork." They trotted for a while and the troll ducked into the dog's thick fur whenever a person was nearby. Max found an opening between the cars and dashed across to the next block. The machines yelled at them in different voices, but Rath was unmoved. "Must train."

He recognized a building on the corner that Diana had taken him to, where she had passed him pieces of something called a scone while he sat in her purse. It was filled with rich smells that he liked—similar to but better than those emitted by the growly machine at home. Another store stood beside it, and after that, a passage extended back between the buildings. It was dark and narrow and foreboding. "Good place for enemies." He gave Max a tap, and they turned into the alley.

Rustling from beneath a large container was accompanied by a scent that made his nose wrinkle. Max growled deep in his throat—the mean growl, not the playful one. Motion blurred ahead, and four furry creatures scampered out, smaller than Max but bigger than Rath. They had brown hair, sharp teeth, and whippy tails.

"Enemies." Max barked his agreement. The troll tightened his grasp on the collar and pulled one of the toothpicks from beneath the point where the bandoliers crossed on his back. "Charge."

The Borzoi launched forward at the creatures, and the enemies scattered. Max turned quickly to follow one, and Rath released his collar. His momentum carried him to the ground, although he added several flips along the way for fun. He landed and held his spear in one hand to point it at the animal nearest him. He dropped his voice and rasped, "I'm your worst nightmare."

The rat charged. Rath held his position and waited for the perfect moment. As it snapped its wicked teeth at him, the troll vaulted forward in a flying somersault and stabbed his foe in the back with the spear. The toothpick broke. Half of it remained in the creature and the other half was still clutched in his hand when he landed. The creature hissed and ran. Rath nodded. "Cowards. One coward down."

A sharp yelp of pain caught his attention, and he turned as a rat slid down the alley wall Max had hurled him into. "Two down."

The dog barked and attacked the third, leaving Rath with the final one. It was more cautious and sidled in slowly. Its tail flicked along the ground and the troll beckoned with his weapon. Without warning, the creature launched forward at the last instant to attack his face, and Rath fell onto his back. The broken end of the toothpick jammed into the ground beside him. The rat scratched itself on the point as it tumbled past and it ran off into the distance on the heels of Max's opponent. Rath discarded the spear, which had now lost its tip as well.

The dog approached and lowered his nose. Rath patted

it. "Max. Good. Good training. Go home." He climbed into his riding position and tapped the dog, then heard something strange. "Max. Stay." He leaned in the direction of the sound—a combination of moans and laughter. He had heard similar things in the movies on TV. He frowned.

"Max. Go. Quiet." The dog moved close to a wall and padded down the alley, blending into the shadows. On the far end, about three Max lengths back from another walking lane, a figure slumped on the ground. He had a blanket over him and wore a hat and gloves with holes in them. Two people stood over him. They were the ones laughing. One of them poked the man on the ground with his toe.

"Max. Big enemy. Need strategy." He whispered in the dog's ear for half a minute. Finally, he was sure that his partner understood. He stood, secured his hold on the collar, and spread his legs wide. Ahead, one of the men spat on the slumped figure. "Loser. Scum. Give us whatever you've got."

Max charged and made no sound at all other than the rasp of his pads on the stone underfoot until they were close. Then, he barked and snarled, and the men turned in alarm.

The troll released his hold on the collar, dashed up his brave steed's head and onto his nose, and shouted, "Launch!"

The dog jerked his head up and to the left, toward the nearer of the two men, and angled at the other one. Rath drew his other spear from behind his back as he catapulted toward his target.

The man's eyes widened, and he raised a hand to slap

the troll away, but it was too late. His diminutive assailant landed on his shoulder and ran around to his back, using his victim's hair to keep himself from falling.

"Ow, what the hell?" the thug screamed. Rath smiled and checked on Max. He'd knocked his foe down onto his face, and stood on him, his teeth locked on the back of his neck. The man struggled and Max growled, tensed his jaw, and pushed the teeth in a little deeper. The man quit moving.

"Coward," Rath confirmed with a nod. The one he tormented now hopped around and swung his hands at where he felt his attacker's feet. The troll dodged them easily and used his acrobatic skills to climb and swing from the man's hair until he was in the perfect position. With a battle scream, he vaulted upward to grab the man's ear, used it to redirect himself, and channeled all his momentum into a stab with his toothpick. There was initial resistance, then none, and the man shrieked when the membrane broke inside his ear.

Rath jumped to his target's shoulder and ran across his back, planning to repeat the process on his other eardrum. The martial arts books Diana had provided had shown many vulnerable areas to attack. He was happy to see it was correct. The man turned toward the brightness at the end of the alley and fled. Rath bailed and landed on Max, then slithered to the ground and watched his adversary retreat. The other man, still trapped by the dog, whimpered.

Cowards.

The troll walked in front of him and the man gasped as the Borzoi reset his hold. He planted his feet directly before the man's left eye and held his spear up. "You stop. Next time, get hurt bad." He stared for several seconds to emphasize his point. "Get out." Max released him, and the thug scrambled away.

A trembling voice emerged from the bundle of rags. "Did I really see that?"

Rath climbed back up Max's fur. He nudged the dog toward the man on the ground, who now sat with his back against the wall and his eyes wide. "Max. Rath. Training."

He patted the dog, and they turned to retrace their steps. Behind them, the man called, "Thank you, little friend."

"Friend," the troll shouted in response.

They made it home without incident and, with some maneuvering, managed to lock the house again. Rath stowed his gear and cajoled Max into opening the fridge for him so he could get some pineapple juice, which was even more delicious than the orange kind. He rolled the can to the living room, stuck a straw inside, and slurped happily as he navigated through the movies on the TV. It was impossible to pass up a rewatch of Judge Dredd, and he hit the play button. The dog flopped onto the floor beside him, and Rath gave him an affectionate pat. "Rath. Max. We are the law."

When Diana returned home from her training, she found the two of them asleep. She smiled softly at the thought of them spending the day relaxing happily together.

This is a good little family.

CHAPTER TWENTY-ONE

Diana shrugged her purse higher on her shoulder as she slipped through the crowd at the Legal Beagle. It was busy, even for Friday, and required a goodly amount of ducking and weaving with one hand guarding her bag. She caught the bartender's eye, and the woman smiled. Julia was a self-proclaimed Capitol Hill washout, a student who had come to intern with a Congresswoman, became an aide, and soured on the whole process. The bar's owner had promised her the opportunity to work toward a stake in the place, and she spent most of her waking hours there. It appeared to suit her if her constant smile was to be believed. The chipper brunette held a finger up and pointed toward the back of the bar. Diana turned, saw Lisa through a gap in the throng, and veered in that direction.

Her friend looked even more attractive than usual in a black dress that showed her off to great advantage. Diana slid into the chair diagonal from her at the square table. "My, you're a little overdressed, but I appreciate the effort. I'm honored."

Lisa laughed. "As if. This is only the warmup for the main event."

"A new flame?"

She shook her head. "Steve continues to burn quite brightly. We're going salsa dancing or something."

Diana grinned. "That's a thing I would definitely like to see."

Her friend stuck her tongue out. "Maybe after I've done it for a decade or so, we can talk."

Diana's drink arrived. She and Julia had an agreement that allowed the bartender to pick something she thought she would appreciate and in return, Diana wouldn't complain too much about the occasional miss. She tasted the beer and smiled.

Another definite hit.

Lisa had an empty wine glass in front of her, and scarlet nails replaced it with a full one before Julia departed. Lisa took a sip, then lowered it and her face took on a slight frown. "That guy's back."

Diana craned her neck as Bryant pulled the door closed behind him. She waved, and the motion caught his attention. He weaved toward them. "That guy is called Bryant, as you well know."

The other woman shrugged. "He still seems like a weirdo with the way he stared at us last time. I'm sticking with 'that guy.'"

She snorted. "I will admit he definitely gave off some predatory vibes at first. But he's okay."

"I'll be the judge of that." Her face brightened, and she adopted a plastic smile. "Bryant, so good to see you again."

He took the chair across the table from her. "You as well, Lisa."

She sipped her wine and smiled sweetly. "Did you research me, too?"

Bryant shot a look at Diana, who immediately found a reason to focus on her drink and stared at the grain of the table's laminate top. "Only a little and only where your interactions with Diana were concerned. We didn't invade your privacy nearly as much as we invaded hers."

Diana coughed into her beer and he laughed.

Lisa shook her head. "Why are you here?" Diana shot her a look and hissed under her breath, but he only chuckled again.

"Life isn't all work. Sometimes, you have to have some fun, too."

From inside Diana's purse, clearly audible despite the sounds in the bar, a small voice cheered, "Fun, too."

Lisa frowned and stared at her friend, who sighed and rolled her eyes. Bryant shook his head with an, "I told you so," expression.

Diana set her bag on her lap and shifted closer to Lisa. She opened it and stared down. "I cannot take you anywhere, Rath." The other woman leaned forward, peered into the bag, and her eyes widened. Before she could speak, Diana touched her arm. "First, relax. Everything's fine. Second, this is Rath. Obviously, he's a troll. He...uh, adopted me."

Her friend looked up, an expression of shock on her face that would have been hilarious in a different situation. "Don't you mean you adopted him?"

Bryant laughed again, clearly enjoying Diana's discomfort. "No, that is not at all what she means."

Rath waved at Lisa from the bag. Diana said, "Rath, Lisa. Lisa, Rath. Lisa is my best human friend." The other woman's lips quirked at the clarification, and Diana's face grew a little heated. Bryant snorted, and she kicked him under the table.

The troll sounded serious. "Lisa friend. Rath friend. Lisa and Rath friends." He appeared thoughtful for a second and added, "And Max. Lisa and Rath and Max friends."

Lisa glanced up, although she tore her eyes away with a clear effort. "So, you run a hostel for wayward creatures, then?"

Diana laughed. "I like to think of us more as a family, but it's not an entirely incorrect description."

Bryant chose that moment to interject. "Why did you bring him? I bet you secretly wanted to reveal him to Lisa."

She shook her head. "He begged to come. I can only imagine what he would've done to the house if I'd refused. It turns out Max is more partner in crime than guardian."

Finally, Lisa seemed to recover her balance and grinned. She turned to Bryant. "So, are magical creatures standard issue? If so, I might think about joining up."

Bryant laughed at Lisa's joke, half because it was funny and half out of politeness. The connection between the two women was so strong, he felt like an outsider. It wasn't surprising. Diana needed someone solid who would push her outside her comfort zone now and again, while Lisa needed someone steadfast to trust. They both had good reasons to be together.

"While we do encounter magic on a fairly regular basis, this one is rare. By the time I realized what was going on, she'd already freed the little guy and it was all over."

Her friend looked curious but Diana waved it off. "A story for another day."

The waitress arrived, and Bryant pointed at Diana's drink. "I'll have what she's having." Lisa, whose glass was only half-empty, surprised him by speaking up. "Make that two. Steve should be here at any moment."

Diana's head didn't quite snap around to face Lisa, but there was surprise in the motion. "Steve is coming here?"

She nodded. "I wanted him to have the chance to meet you. I didn't know that Captain America there would be along, but the more the merrier, right?"

Diana laughed at the joke, and Bryant added his own thin smile. While surprises didn't necessarily bother him, he wasn't really a fan of them, either. There wasn't time to ruminate on it, though, because a guy who looked like he cared a little too much about his image arrived at the table and gave Lisa a kiss on the cheek. He was an inch or two over six feet, had blond hair and a close-trimmed beard, and wore a Nationals baseball cap he didn't bother to remove.

So, what he lacks in initial appeal he further lacks in class.

The newcomer threw himself into the empty chair and stuck a hand out. "Steve."

Bryant shook it, and the other man squeezed a little more than necessary. The agent didn't quite shoot him a dirty look but adjusted his expression to neutral. Steve repeated the process with Diana, and her dirty look wasn't nearly so well hidden. She mastered it quickly and gave him a smile. "Steve, Lisa's told me a little about you, but none of the good parts. What's your deal?"

He launched into a story about himself—something he seemed to enjoy if Bryant was any judge of character. While the man rabbited on, he took the opportunity to snap a picture with his phone and forwarded it to the base. Before Steve had finished his tale—which seemed to go on and on—he had the man's details. These provided nothing of real interest. He did indeed work for a security firm as he claimed. Not one of the better ones, but not the sleaziest, either. Bryant stowed the phone back in his pocket.

Steve turned to him. "Lisa tells me you and Diana work together—something governmental. What do you do?" The agent launched into the ARES cover story—a collective of otherwise independent analysts who consulted on a variety of security issues. The other man gave him a superior smile. "Maybe my firm will hire yours sometime, although we have the best of the best when it comes to that area."

Bryant rewarded him with another thin smile. A tray fell with a loud clang and the table's worth of glasses it had carried shattered noisily. Diana started but mastered herself quickly. None of the others reacted. It was an expected sound in the place.

The agent watched her closely. She closed her eyes once, then opened them again. A hand disappeared into her bag, presumably to give or draw comfort from the troll. As a matter of course, they had hacked her therapists' records, so he knew about her PTSD and how she coped with it—quite well, in his estimation. He felt a twinge of pain on her behalf and wondered what it would be like to face that level of alarm to ordinary occurrences, not to mention magic. In discussions about adding her to the team, her potential issues with magic as a result of the incident were a primary concern. However, he and the others who believed she'd shown the aptitude to handle it won out.

He tuned back into the conversation in time to hear Steve say, "Lisa, you look amazing. Every man in the place will envy my prize."

Her grin turned down somewhat, and Bryant sensed Diana react. He pushed down his own desire to explain to Steve how one ought to treat a partner. She gave the man a fake smile and said, "No question, Lisa is usually the focus of attention. Some of her dates find that difficult to handle. It takes someone truly comfortable with themselves to avoid being petty."

The verbal slap was delivered with no emotion, but it still hit home. Steve bristled and seemed about to reply when Lisa put her hand on his. "Finish up, Romeo. It's time to move. I need to get my dance on."

Diana's gritted her teeth so hard they hurt.

Asshole. Lisa needs better taste in men.

As her friend rose, she touched her arm. "I could probably handle some dancing. Do you want Bryant and I to join you?"

Lisa smiled and shook her head. "Three's a crowd, and four is a downright disaster on a date."

The agent laughed. "Never heard of double dating?"

She turned to him and gave him a real grin. "Listen, I know. How could you *not* be interested in all this?" She gestured down her body. "But you'll have to content yourself with Diana." She yelped as the other woman's foot connected with her ankle.

"Witch."

Diana smiled. "Wench."

Steve slipped his arm around Lisa's waist and nodded to Bryant, then to her. "Pleasure to meet you." He didn't hide his sarcasm well. They left, and Diana watched them every step of the way until the door closed behind them.

"She'll be fine."

She dragged her attention back to the table. "What?"

"I checked him out and found nothing particularly scary. He's a schmuck, but that appears to be the end of it. And I'm sure Lisa has handled her share of schmucks."

Diana released a pent-up breath. "Haven't we all? Present company definitely included."

Bryant's grin showed off his teeth, which were white and perfect. "Hey now. No need to get rude. Or ruder than normal, I mean."

"Bryant?" She said sweetly.

He rolled his eyes. "Yes?"

"Bite me."

"Anytime, anyplace, Sheen." She laughed but it faded when his face clouded over.

Her words formed a question, but her tone made it a demand. "What?"

Bryant shrugged. "I have to talk to you about something. Technically, I'm not supposed to, but I've never been much for technicalities."

Diana nodded. "Me neither. Spill."

Rath sounded equally serious when he echoed, "Spill."

"I'm sure that by now, you've realized that all the BAM recruits possess some form of magic." There was a pause, but her mind filled in the words even before he said them. "Including you."

She leaned back, then forward again, opened her mouth to retort, and changed her mind. "Okay, if we have to have this conversation, I need another drink." She twisted and waved at Julia, who had the server's instinct that ensured she'd be looking at the table at the right moment. Diana held two fingers up and pointed down. The bartender nodded.

"Okay. You're right." She focused on her companion once more. "I've always had a little—moving stuff with my mind and such. But I've noticed some weird stuff lately. How could I not?" She leaned in. "Did you see what happened with that knife?"

Bryant nodded. "Only part of it, and only in a flash. Why don't you tell me what you saw?" She related the story, and he held his reply as their drinks arrived. They each took a deep drink and he nodded. "Telekinesis is often how magical ability first manifests. It seems like it's the most easily accessed way to interact with the world in a non-physical manner. At least that's what the experts say, and it corresponds with what we've seen."

Diana nodded and toyed with the napkin under her drink.

He still sounded serious. "Now you spill."

She sighed. "It's weird. Every so often—like when we went down the stairs and that trap was in front of us—everything slows down for me and I feel a disturbance inside." She kept her gaze locked firmly on the table. Bryant's hand crossed into her vision and touched hers, ever so gently, with only two fingers on the top.

"It's okay, Diana. In fact, it's better than okay. You probably saved my life there." She looked up and he nodded. "The magic techs say it was essentially a firebomb. I would've taken the full brunt of it and my chances of survival would've been minimal."

"You didn't have any inkling it was there?"

He shook his head. "The magic I have access to is mainly active. I have to concentrate hard to use it. You appear to be one of the gifted ones who have some active and some passive."

Diana nodded. "So, I may be able to sense danger?"

"No, you're not Spider-Man or Spider-Gwen, or whatever. It does appear that you're able to sense magic when it's being used, however."

"I'm way cuter than Spider-Gwen." It was a delaying tactic, and she knew it. Still, it worked while she put her thoughts together. She snapped her fingers as revelation dawned. "The sniper used some kind of magic, didn't he?"

Bryant laughed. "You're still not over that one, huh?" He nodded, and his true smile returned. Something released inside at the sight of it. "He says he didn't need to use it the first time since you basically walked into his trap, but he used it after that."

"Which is why I sensed him."

He nodded.

"Do you think I can sense all magic?"

"We can test it if you like."

She looked around. "Here?"

He inclined his head in agreement and she straightened as a mixture of excitement and the retained dread of magic wrestled inside. She quickly shoved the dread where it belonged. "Okay, let's do it."

Bryant nodded, closed his eyes, and raised one finger to his temple. His face scrunched up like he was concentrating. She didn't notice anything and wondered if he were making fun of her. Her focus was so complete that she startled when Rath cackled enthusiastically in her bag. Bryant's eyes snapped open. "Did you feel something?"

She shook her head, confused. "What did you do?"

From inside the bag, the troll said, "Bryant told joke. Funny joke."

Diana frowned. "So, you can speak telepathically with my troll?"

He nodded and Rath giggled.

Sigh.

CHAPTER TWENTY-TWO

The wizard and the Kilomea stood in the shadows of the alley as the woman and her dog exited the sports car and trot the half-block to the animal shelter. The watcher's dark cloaks rendered them almost invisible in the dim illumination. The larger one tensed, ready to lurch into motion, when the other placed a restraining hand on his shoulder.

"We should wait. They'll be more tired and less careful when they come out."

Cresnan frowned at the thin man beside him. "The woman is no match for me, and I'm sure you can at least handle the dog." He wore the familiar smirk that indicated teasing despite the lack of change in tone.

"I could kill them from a distance twice over before you cleared the road."

He folded his arms. "Prove it."

Drisnan calculated time and angles and shook his head. "No. We've seen what results when we underestimate this woman. We'll attack after, when she's thinking about home."

The big one grunted. "She's mine."

"She's ours," his partner corrected. "But you can have first shot."

They withdrew fully into the darkness and settled in to wait.

She was happy to see Doug, as she always was. Max, though, was ecstatic. The Borzoi leaped around and yipped like a frenzied puppy.

The older man laughed with each jump and attempted to avoid the dog's wet-tongued greeting. "Max, my boy, I've missed you. Are you being good? I know you are." He ruffled the fur on the dog's neck, then knelt. A treat materialized in his hand.

Diana smiled.

Doug has a magic all his own.

Max stilled and sat upright, prim and proper in response to the man's gesture. "Now, shake." The dog raised his paw, and Doug rewarded him with a paw-shake and tossed the treat. The Borzoi leaped to catch it and gulped it down in a single bite. He turned and looked at Diana, his tail spinning.

She laughed. "Okay, Max." She unclipped his leash as Doug opened the door to let him into the large play area. It was filled with other dogs chasing and wrestling with one another. The attendant shook his head and followed him inside to separate a pair of growling dogs. Diana opened her purse so Rath could see what was going on.

"Ooh. Max friends. Take home?"

Diana groaned and shook her head. "No, Rath. Our family is big enough as it is. We don't need to add any more members just yet."

The troll remained silent for a moment, and the expression on his face suggested that he was considering her argument. Considering it and rejecting it. "More Max, more training."

She lacked the foggiest notion as to what the troll was talking about and responded by pushing him gently back into the bag as Doug entered and closed the door behind him.

He grinned and she read the "I told you so" in it. "So, Max is working out okay?"

Diana returned the grin. "Yes, he certainly is. He's a great dog. I couldn't have chosen better."

"Maybe it's time you picked a friend up for him."

She shook her head.

Doug, always pushing. Right idea, wrong person.

"My house isn't big enough for any more beings. If I added another, I'd have to move, and I definitely don't have time for that."

"Understandable." He nodded and pointed through the window to where Max chased another dog. Both of their tails whipped in happy circles. "It looks like Max is having fun. You know you can bring him for daycare anytime to play."

"I'll take you up on that. Once life settles down a little, anyway."

Doug grinned. His cajoling was complete. "Okay. I have things to take care of. You can bring Max out whenever you're ready. Watch out for the German Shepherd. He's nippy."

He waved and wandered off, and Rath climbed quickly out of her bag and up her sleeve to tuck in beside her ear. She undid her ponytail and freed her hair so no one would see him from behind, then checked to ensure she knew where all traffic might be coming from.

Rath sounded pleased. "Good doggos."

She laughed. "Doggos? What have you been watching?"

"Crikey Irwins. Real-life action."

"Something tells me canceling cable would be a good idea."

"No fair. Learning."

Diana shook her head. "Yeah, that's what I'm afraid of. An exclusive diet of action content may give you a slightly skewed view of how the world operates."

Rath laughed in her ear. "Max winning. Training is good. But Max tired. No training." She looked and saw Max wrestling with another dog, clearly with the upper hand.

Crazy dog. Crazy troll. Crazy life.

"All right, time to bring this party to a close. Back in your capsule." Rath scampered into her bag as she retrieved Max. He was clearly reluctant to leave but obeyed her command without protest. "Good boy."

They passed through the lobby and of course, Max had to stop and visit the guard at the desk. Finally, they were outside once more, and she yawned. It had been a long day and a long few weeks, and she looked forward to bath and bed. She was about halfway to the Fastback when it happened.

A car passed on the street and it slipped into slow motion and the Doppler sound stretched and warped. She felt a vague sensation of danger to her left and released Max's leash to shout, "Run!" She swung her arm in a wide circle that slid her purse to her hand and threw it forward, then pivoted and dove back the way they'd come.

Time sped up again as a fireball slammed into the brick building beside her, shattered the front window behind the security grate, and triggered the wail of fire alarms. Diana pushed out of her roll, knelt behind a dilapidated fire hydrant, and drew her gun from its holster at the small of her back. A quick look revealed two men, one across the street and the other pounding toward her.

She fired a triple burst at the closing man—no, not a man, a Kilomea—and he sidestepped to avoid them. He was unexpectedly fast. She tried another triple burst and failed to tag him, then fired three at the man across the street, who ducked back into the alley. *Well, at least that's something.* Diana stood, stowed her gun, and readied herself for battle an instant before the huge being arrived.

Rath heard Diana yell and immediately yanked the top of his container shut. He bounced around, was suddenly weightless, and bounced a little more. When the motion stopped, he popped the lid and crawled out of the bag. Max was nearby, positioned between him and the street, and growled deep in his throat. The troll took in the scene and added a growl of his own. "Max. Up." The dog dropped his nose, and the diminutive creature scampered to his usual place on his back to grip Max's collar with both hands. "Must help Diana. Battle calls. Max. Go."

He jerked backward as the dog exploded into a run, barking and snarling as he entered the street. Rath checked both ways as he'd been told, but there was no danger to either side.

Only ahead.

"Unprepared. Mistake. Rambo always has weapon."

The Kilomea was a bruiser who knew how to fight. He threw a punch at Diana's skull that she ducked to avoid, and she jerked up with an uppercut in response. He brought his right arm around to block and followed it with a reversed backfist at her face. It caught her on the cheek, and pain blossomed as her head snapped to the side.

Focus, Diana.

The giant prepared for another punch, and she delivered a front kick to his midsection that knocked him back. She retreated a few steps to open the distance and spat out the blood that had gathered in her mouth. As he advanced, she withdrew at a matching pace toward her abandoned bag. *Maybe Max can bite him.* He aimed another two blows at her head, and she bent backward to evade them. She could literally hear her heartbeat as the adrenaline spiked.

Diana faked another back step before she darted forward to deliver a triple combo—two punches to the ribs and a third hard into the solar plexus. He staggered and coughed, and she had a moment of joy.

Then he grinned. His voice rumbled in a way she'd only ever heard from trains.

He hits like a train, too.

"Agent Diana Sheen. You have become a thorn in our side." He continued to advance and she continued to retreat, feinting every few steps to keep him honest. Her attacker held his arms close, apparently having decided she was worthy of at least that much respect. She wouldn't sneak another combo into his body anytime soon. "Our plan was to kill you quickly. Now that you have made it difficult, we'll have to make it last longer."

"You talk a good game, Sasquatch, but it seems the delivery isn't as good as the words promise. Do you have performance anxiety?"

The bumper of her car appeared in her peripheral vision.

If I can find a minute to reach it, the shotgun in the trunk might work.

The momentary distraction cost her. He lunged forward faster than she'd believed he could and landed a solid punch to her head. She blocked hastily, but the force of the blow catapulted her sideways into the Mustang. When she pushed herself up, there was a dent in the side panel.

She snarled at him. "Screwing with me is one thing, but a woman's car is sacred."

He laughed and spread his giant hands. "It's been fun playing with you, Agent Sheen, but now, it's time to end this. Once you're broken, I'll kill your dog. Then, maybe, everyone in the building you were so happy to visit. Only after they are all gone will I listen to your pleas for death."

Rage burned like lava as it erupted from deep in her core to emerge in a furious scream.

Rath scampered onto the dog's nose and gave the command. "Max. Launch." Doing it while the dog was running was a new challenge, but his acrobatics training served him well.

As he hurtled toward his target, Diana's scream washed through him like a physical thing and a red haze spread across his vision. A ripple surged through his body, starting at his toes and shooting upward, and the world changed. Things grew smaller, distances shorter, and the mage he hurtled toward seemed less threatening.

The troll, now three feet tall rather than the five inches he had been when Max threw him, carried his momentum into a vicious kick at the mage. The swat of magic that would have deflected his smaller form failed entirely to affect his flight. "Nice."

The force of his impact hurled the shocked man backward against the alley wall. The wizard dropped to one knee as Rath backflipped to land several feet away. He stretched his arms and admired the ropey muscles that covered them before he bared his teeth in a fierce grin. "Thank you, stupid man. Rath bigger. Rath better."

He closed on his quarry as the wizard staggered to his feet.

The rage became a living, gnawing, tearing thing, and either the scream or the expression on her face clearly alarmed her opponent. His right hand seemed to glow as it swung in a vicious hook toward her temple, and events slipped into slow motion again. Diana could sense where the fist would land and had ample time to consider and discard potential responses. She eliminated those that would cause further damage to her car, despite the eminent satisfaction that pounding his head into the metal would bring.

Instead, she used her left arm to guide the punch past her face, secured his wrist with her right hand, and yanked the arm straight. She bent her left arm and hammered it into his elbow to generate a satisfying crack as the joint snapped. He bellowed, and she stamped her heel into the side of his knee. His leg buckled and as he fell, a kick to the head thrust him to his knees, dazed. He seemed to immediately shake it off, so she kicked him again, and he collapsed with a low moan. She bound him quickly at ankle and wrist with zip ties, then thought better of it and doubled them. *We'll need bigger zip ties.* With her attacker now secured, she searched her surroundings for Max and Rath. They were nowhere to be seen, and she had almost erupted into a full-blown panic when she heard the scream from across the road.

The wizard fired a series of fire blasts from his wand but

Rath dodged them easily. It was almost a game given how bad his aim was. Or maybe the troll was simply faster in this form. Either way, the battle lacked challenge. He closed with a quick shuffle step and pounded a punch to center mass. For the troll, however, center mass was about the height of his opponent's groin. His adversary screamed and crumpled, and his wand tumbled away, forgotten in his agony.

Rath shook his head in pity at his downed foe. He knelt and looked in the man's watery eyes. "Weak. You should train more."

Stupid wizard.

The ripple shuddered through him again and he turned as Diana entered the alley. Shrinking back to his normal size was much less exciting than growing had been, but perhaps he had enjoyed enough excitement for one night.

She bent to the man who panted as tears seeped from his eyes. "Who are you?"

"You're dead, human."

She slapped him, raising his head off the ground hard enough to hurt but not hard enough to put him out. "I asked you a question, asshole. Who are you? And while we're at it, who sent you?"

Drisnan spat at her. "Kill me if you must, but cease your nattering, woman."

Both Rath and Max growled behind her, and the wizard's eyes widened. She laughed. "Yeah, you're real tough when attacking women, animals, and tiny trolls from a distance. But up close, you're simply another coward." She trussed him like his buddy and stood. "Let's go, you two."

She retrieved her belongings, let Max into the backseat, and restrained him securely with his safety harness. Rath's canister went into its spot in her cupholder, and she climbed in after one last sad look at the dent in her car. Her first call was to ARES to retrieve the trash she'd left behind. She made sure, after a quick glance at the bound giant on the ground, to specify a large vehicle. Her second was to her repair shop. She wouldn't let the Fastback suffer any longer than necessary.

The response team was fast and arrived before Rath and Max grew bored and started to cause trouble. Finally, the necessary tasks complete, she pulled into the street and headed for home. "So, Rath, do you care to explain what went on back there?"

The troll gave her a toothy grin. "Fighting mode."

Diana shook her head with a laugh. If there was a note of hysteria in it resulting from all that Rath's potential for chaos portended, she was sure that neither the dog nor the troll would notice it.

Well, fairly sure, anyway.

CHAPTER TWENTY-THREE

K ergar raised the shot glass to his lips and drank the clear liquid in one burning swallow. He coughed and refilled it from the bottle on his desk. They had opened the rum to share a drink before his lieutenants had left a few hours before to handle the trivial matter of disposing of the woman.

He drank again and refilled once more.

Now, the bottle was half-empty, and he delayed no longer. The dwarf stood and crossed to the warded door, threw the mundane locks, and sent a small pulse of magic to activate the runes carved into the lintel. He returned to his seat and shook his head to clear it, reached down to the bottom drawer of his desk, and muttered an incantation to deactivate its defenses.

Kergar retrieved a sculpture with a wooden base and arms of pure gold that spiraled up to support a purple power crystal. He set it carefully on the surface of the desk, then withdrew the coin from the hidden pocket inside his shirt and raised it to the light to admire the quality of its craftsmanship. The identity of its creator was a mystery. All he knew was that his superior had provided it as a means to travel, to communicate, and as a token of membership. None of his own underlings had one. The coins were reserved for those with responsibility.

And eventually, power. But first, I have to play the game a little longer.

He whispered a series of words in a language never known on Earth and long forgotten on Oriceran. A mist emanated from the coin and rose slowly over the crystal. The vapor gained solidity and brilliance as it caressed the gem's facets. After several moments, it coalesced into the robed form of his superior. He wore an eager expression and spoke before Kergar had a chance to.

"What news?"

He sighed. "Failure, master. Another unexpected wrinkle." He had argued with himself over how closely to stick to the truth but realized he had no way to know whether his superior had been watching. "Your criticisms proved true, again. We underestimated her. Again."

Nehlan's face contorted in fury. His voice was level and controlled, but it was clear that his lack of aggression required significant effort to maintain. "Did I not warn you?"

"You warned me, yes, master." He nodded. "And I warned those beneath me. The strategy was sound based on our observations, but our expectations proved to be optimistic."

The elf frowned. "Explain."

Kergar spread his hands. "The dog is more fearsome than we expected."

His master interrupted him with a cackle.

Shit. He sounds insane.

"The dog? You are telling me you failed because of a *dog?*"

He rushed to interrupt. "Not only the dog, master. A troll. A very violent troll."

The fury diminished visibly as thoughtfulness intruded into Nehlan's expression. "Interesting. And potentially a vulnerability. Good to know. Was it full-size?"

He desperately wanted to say yes. He was reasonably certain, now, that his master had not seen the battle. But the little voice inside—the one that prized survival above all else—cautioned against it. He sighed. "Not full size, no. But very effective." He had watched the battle in real time through a scrying orb and had seen the punch that brought Drisnan down. It had hurt him simply to see it. It was fortunate that Sheen had intervened before the troll could release his full rage on the mage.

His master shook his head. He looked and sounded exasperated. "Did she kill them?"

"No. They are on their way to the human prison."

Nehlan nodded decisively. "Kergar, I will give you a very simple task. This is your last opportunity. You have failed me twice, but our long history together earns you one final chance to redeem yourself. You will ensure that your people do not make it to that place. Rescue them if possible. Kill them if necessary. We cannot allow the humans to interrogate them."

The dwarf nodded, relieved. The fear that had squeezed his chest receded.

His master switched topics and expressions simultaneously and seemed to put the matter behind him.

I am not fooled. I know you neither forget nor forgive. Perhaps our reckoning will need to come sooner rather than later.

"Are the plans finalized for the party?"

He leaned forward, finally able to share some good news. "Yes, master. Identities have been secured, and we have confirmation that all shall be as we expect it to be."

Nehlan gave him a thin smile. "Given recent failures, perhaps you should run through it once for me."

He swallowed hard. "The Oriceran Ambassador to the United Nations is to arrive for the party at seven in the evening, an hour after the dinner portion of the event begins. Drinks are at five-thirty, and our inside people will be in place at least an hour before."

"You have sufficient covers?"

He nodded. "We have secured positions at the hotel during the last month. Some collateral damage was required to create opportunities."

The elf waved his hand. "Continue."

"As I said, the ambassador arrives at seven. He will enter through the front door and immediately move to the stage to begin his speech. The vice president arrives at seven-thirty, along with an increased security presence. This gives us a window of thirty minutes in which to act. We plan to strike immediately after he begins his speech when everyone has settled in and believes they are safe."

His master nodded, seemingly content with the arrangement. "And your exit route?"

"Once we have the ambassador, we have our choice of three exits. Cars in the street are our fallback, and a departure from the roof is our first backup. If all goes well, we will go out through the kitchens and through the basement tunnel that connects to the company's other property a block away. Of course, this assumes that they have blocked our ability to create a portal."

Nehlan grunted. "The humans have shown this ability before. We must expect them to use it. You've ensured that the tunnel is passable?"

"We have." He nodded confidently. "It is a relic of a time gone by when the wealthy owners needed a way from one place to the other without appearing in public. The tunnel was well constructed then and holds up now. It will be a little beneath the ambassador's station, of course." He risked a chuckle.

His master's frown indicated he wasn't at all impressed. "Just so we're clear, remind me what happens if the ambassador dies."

Kergar swallowed the painful lump that appeared in his throat. "I die."

"And?"

"All my people die."

The elf smiled coldly. "Where the humans are concerned, kill whom you must but no more. Once they know their place, they will be useful partners." His emphasis on the word left no doubt that it would not be an equal partnership. Kergar was also fully aware that Nehlan couldn't care less about the people of Earth but was appropriately worried about limiting the exposure of the Remembrance. A mass killing would draw far too many eyes to them.

He nodded to acknowledge the instruction, then sighed

and asked the question that prudence required. "What of Agent Sheen and her organization?"

His master laughed. "I think we can expect a show of force from them at this event, don't you?"

"Certainly so. What if it's a trap?"

The elf shrugged. "Sometimes, the only way to deal with a trap is to spring it and turn it back upon itself. Perhaps you should consider ways to accomplish that."

There was one more question he didn't want to ask. He seriously considered ending the conversation but sighed again and gave in to the necessity. "Will you join us, my lord?"

His master didn't reply and simply sat in silence, his expression thoughtful. When the one-minute mark passed, he inched his hand toward the device to verify that it was still working. Finally, the elf sighed. "No, I will not. I will, instead, trust you to not fail me again. It is imperative that the ambassador be unavailable for a time."

The dwarf wasn't sure what the ultimate plans for the ambassador were, but after seeing the mentally dominated humans at his master's home, he thought he might have an inkling. He nodded. "Very well, master. I believe that we are prepared for this and that you will have good news in short order."

Nehlan's gaze bored into his lackey's. "Do not fail, Kergar. Better you should die in the attempt than come back to me with anything other than success. There are worse fates than the gentle slide into death, and I will ensure you experience every one of them should you fail."

Kergar stuttered "Yes, master." The image faded in an instant. He had restored the coin to his pocket and locked the warded drawer against all intrusions, both mundane and magical, before he gathered the courage to speak. "Asshole."

He pushed himself up on shaky arms and took several deep breaths before he left the room. An upward gesture armed his wards and another downward tripped the locks. He clutched the bottle and shot glass in one hand and made his way unsteadily to the bar. It was filled with the usual crew, the seats reserved for Cresnan and Drisnan conspicuously empty.

The bartender wandered over. "What's up, boss?"

He emptied his glass in a single swallow and refilled it. Enthan looked hazy, and he smiled at the wavering wizard. "It appears we can't afford any more setbacks, or many lives are forfeit."

He nodded his understanding. "What can we do?"

"I need you to send our most skilled operatives out on a shopping spree. Find rich homes, steal expensive things, and turn them into human currency. Use it to buy the best mercenaries available."

"The ones we hired before were the best available."

Kergar shook his head and pointed a swaying finger at the bartender. "No, they were the best not currently contracted. Enough money can convince someone better to break their agreement and join us. Put the word out quietly and see who we can find. Worst case, we go back to the tried-and-true."

Enthan grinned. "Kidnapping and extortion?"

"Everyone has someone or something they love. It's only a matter of finding their pressure point."

He nodded and emptied his glass, then abandoned the

empty bottle on the bar. "See that the burglaries start tonight. We need our soldiers within two days. Two days after that, we make a bold move that puts us in a good position with those above. And, maybe, those above them."

And, if we're lucky, maybe we'll have the chance to kill Sheen where her dog and troll can't protect her.

CHAPTER TWENTY-FOUR

Diana set her bag carefully in the backseat of the SUV and secured it with a seatbelt. She looked inside to make sure Rath was okay and he gave her a thumbs-up. She slipped into the passenger seat and buckled in. Bryant stared at her with an annoying grin on his face.

"Shut up. Drive."

He laughed and pulled out into traffic.

She blew out a breath. "Thanks for the ride."

He nodded, then could no longer resist. "You did it with your head, didn't you? And it was a huge dent, wasn't it? So vicious the car won't even run anymore, right?"

She slapped him on the chest with the back of her hand. "Jerk. No."

He chuckled one more time before he sobered. "We didn't anticipate an attack on any single one of us. Maybe we should have, but then again, it's a bold move."

"Bolder than trying to detonate a Starbucks?"

"You do have a point."

She swiveled in her seat to face him. "Is everything set with my requests?"

Bryant switched lanes and glided smoothly into a left turn. "We have eyes on your parents and Lisa, plus their homes and yours. Your FBI mentor helped us out with that one."

Her relief at the news allowed her stomach to unclench for the first time since the attack. "Good. Thank you."

"It's no more than you deserve." He shrugged. "I'm surprised you didn't bring the dog, though."

Diana rolled her eyes. "Max is perfectly happy at the shelter daycare, especially since he got to ride in with Doug. Plus, Rath likes visiting the other dogs. Don't you Rath?"

A small voice from the backseat said, "Yes. Partners. Must train."

Bryant looked quizzically at her.

She shook her head. "So, what's the deal with the party?"

"Our analysts say that it's too good an opportunity for them to pass up. A chance to strike at the Oriceran ambassador and the Vice President in one spot? It has to be on their radar."

"What do they have against the ambassador?"

He shrugged and spun the wheel into the next corner. "It seems like they're mainly interested in gaining power and prestige. Having the ambassador in their grip would give them both in the eyes of the criminal underworld on both planets."

"Oriceran has a criminal underworld?"

"Eh. Not really. But they do have a few who are not

fond of the current arrangement and think power would rest better in other hands."

That sounds familiar. Different worlds, same issues.

"So, they'll strike at the party."

"We certainly think so. The thing is, it'll be crawling with Secret Service since the VP will be present. We won't be able to go in with our usual gear."

"That seems a little dangerous." She frowned. "We won't be unarmed, will we? Because that would be dumb."

He scoffed. "Of course not. We'll be disguised as Secret Service agents with authentic IDs and everything."

"Well, at least we'll get to carry a gun. Although, I've gotta tell you, these guys absolutely deserve the business end of a rifle." She pictured the Kilomea and scowled.

I hope he hates the prison food.

"It's not all bad, though. I said without our main gear. I didn't say without *any* gear."

He swung into a parking spot near the unmarked door that led to the base. "Kayleigh and Ems have worked on some things for us. Let's find out what they have."

Emerson beamed like the father of a newborn. Arrayed before him on his office desk were a bunch of strange-looking bullets and a box. He smiled at them. "Diana, Bryant, good to see you. Did you bring Rath?"

Diana grinned at his eagerness to see the troll. The little fellow was apparently equally excited, as he jumped out of the bag and ran up her arm, then did a somersault onto the table. The agents both laughed. "Yes, we brought him."

Emerson pointed at the troll. "I have some things for you, little guy." He looked up at the others. "Kayleigh has things for you after that. But I wanted to handle this one personally."

He opened the box and withdrew a tiny armored chest piece, very similar to their tactical gear but in miniature. He held it out, and Rath stepped forward. Ems lowered it over his body and fastened it in place. The troll turned this way and that and admired the vest. "Good defense. Fighting mode."

Diana hesitated, then said, "Uh, Ems, you're aware of his size thing, right?"

The man was already digging in the box again, but looked up, momentarily startled. "Size? Oh, yes. Trolls grow. Right. On their own, or something about their bonded partner's emotions, right?" He didn't wait for an answer. "It's Velcro. When he grows, it will simply fall off him." He pointed at Rath again. "Try not to lose it, okay? Actually, I have a thing that might help with that."

He drew a belt from the box, complete with a number of attached pouches and a holster on each side. It was too big for Rath in his current form, so Ems set it on the table beside him. "This is for when you're bigger. Perhaps Diana can keep it in her purse for you." He looked up and she nodded. "It's has a fair amount of fun stuff in the pockets, all appropriate to your size when you're in—what was it called, fighting mode?" The troll nodded with a big grin.

Emerson grinned affectionately at the tiny creature. "Yes, good. So, you will find some seriously cool stuff in there. And you might discover a use for these, too." He withdrew two squat cylinders and slipped one into the holster on the right side of the belt. The other, he gripped between his fingers and flicked to extend the small collapsible baton to full length.

"Ooh." Rath's eyes brightened and he made to touch it, but Ems withdrew it hastily.

"Be careful where your hands go, little guy. It's a stun baton. That stick will deliver a few electric shocks before you have to recharge it."

The troll clapped with glee. "I am the law."

They all laughed, and the technician dipped back into the case a final time. "I have one more thing for you. Well, actually, two more things." He extracted a pair of slender needles with ridging on one end. "You're a little small for true swords, but these are wickedly sharp and made from virtually unbreakable carbon steel. They go into your vest like this." He slid them down into an X-shaped holder mounted on the back. Rath reached over his shoulders and drew them to brandish the blades as he battled invisible enemies. He tried to sheath them but couldn't quite manage it, and Ems took the weapons from him with appropriate gravitas. "It will come with practice, like all things, my friend."

"Rath. Emerson. Friends. Thank you. Must train."

Diana swept the belt and batons into her bag, and Rath followed with a yell and a leap. She shook her head. "Thank you, Ems. And especially, thank you for not giving him a gun."

He raised an eyebrow. "A troll-sized gun. That *is* an interesting concept. Let me start some sketches."

She rolled her eyes and he laughed at their backs as they departed.

Kayleigh awaited them outside and waved for them to follow her to one of the central tables. "Okay, we've worked hard to have the stuff ready for all the team members, but those in the main room have priority. First, this." She held a small pistol up.

"Ruger?" Diana asked.

The woman nodded. "Our police contacts tell us it's the best backup weapon. And we've made it better." She swung the cylinder out to show that it was filled with the bullets that had littered Emerson's desk during Diana's last visit. Closer inspection revealed that runes covered the visible surface. Diana looked up in confusion to see Bryant's nod of approval and Kayleigh's wicked grin. "Those are anti-magic rounds. Their shields won't work nearly so well against them."

Bryant pulled one out and examined it. "For something so small, it's amazing what a difference it can make. We have to find the traitor in our midst who is helping divert our shipments."

Kayleigh nodded, scowling. "I've been wondering if it could be a gang wanting to take out their magical rivals."

"Doesn't matter, either way we have to be ready to take care of business."

"You're right and Ems thinks he has a potential work-around. A way to manufacture them in-house—or at least in partnership with those who developed the bracelets. The magic techs are working on it with him." She didn't quite smother the note of derision at the reference to her magical counterparts. "Anyway, you each get one and an ankle holster to go with it." She passed the items over.

"Next up, new vests." She led them to a mannequin that

wore a strange-looking thin Kevlar vest. Kayleigh gestured at it. "So, it has a ceramic lattice that will help dissipate force even better than a standard vest does. It still won't do much against blades, though. We're working on that." She pointed at four patches, each set with a clear stone in the center. "These are magic deflectors. You'll be able to wear the vest under everyday clothes relatively easily, which might come in handy." She looked pointedly at Diana.

The agent raised her hands. "I'm all for defenses, but I think a fireball has the potential to cook you regardless of whether it's from a flamethrower or wizard."

Kayleigh grimaced. "Yes, dodging is probably still the best option where fireballs are concerned in case it overwhelms the defense. These should work against other kinds of magical attacks, though. Force, shadow, and possibly against magical creatures if they touch them. We haven't tested the last one yet."

Bryant chuckled. "Hear that, Rath? Keep your hands to yourself."

A small, "Definitely," came from her bag, and they all laughed. Bryant asked, "Is it only me, or has his speaking improved?"

Diana rolled her eyes. "Not only you. At home, I can't get him to shut up. He practices constantly."

"Now look at this," Kayleigh interjected. She pointed at a flat piece of what looked like very flexible metal that ran over the vest, up and down the sides, around the anti-magic deflectors, and crossed over the shoulders and around the back. "This is an extra guard against electricity. If you are struck, this channels the current and lessens it with each resistor until they're all popped." She pointed, and Diana bent forward for closer examination. Sure enough, there were tiny little beads set into the metal at intervals. "In testing, it's taken a few strong blasts. It might even handle actual lightning, but let's not find out, okay?"

Diana straightened. "Kayleigh, these are awesome."

The tech smiled, led them over to another table, and handed them each a pair of flattened canisters, similar to the pepper spray grenades.

Bryant whistled. "It's all the toys today, isn't it? Sonic grenades?"

She confirmed it. "We only have two for each team member right now, but we're working on getting more. This is the one area where our lack of government affiliation hurts us. We have to find our own channels."

He nodded. "There's more benefit to that than harm, though."

"Absolutely. Also, these." She handed them each a case. Inside were earpieces cast from molds of their ears to ensure a perfect fit. "These replace your old ones. They have all the same functionality but can take a signal from the sonic grenades to adjust before they go off, exactly like the flashbangs."

Diana nodded. "I know this is a stupid question, but is there any chance of an earpiece and a comm for Rath?"

"Earpieces, for his small form, probably. Obviously, they can't grow with him, though, so we'd have to make a second pair and rig something to carry them. The good news is they'd simply fall out if he got bigger." She pulled her phone out and made some notes. "Rath, can you come out here, please?"

He bounced up onto the table and Kayleigh pressed a

few more buttons. "Okay, hold still." She held her phone near his ear, and red lasers emitted and traversed the side of the troll's head. "Good, I have that one 3-D modeled. Let's do the other." When she was done, she looked at Diana. "We'll have to do this again sometime when he's bigger."

It's not like I can simply switch it on.

"I can't really make that happen on purpose yet, and I don't get the impression that he wants to do it on his own. You have to admit, he looks fantastic at that size."

Rath added, "Fantastic."

Diana shook her head. "We'll have to wait for an opportunity to present itself."

Kayleigh grinned at the troll. "Good deal." She turned to Bryant. "I need about five minutes more with Diana, but you're free to go. The boss wants to see you."

Bryant smirked at Diana. "It's difficult being so important, you know?"

"You mean like when people need to constantly check and make sure you're not screwing everything up? It must be."

Laughter rose around the table.

Point to me.

He shook his head, but the smirk didn't vanish. "Well, you'll have to wait for me since you damaged your car by cleverly being hurled into it. Way to distract him."

Another laugh from the table made her scowl.

Okay, one to one.

She was about to deliver a much more scathing comment when he wisely turned and walked away. Kayleigh led her into a small office about half the size of

Emerson's and gestured her to a chair. The tech sat on the other side of the shallow desk. "Okay, I have a few more presents for you. First, this." She slid a pepper gas grenade to her to replace the one she'd used.

"You should know it worked great. It kind of sucked for me, too, but I was ready for it. He definitely wasn't, and it took him right out of the fight."

The woman clapped with real satisfaction. "I knew it would be useful. And it's much cheaper to make than a sonic grenade. I'll get some more under construction." She reached below her desk and pulled out the most amazing objects yet—a pair of fashionable black ankle boots.

Diana's eyes went wide. "They're lovely."

"I know, right? But they're also awesome." She tipped them on their sides and pointed out the features. "Ruger fits in here, on the right side of the right boot. On the other side, we have this." She looped her pinky through a small ring and pulled. A stiletto as long as the boot was high slipped out from the inside. She swung it to settle it into her hand. "Triangular, carbon fiber, and ceramic. A nasty little bugger. You can do some serious damage with this." She handed it over, and Diana held it up, marveling at its light weight and vicious point.

"You give good presents."

Kayleigh laughed. "Now, the left one is more boring. It only holds these." She used her index fingers again and caught the loops to withdraw two flat blades. "These are throwing knives, perfectly balanced. You'll want to practice with them as they're a little different than most. They're also carbon fiber and ceramic, so metal detectors won't sense them."

Diana shook her head in appreciation. "These are excellent. How did you know what I liked?"

The woman leaned back and laughed as she lifted her own pair of identical ankle boots to the table. "We can always spot our own kind."

Diana laughed and nodded. She took the boots and slid them on, then stood to walk in them. "They're perfect." She turned to Kayleigh. "How are they perfect?"

She shrugged with a smile. "I measured your feet when you stood on the scale in the locker room."

Her voice was a little too sharp as she replied, "Seriously?"

Kayleigh didn't sound apologetic in the least. "Data is everything, so we always get what we can. Within the bounds of reasonable privacy, of course."

Diana shook her head, then shrugged. "Well, I guess I can't complain since it scored me a fantastic pair of boots. These may already be in my top four or five."

"We'll have to compare notes sometime."

"We can make a day of it. Show off our stashes and maybe go on a little shopping spree."

The tech grinned like she'd just been invited to the prom, only better. "It's a date. Oh, and by the way, try not to get killed or anything. The ones I'm prototyping now are twice as good. You'll want to be around for them."

"If that's not a reason to live, I don't know what is."

CHAPTER TWENTY-FIVE

S howtime. Diana took a deep breath, made sure Rath's capsule was securely attached to her belt, and stepped into the dining room.

The hotel was one of DC's oldest and managed to convey an old-world charm despite the monitors on every wall and the modern lighting that replaced the elegant chandeliers. The dining room was set banquet style, with round tables of eight and ten populated by upper-level politicos. Admission to the event started at four figures, with some paying five for access to the ambassador and six to add the vice president. All were listed as political donations, of course.

She heard a soft growl, muffled by the canister, and patted her hip. Ems had added a small angled mirror so Rath could see what went on around him, and she pictured the troll reviewing each detail greedily. Every new Earth experience seemed to entrance him.

We're probably a tough bunch to figure out. Political stuff, especially.

TR CAMERON

Diana walked a slow circuit of the room and kept the bored-agent expression they taught at the Academy on her face—not aggressive, not dismissive, merely casually interested. She made a discrete inventory of her gear as she paced. Her Glock was comforting in its shoulder holster with its spare magazines on the opposite side and weight balanced exactly as it should be. She wore a jacket specially tailored to conceal the rig and had left it unfastened so it wouldn't betray the magazine pouches on the back of her belt that held the sonic and pepper grenades. Rath rode on one hip, and a flashbang rested on the other.

She'd worn the boots Kayleigh had provided her more or less since the moment she'd received them. When the elderly men who ran the antique shoeshine stand in the lobby remarked on them, she'd given in and stopped for a shine. They'd professed no special knowledge of the night's event and encouraged her to make a good shine part of her daily routine. If they noticed the knives or the gun that were reasonably well hidden by her pant legs, they didn't acknowledge them.

Those guys have probably seen everything.

Calm but alert, she flicked her gaze across the room and to where Bryant kept pace on a diameter line from her position. Three BAM agents were present, along with a ton of Secret Service. The team's face, Trent, posed as a statie again and made the rounds of the tables, seemingly immune to the annoyed stares of those not interested in his networking efforts. He really was very good at being annoying.

He might be a decent match for Lisa, after all. Certainly better than Steve, anyway.

Diana suppressed a snort.

The edges of the room were concealed with black pipe and drape, and she made it a point to check behind them at every break in the fabric. It was attractive but would allow enemies to position themselves out of sight. She raised her smartwatch, which acted as a comm when they couldn't wear throat mics. "The drapes concern me."

Taggart's voice was reassuringly crisp in her ear. "Our advance team felt the same. They planted wireless cameras at the corners. We have eyes on the gaps."

At least the comms work well.

She frowned. "Good enough resolution to distinguish friend from foe?"

A pause followed, and Taggart replied, "Iffy. I'll mention it to the Service."

Diana let it drop. As long as someone was on it, whether ARES or Secret Service, she could put it into the routine check part of her mind. She turned left to walk the front of the room. The six-figure-folks were clustered around the frontmost tables and shared common qualities —fashionable men, glittery women, and all with the hungry look of people with a purpose. Exactly what you'd expect. The stage was raised three steps off the floor, and a thick podium stood to house left, swathed in spotted illumination that displayed the seals of the Oriceran consulate and the United States.

Bryant's words sounded as if he stood next to her, even though he still paced at the back of the room. "I like nothing about this."

Taggart's response was instant. "When do you ever like anything, Bryant?"

He didn't rise to the joke, which worried her more than any words that might follow. "There are some people at these tables who read wrong to me. They're harder than those around them."

She made another turn to the far side of the room and saw what he meant. At the nearest table, eight of the guests struck her as normal DC types. Dedicated politicos who kept fit, maybe even were true gym rats, but all only to look pretty in service of their careers. The other two, seated side-by-side, seemed more solid, both physically and in the attitude they presented. The pair caused her inner voice to take notice in a way that their tablemates did not.

Diana raised her left hand and touched the tiny protrusion on the side of her AR glasses. A high-resolution still image of the couple uploaded to one of the high-speed wireless receivers they'd planted throughout the hotel's first floor and forwarded to the mobile command post parked a block away. There was a brief delay while the techs did their work, and she checked her watch. Six fifty—ten minutes until the ambassador should arrive and forty until the Vice President threw the place into lockdown. One of the team in the bus was responsible for tracking their arrivals, and his young voice provided updates every few minutes. All signs suggested that both would arrive on time and as planned.

After three minutes of pacing, a tech's voice rose, young and excited over the line. She had a little Boston in her accent but not enough to distract. "Okay, those two are currently listed as principals with Alpha Dog security consulting."

Diana turned her laugh at the ridiculous name into a discreet cough. "Seriously?"

She could hear the matching amusement in the tech's voice. "The security companies are subtle, right? Anyway, they seem legit, but have also been tagged as being in the employ of some questionables."

"Oricerans?" Bryant asked.

"Wait one." The channel was quiet for a moment and when the tech returned, she sounded a little more serious than she had before. "No Oriceran connection in the records, but they apparently have been linked to some really questionable ops. Their most recent press release includes a mention of working for Bloomten International —which, if you dig deep enough, is associated with some of the contractors the government hammered for looting overseas."

Diana deliberately made no effort to look at them but scanned the tables ahead as she turned the corner at the back. "So, scumbags."

Her partner agreed. "Scumbags who have unexpectedly turned up at a thousand-dollar-a-plate event with some seriously high-profile VIPs."

Taggart sounded concerned but calm. "We're getting pictures of everyone and running them through now."

Bryant peeked behind the drape across the way before his gaze returned to the room. "Why didn't we flag these guys at the checkpoint?" The Secret Service had agreed to use ARES equipment to screen the guests as they entered the dining room. It included the same sensing suite as the base, plus facial recognition through every government database ARES had access to either legitimately or through back doors.

Taggart clearly wondered the same thing. "They either didn't come through—which is almost impossible—or they did something to defeat that security. We have no record of them entering through the checkpoint."

Bryant's voice was a low growl. "I see at least eight more paired up that seem out of place, plus a few more questionable folks who look like they're flying solo. We should abort."

The SAC was decisive. "Not a chance. We don't have that power. Only the Service can call it off."

"Convince them." Diana couldn't remember hearing such weight in the agent's voice before.

"I've suggested it and they refused. The VP won't do it."

Bryant's anger was palpable. "Idiot." ARES personnel were almost entirely apolitical. They didn't care who held the offices, they merely wanted them to make smart decisions. Unfortunately, they were frequently frustrated in that desire.

Diana decided to cut through the center of the room and take a closer look. Ahead of her, a server stumbled as one of the boisterous diners threw his arms up with a giant belly laugh. She grabbed the woman to steady her and kept her from dropping the tray. The server smiled gratefully and moved on. The matching smile vanished from Diana's face as soon as she turned away, and the cold metal on her right wrist pulsed bolts of alarm through her. She raised her other hand to adjust her hair and whispered "Illusion present. I think it's a server."

To their credit, neither the ARES agents nor the Secret

Service in the room reacted beyond a tightening of expressions and subtle moves to put their hands closer to their weapons.

If one could whisper a scream, Bryant certainly did so. "Boss—

"Negative, Bry. They won't do it." The agent cursed and Taggart continued. "You two and Trent take paths through the tables. We're tracking your movements. Any time you get a reading from your bracelet, tap your watch."

They complied, and a map of the room appeared in the far right of her glasses. It showed blues of varying hues depending on whether one, two, or all of them identified the presence of an illusion.

Bryant's voice registered even more concern, which she would have thought impossible. "That's a lot of blue. It probably explains how they got through the barrier at the checkpoint. We need to add the bracelet tech to our scanners."

"Noted," the SAC replied.

Even ARES misses stuff sometimes, apparently.

The voice that had marked time entered the conversation. "The ambassador's out of the car and on the way to security."

Bryant and Diana moved to their assigned positions for the event, taking opposite sides of the room about a third of the distance back from the stage. They faced the center and observed the diners through their glasses switched to fisheye to provide a wider range of vision. These would sense any substantial motion by the wearer and eliminate the distorted view if action was necessary. The crowd gave a standing ovation as the ambassador walked onto the stage and waved to them.

Rath intruded at the edge of her hearing. "Ooh."

The ambassador stepped up to speak, and the crowd settled back into their seats in a wave.

Suddenly, the lights went out and the backup lights kicked on an instant later. Many in the crowd laughed nervously, but not those who had remained standing. These men were already on the move.

The backup lights extinguished and plunged the room into darkness.

Shit.

CHAPTER TWENTY-SIX

Her glasses rendered the room in shades of green and gray as they switched to night vision mode. The people they'd identified at the tables were still on their feet and their hands dipped into pockets, under jackets, or into purses. Several of the workers had dropped their trays and were in deliberate motion as well.

"Some servers are hostiles."

Her Glock cleared its holster, and she twisted toward the front. The six-figure tables held no apparent enemies.

Even criminals have budgets.

Her area of responsibility was the left side of the room, so she found the first likely target on that side and lined the shot up. He hadn't drawn a weapon yet, and her innate caution wouldn't allow her to squeeze the trigger. When a gun appeared in his hand, however, she didn't hesitate. She put a round into his hip, another into his back, and the third into his shoulder. In almost the same motion, she adjusted her aim to the woman beside him, who had drawn her own pistol from the patent leather clutch she carried.

Diana struck her twice in the arm and once in the leg as the target tried to change position for a better angle. The man fell to the left, and the woman crumpled to lie across the table.

The room filled with screams as the chaos built. Diana distantly registered the familiar gunfire of Trent and Bryant's weapons. The BAM pistols all sounded slightly different than the off-the-shelf models, thanks to Emerson's tinkering. She sought the next target and kept one eye on the ambassador's security team as they rushed him toward the far end of the stage. In that instant, three things happened simultaneously. First, the Secret Service responded and fired at obvious targets behind her. Second, the ARES team members positioned outside the doors flooded in. There were contingencies for most situations, including power loss, and barked incantations preceded orbs of wizard light that blazed up to hover at ceiling height. The space was bathed in a cold glow.

The third thing was not nearly as positive. On the stage, from the exit point the ambassador's team had chosen, a pair of dark figures appeared. A fireball and a bolt of force eliminated the guards in an instant. The ambassador raised his hands to cast a counter attack, but tendrils wound around him, yanked his arms tightly to his side, and covered his mouth. He floated through the door a foot off the ground, preceded by at least one enemy and trailed by another who backpedaled to guard against intervention but otherwise passed on the opportunity to join the fray.

And you think nobody noticed, scumbags?

"They've taken the ambassador, house right front." Diana immediately flowed into a run and shoved through the panicked crowd to leap onto the low stage and pound after them. Bryant was a couple of steps behind her when she reached his side of the room, and she imagined Trent would be on his way as well.

Taggart's calm voice cut through the surrounding din. "Squad one, secure stairwells and elevators. Don't let them go up. Squad two, cover the front and back exits. Secret Service will take care of the dining room and the sides of the building. Sniper teams, check in."

The sleepy voice of Tara Brenner, the most wicked shot on the team, replied first. "Sniper one, no activity in front."

Johnson's smooth tones followed immediately after. "Sniper two, three unmarked SUVs approaching the back."

There was a pause, then Taggart answered, "Drones have them in sight. They're not Service or us. Take them out."

Diana reached the edge of the stage and through a gap in the drape, saw the corridor beyond. She waited until Bryant arrived, then pointed at herself and held a finger up, and he nodded. A crouching sidestep into the hallway with her pistol extended revealed no enemies. She stood and rushed toward the double doors to the kitchen a dozen feet ahead.

"Cars immobilized," Johnson reported. He sounded bored at first but ended on a hopeful note. "Weapons free?"

Taggart was quick to reply. "Negative. FBI and DCPD are on the way. We have the runners tagged with the drone. Unless they attempt to intervene, let 'em go and focus on the building."

"Affirmative." The sniper sighed regretfully.

She barged into the door to the kitchen and plowed

through without slowing. This section seemed to have escaped the blackout and the ugly florescent lights above threw everything into harsh definition and the staff stood with hands raised. "Where'd they go?" she shouted. Fingers pointed toward a side exit that headed toward the interior of the building. She kicked it open and stuck her head through to discover an immediate left-hand turn and stairs down. *Damn. Why would they trap themselves in the basement?*

Cautiously but quickly, she began her descent and kept her pistol trained ahead. "They're headed down. Are there exits below?"

"Checking," the SAC replied. Diana reached the bottom of the stairs, which ended at another door. This one felt more dangerous for some reason. She removed her jacket to ensure quicker access to her gear and met Bryant's eyes as he did the same. He nodded his readiness. She patted Rath's cylinder to make sure it was still with her.

"There's nothing on the blueprints other than the freight elevator," Taggart said,

Johnson added, "And no activity where the elevator opens onto the alley. I have eyes on it."

Diana shook her head to clear the impatience.

Fine. whatever. Let's do this.

She pounded her foot into the door to open it and darted through. The first thing she noticed was the size of the basement. The room was probably a little larger than the dining room. Pallets of wrapped supplies covered both sides to leave an irregular lane between them. It was wide enough to accommodate the small forklift parked against the wall in a nearby corner. The second thing she noticed was the glint of rifle barrels in the instant before the clatter of weapons fire began. She skipped to the right, ducked behind a stack of boxes, and crouched as soon as she was out of their line of sight. Bullets punched through the cardboard above and rang against the metal of the forklift beside her.

Bryant crouched on the opposite side of the room behind his own tower of sight-blockers. The initial salvo of bullets slowed to a stop, and the echoes bounced around until they, too, faded. He pointed at himself and slashed a hand to indicate the middle lane. She nodded and he started the count using his fingers. At one, she crabbed out, fired blindly down the alley, and squeezed the trigger steadily to cover his advance until her gun clicked empty. Diana scuttled back against the wall and hoped the depth of the obstruction would hide her from return fire. She ejected the magazine, replaced it, and racked the slide automatically.

Her partner's gun barked, and she dashed out of her own position and scanned frantically to find cover. There was none so Diana increased her speed as she flashed past Bryant and flicked the selector to burst. Ahead, two adversaries with rifles stepped clear of their own protection on either side of the lane. She extended her gun arm, dropped into a slide along the rough concrete floor, and pulled the trigger as rapidly as it could respond, her aim focused on the one on the right. Her bullets stitched a diagonal across him and catapulted him back before he could fire. She thrust both her arm and her will out and pictured the other gunman's rifle barrel rise to the ceiling. His bullets went high as the muzzle tilted, and Bryant fired the fatal shot.

She pushed up onto trembling legs and blew out a breath to steady herself. "Too close."

Even in the heat of battle, he managed to tease her. He imitated her voice. "You didn't tell me you had magic."

She raced forward to flank the doors out of the room, and he matched her on the opposite side. "You lied first," she whispered. "Also, bite me."

Taggart's interruption was startling. "Focus, people. We have a team coming down after you, Bryant, Diana."

"Tell them to go faster." Diana bulldozed through the door and her slow-motion magic spider sense saved her. She threw herself to the ground as a thin beam of confined flame speared through the space her skull had just occupied. The fleeting look she had of her assailant's face as she rolled to the side filled her with rage. She growled. "It's the skinny fuck who tried to kill Rath. I bet the bastard giant is here, too, since they seem only to come as a set. Why the hell aren't they in the Cube?"

After a brief silence, Taggart spoke roughly, his voice a strange mix of angry and apologetic. "The transport was apparently ambushed on the way. The team at the prison thought it would be a good idea to do their own investigation before they reported it."

Forgiveness was not in Diana's wheelhouse at the moment. "Mark them down for a boot to the head." She raced in pursuit and the blood pounded in her ears as she yelled, "Get back here, scumbag!" Rath's cannister shook violently at her hip and snapped open. He leapt out and to the side, already starting to grow. By the time she reached the corner the wizard had fled around, the troll ran beside her, a fierce grin on his face.

"Fighting mode."

"Let's kick some ass, Rath."

She was ready for it when they rounded the turn and saw the two who'd conspired to damage her car standing side-by-side. Rath angled toward the skinny mage, who blanched at the sight of him but still launched streams of flame in his direction. The troll bobbed and weaved and laughed with what could be called fiendish delight. He made it close enough to jump and launched into a two-footed kick that would've done Jet Li proud. The mage yelled, "Not this time!" and flicked his wand.

A shimmering wave struck him, and he hurtled into the wall at his side before he dropped hard. Diana ground her teeth and emptied her pistol at the huge figure in front of her, but he dodged most of them and laughed at the ones that did strike home. She thought briefly about going for her backup gun, but building rage pushed her to use her fists.

Besides, I might need the anti-magic bullets later.

The skinny man was already racing from the room. Bryant called, "I'm on him," as he barreled past.

Diana holstered her weapon. "Okay, big boy. Let's see if you're any better in round two." In her peripheral vision, she saw Rath flip to his feet. Thankfully, he looked none the worse for wear. She yelled, "Help Bryant!" as she ducked under a wicked hook from the muscled mountain and threw a low X-block against the body jab that followed. She attempted a wrist lock, but he pulled away before she could apply it. The move opened his ribs, and she powered a quick step-sidekick into them and drove him back a half-foot.

Shit. That should have put him into the wall.

She danced back as he threw a series of kicks with a wide grin. He rumbled at her and condescension dripped from his words. "I underestimated you before, but not this time. You'll have to do better than that, little girl, if you want to save your partner and your pet."

Her anger impelled her forward, and she attacked with a furious combination of body punches and a kick to the shin. He weathered them all and spun an elbow at her face. When she dodged, he drilled his own sidekick into her. The Kevlar blunted the impact enough that her ribs didn't break, but the sharp pain suggested that at least one was cracked. He was on her before she could recover, landed two body blows against her blocking arms, and brought an ax kick down at her shoulder.

Diana took the only option, which was to fall and roll under his descending heel to save her collarbone. She scrambled back as he stamped at her and managed to swing her legs around for an ankle sweep. It didn't connect but it forced him back long enough that she could use the momentum to climb to her feet. He still wore the grin. Frustration flowed through her, and she embraced it, picturing Rath and Bryant in trouble. Her fury climbed. She absorbed it hungrily and packed it into her flesh, visualizing it as a pool of bubbling red power waiting in her core.

"You should've chosen the Cube, asshole." She rocketed forward and feinted low. When he flinched to block, she launched upward, snapped her foot out at the perfect moment, and channeled the waiting power into it. The combination of momentum, muscle, and magic struck his chest right of the center line. His ribcage buckled and caved in, and her momentum thrust him back and crushed him between her knee and the wall to maximize the damage. She landed poised and ready to deliver a finishing blow, but he only coughed blood and slumped without a word. His eyes were wide with pain and shock.

She shook her head. "Threatening people I care about is a bad idea. If you survive, I'm up for round three any day, any time." Then, she ran for the exit.

Bryant followed the passage through several twists and turns before it finally ended in a small room with a heavy old door that swung closed as he entered. In front of it stood the wizard who had blasted Rath and he looked furious. The agent emptied his pistol as he closed but the mage waved his wand disdainfully to deflect the bullets.

"Idiot." He sneered and twisted the wand to release a strange shimmer at his adversary. It was different than any force or fire attacks Bryant was familiar with and seemed flatter and more solid. His brain finally put the pieces together and decided it was most like the blade of a longsword.

Bryant dropped in a panic as it swished dangerously above him. The mage laughed, and the agent heard the roar of the fire before his brain could anticipate the follow-up attack.

"*Scield!*" A sphere of protection surrounded him in an instant.

I owe Kienka double for delivering the charm early.

He had barely managed to attune it in time and had, in fact, only finished the process on the trip to the dinner.

Fire washed over him but didn't pierce his protection. He bounced back to his feet in time to register the warning as the wand flicked at him once more. A physical blow shuddered painfully when the shimmer met the edge of his shield and knocked him to the side. He turned it into a roll to avoid another fire blast. Panic lapped at the edges of his mind as the time remaining on the shield—kept by careful count in his head—descended into single digits.

Rath saved the day. The troll careened into the room as fast as his short legs could carry him. In seconds, he had closed the distance before the man noticed him. His arm was cocked, ready to deliver a vicious blow, and his target flinched and redirected all his power at this new enemy. Rath slid under the fire and followed it with a diving tumble over the blade of force that even the most cranky Olympic judge would have respected. The mage scampered to the side to put some distance between himself and the angry creature.

Bryant grinned as his shield fell. He primed the sonic grenade, yelled, "Rath!" and threw it at the mage. The troll dropped into a tightly curled heap on the ground and shielded his head with his long arms. The agent's earpieces reduced the noise in the room to virtual silence as the sonic grenade emitted its activation pulse and detonated.

Unfortunately, his warning to Rath had also alerted the wizard. He responded and a blast of force intercepted the grenade and bounced it back, resulting in minimal impact to himself and none to Bryant.

Waste of a good grenade. The agent switched magazines

and tried the bullets again, this time to cover Rath's actions. While the mage blocked the rounds, the troll curved out of his vision and attacked from behind. He vaulted onto the wizard's back and used his hands to claw at the enemy's eyes.

Bryant had to admit the wizard's reflexes were deceptively quick, given his scholarly demeanor. The man ducked his head and took the scratches on his forehead. Blood flowed, and he screamed in pain or anger or both. He thrust his wand forward, and Bryant braced himself against the impending force blast. Instead, the mage rocketed backward and slammed the troll between himself and the wall. Both fell to the ground, dazed. They recovered simultaneously, and the man drew a runed blade from behind his back and slashed viciously at his adversary. Rath scrambled away, found his feet with a backward somersault, and easily avoided the frantic swipes. The familiar toothy grin looked far more ferocious in his larger form.

"Enough of this," Bryant muttered and drew his backup weapon. He sighted carefully and calculated the mage's path as he stalked toward the troll with the dagger raised. Aiming for a headshot was purely reflex, and the agent shifted the barrel down at the momentary thought that a prisoner might prove valuable. He pulled the trigger twice. The mage reacted immediately to the gun's soft bark and threw up a shield in an awkward cross-body movement. The anti-magic bullets sliced through the barrier and pounded into his leg at knee and thigh. He screamed and fell.

Rath attacked and delivered a boxing combination that

looked suspiciously like something Rocky had used against Ivan Drago. He stood over the downed mage and grinned.

Bryant shook his head and retrieved some zip ties from his back pocket. "Tie him up, Rath. I'll go after the ambassador."

The troll nodded and caught them out of the air. "Bryant. Rath. Diana. Team."

"You got it, big guy." He re-holstered the Ruger and grabbed his Glock, ejected his part-empty magazine, and swapped it with his last full one, then opened the heavy door. Beyond was a dusty tunnel with two sets of footprints in the dirt. It was only as he pounded along the passageway that the image of the ambassador floating from the room entered his mind.

Reinforcements. Shit.

CHAPTER TWENTY-SEVEN

Diana burst into a smallish room in time to see Bryant vanish around a corner in the dimly lit corridor ahead. She skidded to a stop at the sight of Rath applying zip ties to a crumpled wizard. His three-foot size was still a surprise every time she saw it, accustomed as she was to his normal stature. "Is Bryant okay?"

The troll nodded. "Bryant and Rath strong. Stupid wizard weak."

"Excellent. I'll go after him. Oh, wait." She fished around in her front pockets, withdrew Rath's batons, and threw them, and he caught them with a grin. He flicked one open and poked the figure on the ground before him, then laughed at the resulting snap and sizzle. The smell of ozone wafted through the room.

He looked at her with a wicked grin. "Had to test."

Diana shook her head. "Of course. You can't go into battle with a weapon you don't trust. Catch up when you're done." She drew her pistol, bolted into the corridor, and activated her comm. "Bryant?" There was no reply. Even the subtle carrier sound of an empty channel seemed to be missing. She took the turns and curves of the passage at breakneck speed on the assumption that he would have identified any traps along the way or enemies lying in wait. After a few moments, she caught up in time to see him peek around the corner before he entered a wider space.

Angry voices echoed, but she was too focused on running to make sense of them. She lurched into the room to find Bryant with his pistol aimed at the enemy closest to the ambassador and an outstretched hand directed at the room's other occupant.

The agent sounded smug. "What was that you said about two on one?"

The dwarf who stood beside the ambassador swiveled to target Diana. Arrogance dripped from his words. "No matter. You're both human and easily defeated."

She aimed her gun at him and snaked the other hand behind her back to palm her pepper grenade. "That's what the other two thought. It didn't work out too well for them."

The wand-wielder in the far corner barked a laugh. He was of normal height but ugly. It looked like someone had stood on his face and pushed it inward. "Disposable soldiers. Their skills are much less than ours."

Bryant shook his head. "If you try to leave, you're dead. If you don't, our reinforcements will be here in short order. You're stuck. How about you put your weapons down? Nobody has to die here today."

The dwarf gave him a thin smile. "Failure *is* death, human."

Time slowed and Diana moved. She threw the pepper

grenade at the wizard across the room, not trusting the ambassador's ability to breathe while trapped in the massive tentacles that encased him. The dwarf summoned a bolt of darkness that raced toward her even in her adjusted vision. She pivoted back on her right foot, knowing she couldn't dodge all of it but hoping to at least evade some. Her gun barked, and with his attention focused on the ambassador and the attack, his hasty shield activated too late. A bullet caught him in the right upper arm, and he cowered and raised his left hand instinctively to cover the wound. She caught the glint of metal. *Does everyone but me have one of those stupid bracelets?* The tentacles began to uncoil, and she had a brief moment in which to enjoy her success before the shadow bolt pounded into her.

Four loud pops erupted as the anti-magic deflectors on her vest were consumed. Each felt like a jab from a skilled boxer and she stumbled in the direction of her pivot. She spun to the ground with a cry of surprise and pain. Her magical perception fell, and Rath moved at real speed when he bounded over her prone form on his way to the foe who had attacked her.

Across the room, Bryant fired bullets one at a time to keep his opponent pinned in place. The wizard extended his arm and yelled a command, and lightning flared from his wand. One multi-forked blast burst into Bryant, dropped him to one knee, and turned the deflectors on his vest black. Another caught Diana. The icy needles stabbed at every nerve and pinned her to the ground as she rolled onto her arched back with a shout, this one more of rage than pain.

She heard the pepper grenade detonate and the lightning fell away. Rath flung himself at the dwarf, who now wore a look of absolute fury. He made a scooping motion, and the troll was lifted and thrown to the far side of the room. He managed to position his legs and landed in a skid, then seemingly realized for the first time that a second enemy was present.

One that coughed and gagged from the pepper spray.

One that was only a few feet away.

With a loud bellow, the troll hurtled at the wizard and smacked his forehead into his target's nose. An echoing crunch confirmed the effectiveness of the strategy.

She heard chanting as she pushed herself to her feet. The dwarf opened a portal behind the ambassador, who swayed senselessly although now tentacle-free. Bryant shouted a word she didn't recognize, and the opening collapsed on itself. He cried out, and she turned to see him grip his collarbone.

The dwarf snarled defiance. "There will be another time, humans. Count on it." He fled down the corridor and Diana stumbled after him, firing with each step.

Her bullets sparked off a vibrant shimmer that encased him, and she cursed. Her gun clicked empty, and she resisted the urge to throw it at him. She closed the distance as her gait steadied, his shorter legs no match for her enraged sprint. There was an intersection ahead, and she saw him pass the opening to the left and continue. She put her head down and added a burst of speed.

The blast of force that struck as she crossed the intersection careened her into the wall and pinned her off the ground. Her gun fell from numb fingers to clatter on the cement floor. The figure ahead had vanished, and she fought to turn her head to the left against the giant hand that now crushed her. The dwarf stood there, smirking, in the center of what appeared to be a library. His right hand was extended toward her, and his left pointed at the floor. Tendrils emerged from it and slithered toward her like snakes. She noted, far too late, that the bracelet on her wrist had been icy cold and now faded to normal.

He twisted his right hand into a fist, and the force pushed harder to grind her shoulder blade against the wall. She snarled at her own stupidity. An answering growl echoed from the direction from which she'd come and she knew Rath was on his way.

I only have to hold out.

The dwarf couldn't resist taunting her as the first tentacle encircled her calves. "We should have plenty of time to make it out of here before your friends find their path through my illusions. Once the tentacles have you, we will retire to a place where we can spend many an hour getting to know one another very well indeed."

"Let me go and I'll show you everything you need to know about me, asshole." She panted against the pain. He laughed, and the tentacles climbed higher. Diana tried to summon a clever comment, but he increased the pressure and a scream of rage emerged in its place.

Rather than overwhelm her senses and force her to fight for control, the surge of emotion did something unexpected. Suddenly, she sensed the edges of the spell that held her. She imagined the cone that emanated from his hand and the steady pulses that ran through it to press her against the wall. It materialized in her vision exactly like another augmented reality overlay. A familiar pressure pushed inside, the same one she unthinkingly blocked by well-practiced reflex whenever it occurred. Her inner voice suggested that since she was about to die—or about to be taken away for the extended torment of being in the pretentious scumbag's presence—maybe it was time to quit fighting herself so hard.

Frustration marshaled against the suggestion immediately, and she realized with a shock of insight that her instinctive defense wasn't all strength as she had believed it to be. For the first time, she saw the fear woven through it, cleverly disguised and subtle in its influence. That fear had been part of her since the first time her magic power erupted and blasted apart a toy that had vexed her seven-year-old self—and the table it sat upon.

That same fear had lain mostly dormant as long as she stayed away from magic. When the squad was attacked in Atlanta—when *she* was attacked in Atlanta—it rose in secret and masqueraded as rationality to convince her once again to squash her inner power for fear that she would lose control of it.

You've seen what magic can do, it had whispered then.

All that self-analysis passed in a flash. With an act of will greater than any she remembered and fueled by her anger at the self-deception, she released the mental doors on her mind that she'd strained to hold closed. The magic exploded from her and traveled the channel the dwarf had created between them. He shrieked as the backlash of raw power fueled by Diana's fear, anger, and self-loathing shattered his hand.

Diana fell to the ground and stretched her arm out to summon another force blast to end the fight.

It failed to materialize.

Shit. So much for control.

She extended her other hand and pictured his feet flying out from under him, then yanked it toward her. The telekinesis still worked, and he fell hard on his back. She tried to rise but stumbled. Her legs were too weak to stand. He rolled and scrambled to his feet, raised his functional hand with a scream, and snapped it forward. She saw the ball of energy rocket toward her and knew there was no chance she could get out of its way.

Fortunately, she didn't have to. Rath jumped in front of her and absorbed the blow, crouched as he weathered the blast, then straightened with a yell. He erupted in a blur of motion and smashed at his attacker with his batons. Sharp cracks punctuated the blows that he rained on the dwarf's legs and arms. The Oriceran managed another weak blast as he fell, which sent the troll into a violent head-over-heels tumble to slide into the wall beside her.

The dwarf's mouth was bloody, and a shard of bone protruded from the arm above his ruined hand. He coughed, and it sounded like something was broken inside him. "At least I'll have the satisfaction of taking you with me." The air surrounding him glimmered. The pressure in the room increased, accompanied by a buzzing that grew in volume with each passing second. Diana couldn't stand, so she did the only thing she could think to do. She flopped onto her stomach, drew the Ruger, and extended it ahead of her. Contact with the floor helped to steady her trembling hands.

She squeezed the trigger six times and anti-magic bullets struck the dwarf again and again. As he jerked and writhed with each impact, the noise and pressure continued to build.

She looked at Rath, and her inner floodgates opened, filled with regret they wouldn't have more time together and vicious anger at the mage who had stolen it from them.

No, not only anger.

Raw, primal fury.

Diana fell into it, snatched handfuls of the molten emotion, and bound it into a shell around her. Her last conscious effort was to use the final physical energy she possessed to throw herself forward and curl around Rath.

The dwarf's death spell detonated and shattered the stone walls of the room to spray shrapnel in all directions. The furniture instantly splintered, and they were caught in the maelstrom of whirling destruction that decimated everything it touched.

Fortunately, it couldn't reach either Diana or Rath. A bubble of translucent ruby force surrounded them and resisted the onslaught. Finally, the tornado died as suddenly as it had started. Diana's rage abandoned her, and the shield dropped.

Rath looked at her with a joyful grin. "Diana. Fighting mode. Is good."

When Bryant finally reached the room, he was stunned by the destruction and shocked at the damage the dwarf had taken. The most alarming thing of all, though, was the sight of Diana and Rath lying on their backs, twisting and writhing in spasms of uncontrolled laughter while shredded book pages floated around the room like snow.

CHAPTER TWENTY-EIGHT

Bryant braced himself for the impending noise. Taggart squeezed the trigger smoothly six times and emptied his backup Ruger into the humanoid target at the end of the pistol range. Even through the earplugs, the gun's reports were startling in the small space at the back of Ems' domain.

The bullets had made two tight groupings, three in center mass and three in the forehead. The men removed their hearing protectors. "Nice shooting, boss."

Taggart grinned. "Some things, you never forget."

He aimed the gun skyward and flicked out the chamber to allow the cartridges from the safety rounds to fall into his off-hand. "One more set, I think." He turned the table, gathered up six rounds, and slotted them into the cylinder's chambers. "So, do you have any thoughts about the mission you didn't include in your official report?"

The agent shrugged as he considered the question. "Not really. It was a bad situation, but we did well, regardless. The new tech was a vital piece of it, though. We need to make getting anti-magic bullets a priority. Find out who has them and why." The SAC waved his hand as if to say, "Heard it before, move on."

Bryant complied. "Diana did great, as did the rest of the team. No areas of specific improvement necessary. Merely more of the same."

Taggart spun the cylinder. The ratcheting was soothing. "And the troll did well?"

He rolled his eyes.

Of course Taggart found out about the troll.

"Rath was great, too. He will keep Diana on her toes even better than I could."

The other man barked a laugh. "She has certainly landed in the thick of it, magic-wise."

Bryant endured a moment's discomfort before he decided some secrets weren't important enough to keep. "I talked to her about her magic."

"I wondered if you would. It's good that you did. That shows strong leadership in the face of questionable policies, even if they're mine."

The agent laughed. "I learned from the best, boss. Anyway, she's likely to be even more powerful than we thought. The early warning thing, some telekinesis, and..."

Taggart looked sharply at him as he swung the cylinder closed with a *click*. "And?"

Bryant shrugged. "She hasn't really talked about it, but from what I've seen, there seems to be a randomness to her magic that is unique. She claims to have had only telekinetic power, but I definitely saw her use force magic at one point. I'm not sure, though. Maybe she couldn't tell the difference, or maybe she doesn't want to talk about it until she gets the hang of it. Either way, there's something there."

The SAC nodded and looked extremely satisfied that his instincts had proven correct. Again. "That'll make your job even more fun." Bryant laughed in response. "Are you ready to get started?"

"As ready as I'll ever be," the agent said. "We'll need every one of those offices up and running as quickly as possible."

Taggart paused, one earplug already inserted. "And if what we've seen with this bunch of scumbags is any indication, we'll need to apply what you learn in the Northeast to the rest of the country sooner rather than later." His companion nodded as Taggart finished inserting his earpiece and turned back to the target. He raised the Ruger and put six rounds into the target, one into each arm, and the remainder created a diamond pattern on its face.

Bryant shook his head. "Yep, you've definitely still got it, boss."

Diana found Kayleigh waiting when she entered the core and rushed to share her appreciation. "The boots are awesome. The Ruger pulls clean every time. And they go with everything I own."

The tech laughed. "Of course. I would never go half-effort on something as important as custom footwear."

"And rightly so."

She tapped a button, and the transcript of Diana's after-action report spat out onto one of the displays. "I think a sonic grenade would've worked out better than the pepper spray."

The agent laughed in appreciation of the brash comment. "You may be right. Maybe you should join us in the field and do some experimentation yourself."

Kayleigh held up her hand and backed away a step. "No way, not a chance. I'm a learner, not a fighter."

Diana folded her arms. "Learn to fight, then. I bet you'd be great outside the lab. In Pittsburgh, say."

The other woman laughed again and looked ready to offer another counterargument, but the core's main door opened and saved her from having to reply.

Oh, I'll get you, my pretty. And your little dog, too.

Diana turned to Bryant and Taggart. "Howdy, gents."

Bryant smirked at her. "Howdy yourself, Special Agent in Charge Sheen."

She grinned.

It does have a nice ring to it.

Taggart ignored them both and addressed Kayleigh. "Can I see the chart in one half and the coins in the other?" She nodded and activated some buttons on the display table.

"Coins?" The happy note in Diana's voice had been replaced by concern. Taggart gestured to the display where front and back images of two matching coins appeared on the screen. She peered closer. "They're truly identical, not merely similar, aren't they?"

He nodded. "They are. The tiny hope that we might be facing solo actors—or at most, a very small group—seems to have been put to rest."

She frowned. "Why is that?"

Bryant answered. "One person with the coin would be strange since it's a lot of work to go to for whatever they wanted to accomplish. There would be easier ways. If there were only a small number, we'd expect some differences in them to indicate that a limited amount of effort went into making them. I mean, if you only make a handful, the motivation to strive for perfect uniformity is minimal."

"Unless the uniformity is necessary to make the spell or mechanism or whatever work," Kayleigh chimed in.

"Granted. But we can't afford to think best case, right?" Everyone nodded in response. "So, it's likely there are more of these floating around."

Diana stared at the image but no answers came. "Where was this one?"

"On the dwarf who went kaboom." Bryant mimicked an explosion with his hands. "Despite being at the origin of that destruction, the coin was completely unharmed."

She released a sigh to relieve the tension inside her. "Okay, so in practical terms, what does this mean for us?"

Taggart shrugged. "Well, by itself, nothing. But in the context of the rest of our discoveries, probably a great deal." He swiveled his head to Kayleigh. "Can we see the Twisted Lizard, please?"

An image of a building that was more charcoal than actual structure displayed. "This bar burst into flame immediately after the incident at the hotel. It burned exceptionally fast and hot, so the fire department is calling it arson. Our teams went through after the blaze was out and found everything in the place destroyed except for a single pristine desk drawer."

"A fireproof desk drawer? Is that a real thing?" Diana

asked.

Bryant chuckled. "Probably not, but a heavily warded and protected one apparently is."

Taggart nodded. "It took the magic techs a while to undo its defenses, but when they did, this was inside." He gestured, and an image of a metal spiral supporting a gemstone replaced the destroyed bar. The golden twists were attached to a dark wooden base.

She stared at the gem, which was unharmed and happily aglow despite having been through the destruction of the building around it. "What is it?"

The SAC sounded worried. "We're not positive and are sticking with passive tests at the moment. Frankly, we're not yet desperate enough to try putting it together with the coin to see what happens. Our best guess is that it's for communication, or perhaps it's a sensing tool."

Bryant sounded equally worried. "Or maybe it's a doomsday device. I hope you keep the coins in a different part of the building from the stand. Hell, in a different building altogether."

Taggart chuckled. "We have it under control. Don't get your boxers in a twist."

"Boxer briefs, actually," the agent snarked.

Diana waved her hands in front of her eyes. "Entirely too much information. How about we talk about what the symbol means instead?"

Taggart looked uncomfortable, an expression she'd never seen him wear before. "There's no exact match to it in any records. Not ours or Oriceran's. However, it does have resonance with an important icon from the past." Without being asked, Kayleigh called up another image.

"An infinity symbol? The number eight? What?"

He didn't laugh at Diana's comedy. "That symbol was used by the followers of Rhazdon, an evil leader who tried to create a power base in opposition to the rightful rulers of Oriceran. She is directly responsible for the creation and dissemination of any number of artifacts that have appeared on Earth."

"Two hundred and eight artifacts," Kayleigh interrupted. Taggart held a palm up in acknowledgment.

Diana frowned. "So, she's our target?"

Bryant shook his head. "You need to brush up on your Oriceran history, Sheen. Rhazdon and her followers were finally defeated a couple of decades ago."

"So, what are we worried about then? Ghosts?"

Taggart sounded uncomfortable, too. "We think it's too similar to be a coincidence. Whoever is in charge of this group is invoking her memory for some reason. Whatever that is, it's unlikely to be good for us."

"Well, at least we can sweat the Kilomea for details once he gets to the Cube."

The SAC nodded. "You can take care of it personally since you've developed such a rapport with him." She snorted. "Next week, you're on your way to your new gig."

Diana grinned. "You mean I won't get to see Bryant every day anymore? That's truly a sad, sad moment."

Bryant smirked and put his hand on his heart. "Diana, I didn't know you cared."

"For him," she finished. She received the expected laughs and beamed at her comrades.

That's Special Agent in Charge Diana to you, pal.

CHAPTER TWENTY-NINE

The Legal Beagle was packed, even more than usual for a Friday night. Nonetheless, they'd been able to claim their favorite pair of seats at the end of the bar, and the trio of bartenders kept their drinks fresh without the need for instruction.

Diana wrapped up the tale of the fight at the hotel and the rescue of the ambassador. "So, that worked out okay."

Lisa nodded, her eyes a little wide. "So Rath protected you? Not the other way around?"

She laughed. "We're a team. We look out for each other. Exactly like you and me."

Her friend chided her with a *tsk*. "I'm not sure how you'll manage that from Pittsburgh."

The agent rolled her eyes. Lisa had poked her about the impending relocation all evening, even though she understood the situation perfectly. "There will be eyes on you. And I'll be back whenever I can to make sure you don't destroy my house."

Lisa laughed. "Hopefully, you're a better landlord than

you are a friend. Or a home renovator. Or, really, better than you are at most things, I guess."

"Maybe we should discuss some sweat equity."

"Please. Construction is not my bag, baby."

They shared a laugh and paused to sip their drinks. Diana had ordered a thick double IPA, and the other woman drank a seasonal ginger cider she claimed to love. Lisa lowered her voice. "Why didn't you bring Rath?"

Diana shook her head in exasperation. "I offered but he refused to come. Apparently, Max 'must train.' Frankly, I fear whatever the two of them get up to at home. There may not be a place left for you to move into."

Lisa's reply was preempted by a harsh slur from beside her. "Well, if it isn't the tramp and her frumpy friend."

They turned together to face Steve, who was clearly drunk and visibly angry. Lisa had confided to her earlier in the week that they'd broken up, but she'd played it off like it was amicable. The man's attitude offered a different version of that parting.

Diana twitched and her mouth opened to tell him exactly what he could do with his inebriated idiocy, but Lisa stopped her with a hand on her arm. Her voice was chilled but reasonable. "Steve, we discussed this. I'm not ready for the level of commitment you seem to want, and we're far from a perfect match, anyway."

He pointed a finger, and Diana resisted the urge to break it and use it to slam his face into the bar. The pictures in her head were momentarily pleasing, though. His words emerged in an accusing snarl. "You were never honest with me. You lied."

Lisa frowned. "You heard what you wanted to hear and

saw what you wanted to see. We had some fun dates. Don't ruin it with this nonsense." Her voice hardened. "Now go away, or you'll get yourself thrown out."

The third bartender—who doubled as the Beagle's bouncer on the rare occasions it was necessary—hovered nearby. Steve recognized his presence with a visible recoil, and he backed off with a parting, "Yeah, right. Whatever." The name he muttered under his breath made Diana want to continue the discussion with her fist.

Lisa turned back to the bar. "I thought it was the female of the species who was supposed to be all possessive. Every man I date wants to marry me within a week, it seems."

Diana laughed. "That's really not a problem for me. I guess there *is* a benefit to not being the shining star after all."

Her friend sighed and Diana watched her banish the incident from her mind. "So, I can move in next week?"

"Yep. Rath, Max, and I will head up Monday. Bryant will meet us and show us around. On Tuesday, the real fun begins."

Lisa leaned back as if seeing her for the first time. "Special Agent in Charge. Bah. You don't look the part."

She ordered one more round of drinks. "I will probably have to dress up more often for the new gig, so if you think I'll wear anything other than jeans and sweatshirts between now and then, you don't know me as well as I thought you did."

Well, and the boots Kayleigh gave me, anyway. I guess I'll need to find a good shine spot in Pittsburgh.

They spent the next forty-five minutes in quiet conversation, as comfortable and easy together as always. Her imminent departure wouldn't stop them from texting and talking, and they'd committed to getting together at least a couple of times a month. Diana wasn't willing to lose her connection to DC, even though she eagerly anticipated the move north and all the challenges it would bring.

As they finished their drinks, a still-seething Steve stormed through the crowd and slammed the front door behind him. The women exchanged glances and Diana asked, "Do you think he'll let it go?"

"Before tonight, I would've said yes. Now, I'm less sure."

"I can hang out with you until your lift gets here and make sure you get away safely."

"You can't watch me forever. If he sees us together, he'll wait for another opportunity—assuming he plans to do something, anyway. We're probably worrying for nothing. Steve's a talker."

"You never know, though." Diana thought for a minute, then nodded, her decision made. She gestured for the tab. "Okay, let's find out if he's up to anything or not. Here's what we'll do."

Fifteen minutes later, Lisa left the building by the front door. She turned toward the pickup spot she always used when carless, far enough away from the front door to avoid the second-hand smoke. As she passed the small alley that ran beside the bar, Steve's voice called to her and sounded remorseful. "Lisa, I only want to talk to you." He slurred half the words, and she shook her head in sadness at his stupidity.

Why can't people treat one another better?

She turned into the alley as Diana had instructed her. They had correctly concluded he wouldn't be bold enough to confront her on the street.

Steve stood about six feet in, his back against the right wall and his hands in the pockets of his peacoat. He spoke before she could, and his breath misted in the cold air. "I'm sorry for how I behaved inside. Sometimes, I get a little too invested, I know. It's just...I'm sure we could be good together. It's hard to let go."

Lisa nodded. "I accept your apology, Steve. I hope you find the right person for you. Truly." She turned to leave, and his hand immediately grabbed her wrist.

"I already have, Lisa. Give me another chance." He smiled as his arm encircled her waist from behind. "I know I can make you happy."

One last try.

"I've made my decision, Steve, and won't change my mind. Now please, let go of me." He tightened his grasp, and she sighed. With a rotation of her arm and a quick yank against the place where his index finger and thumb met, she broke his hold and stepped away.

His eyes betrayed his surprise, and he took a couple of staggering steps to put himself squarely in her path to the street. "No, Lisa—look, let's talk about this rationally."

From behind her, Diana's voice rang out over the sound of the back door to the bar slamming shut. "I believe the lady asked you to leave her alone, Steve. Walk away before you find yourself in cuffs."

His face twisted with anger and dislike as he looked past her at Diana. He bumped her shoulder as he strode past, apparently having made the incredibly foolish decision to confront her friend. Lisa sighed again. *Idiot. You'll wish you'd left.*

Diana leaned against the bar's outer wall, one leg crossed in front of the other, and watched him approach. It was cold, and she kept her hands tucked into the pockets of her leather jacket. There was no reason to think he was carrying, and she had no fear of his ability to fight unarmed given his alcohol intake. He appeared angrier with every step and clearly built himself up to confront her. She'd seen that particular routine before many times.

When he got within skip-sidekick range and opened his mouth to speak, she held a hand up and snapped, "Shut it." She straightened as he blinked in surprise. "I trounce people twice as big and three times as smart as you on a regular basis. You do not want to do this. What you do want to do is turn around, walk out of this alley without so much as making eye contact with Lisa, and go home to sleep it off and *never* bother either of us again. Any other choice will end badly for you."

He frowned. She watched the emotions whip across his face—first fear, then anger, then defiance as he convinced himself he could handle her.

Predictable.

His voice was condescending. "You think you're tough because you have a gun." He searched for what to say next, and she laughed inside.

And a knife, and two other knives, asshole, but who's counting?

He finally came up with it. "Only a coward hides behind weapons." She gave a lazy grin. He'd made his choice, and she was more than ready to deliver his reward. "I know all about you, *former* FBI Agent Diana Sheen," he sneered. "But you're not with the FBI anymore, are you? So all your posturing is a lie. You have no more authority than any other random bitch."

Her eyes narrowed as she took two steps toward him, and she made an internal note to have his business checked out more thoroughly. He shouldn't know that, and Lisa wouldn't have told him. On the outside, though, she merely widened the smile. The perfect quote for the situation popped into her head. "Are you gonna bark all day, little doggy, or are you gonna bite?"

You can never go wrong with Mr. Blond.

He bit. After a quick step forward and a feint with his left, he swung a drunken right hook at her head. She took a step back and swept her right arm across her body and outward in a circle block. Her hand slid down to grab his wrist and she used her left palm to lock his elbow. She put pressure on the joint and he squealed in pain as she forced him to his knees. Diana shook her head. "Even if you weren't drunk, you couldn't connect with that punch—too slow and too obvious. To quote a friend of mine, you 'must train.'" She gave the elbow one more push to emphasize her point. "I'll release you, and you'll walk away. If you don't, I'll call the police."

She stepped out of range, and he staggered to his feet

and brushed his pants off. He wore regret on his face, but it was so overdone that she knew it was a lie.

Save us all from drunks with delusions of competence.

At a slight movement over his shoulder, the corner of her mouth twitched up. He saw it and immediately took offense. "I'll teach you to laugh at me, you—"

Whatever he was about to say turned into a choked gasp as Lisa's foot rocketed up between his legs from behind and dispelled the illusion that he was in any way equal to the moment. He fell hard, curled up protectively, and keened pathetically.

The two women looked at him and Lisa said, "I'd better never see you again, Steve. Not at my work, not at my home, not at a restaurant, and not at the Beagle. If you see me on the street, you run the other way. In fact, you should consider moving."

Diana nodded. "Because if she does see you again, you'll go down for assault. I'll write it up today. How will your company react once you have a criminal record?"

He only whimpered as they walked away. Lisa talked animatedly about how she could've made the kick better. Diana reassured her it was just fine.

CHAPTER THIRTY

The doorbell rang and Diana checked to ensure it wasn't a miscreant. Bryant was on her landing again and stared at the camera with a goofy grin.

So, kind of a miscreant.

"Rath, Max, let Bryant in." The pair were in motion before Rath realized the implications of the request. He looked around guiltily and Diana laughed. "Teeth marks on the door handle. Plus, the camera records people going in and out. Once I noticed the scratches, I checked."

The troll cackled. "Training is important."

She shook her head. "I have decided it's beyond useless to try to stop you. At least you can look out for each other. And it's not like you couldn't simply grow bigger and open it yourself." The doorbell rang again, and she waved her hand. "Go." Moments later, Bryant entered. He was dressed for comfort in jeans and a Captain America T-shirt. She laughed. "If only Lisa could see you now."

"Right?" He grinned and tipped his head to the side to indicate Rath and Max. "Nice concierge service."

"They don't pay rent so they have to contribute somehow."

Rath vaulted onto the counter with an acrobatic leap from the dog's back via a cabinet handle. "Max. Rath. Guard."

"I'm kidding, Rath. Now move." The troll scampered out of the way as Diana took a large pot of bubbling pasta from the stove and dumped it into the colander in the sink.

"Mmmm, Max," the diminutive creature enthused.

Diana laughed. "It's not macaroni, it's farfalle, but you can certainly pile as much cheese as you want on it."

He corrected himself. "Mmmmm. Far-fall-ay." He stretched each syllable out.

She gestured at the small table, which was already set with three places and held a steaming bowl of homemade pasta sauce.

Once she'd wiped her hands, she threw the towel on the counter and visited the fridge for two bottles and a can. She handed Bryant the beers to open and put the can in front of Rath's place. They sat and busied themselves with dinner, putting dressing on salads and spooning sauce over plates of pasta before they teamed up to prepare Rath's portion.

Finally, they were done, and Diana and Bryant broke into simultaneous laughter. She shook her head. "Well, this seems awkward. Why is this awkward?"

"I blame Rath."

"Nope," the troll piped up.

Diana raised her beer bottle to her lips and took a bracing sip. "I guess we've never had a purely social moment, have we?"

He shook his head. "It's a first, all right. And the last for a while, at least in DC, I guess. Are you all ready to relocate?"

She nodded. She'd live out of suitcases while she got organized in Pittsburgh and there wasn't really all that much to pack. "Ready, able, and downright excited to see what's next."

Bryant nodded approvingly. "There'll be more magic stuff there, at least until you clean the place up. Are you okay with that?"

She finished chewing the bite in her mouth—the *sauce could've used a little more salt*—and swallowed. "I have a handle on it. It's all good."

He swiveled his head. "How about you, Rath? Are you ready to move?"

The troll nodded solemnly. "New places to train. Maybe more Max." The Borzoi chose that moment to bark and signal his apparent support for the idea.

Diana pointed at Rath. "No, no, *no*. We are not getting another dog. The place we're renting is smaller than this one. You guys would wreck the place."

Rath shrugged with a smile that was not at all apologetic. "More training. Get better. Help Diana. Help neighborhood."

Bryant nodded. "I've always wanted to ask, Rath—how did you get locked in that cage, anyway?"

The little troll gave a tiny shrug. "Fell asleep home. Woke there. Not sure."

The agent turned to Diana. "Guerre probably planned to sell him—or worse, to train him as support for his work."

"One more reason to be happy he's locked up. Is there anything else important before Monday?"

Bryant frowned. "You know, garlic bread would be good with this."

She rolled her eyes. "No one needs carbs with their carbs. I'll throw some meatballs in a roll for you before you go, how's that?"

"Who knew you were so domestic?"

"The amount that you really know about me can fit in a thimble, Bryant Bates."

Mirth burst out of him in a laugh and grin. "So, you found out. And I'd been so careful."

"It helps to be friends with the right techs." She raised an eyebrow. "Should I call you BB, then?"

He offered her a flirtatious smirk. "You can certainly call me baby if you want, but you probably want to avoid it at the office. What with the rules against fraternization and all."

She groaned. "There are no such rules. You're such a liar. Anyway, back to Pittsburgh."

"There are baddies at the Cube from all over the Northeast, people we need to examine more closely. It's expected there'll be some from the mid-Atlantic as well. And naturally, they're the worst of the worst."

"Who's in charge?"

Bryant gave a dark laugh. "Technically, that's one of the things on my plate. But since I'll travel a lot, I don't expect to have all that much to do with it. The warden is sharp, and before you ask, no, she wasn't involved in the earlier snafu. She hadn't started yet. She's made a name for herself in a number of different government agencies, and this is a step on her ladder to heading one of them, eventually." Diana nodded. "Fortunately, she'll have access to a support team right in her backyard."

Diana lifted an eyebrow. "Any other surprises?"

"Nothing you haven't heard about already. Do you plan to launch both the BAM office and the bounty hunting agency right away?"

"I have a thought about that, actually. Rather than calling ourselves bounty hunters, let's go with security consultants. We can still hunt fugitives, but that might provide access into places we might otherwise not get into."

Bryant nodded. "I like it. We've bought some space in the Strip District. It used to be a warehouse but now, it's empty. The front section can be set up as the public face of the company with a little renovation, and the back is completely open. It should make for a great training spot."

"Will I have the budget to outfit it?"

He had the decency to sound at least slightly regretful. "Not at first. And you'll never be rolling in money. Even though we bring a lot in through our cover companies, our expenses are high."

She shrugged. "Same old, same old."

Bryant grinned. "But with the security agency, you can create another stream of income. Get some contracts. Maybe hire some folks who aren't part of the other side of the house."

She frowned at him. "So what you're saying is that I need a second job to get the funds I need to run my first job?"

"Welcome to Black-ops Agents of Magic, Special Agent in Charge Diana Sheen."

They laughed comfortably and spent the rest of the evening watching action films—this time, *The Expendables* series, which brought together some of Rath's favorite actors. As usual, the troll grew sleepy before they did and curled up. His last waking comment was, "Bryant. Diana. Max. BAM. Is good." He paused and gave everyone a sleepy smile. "We are the law."

Diana grinned.

A new Sheriff's coming to town, Pittsburgh. And she's bringing some kick-ass deputies. You are most definitely not ready for this.

The story doesn't end here. Diana's adventures continue in
Agents of Mayhem.

AUTHOR NOTES - TR CAMERON

MARCH 4, 2019

Thank you.

Thank you for reading the first book in the Magic Ops series, and for continuing on to the author notes! I hope you had as much fun reading the tale as I had writing it.

From the first Oriceran book, I was hooked on the Universe's vision of magic and the conjunction of two worlds / cultures. But what really got me was the action-adventure of it all, the strong heroines and heroes, and the dominant thread of good vs. evil. Plus, the humor.

I live for that stuff.

As this series rolls along, several cool characters will join the team, each bringing their own unique perspective to the mix. No more animals or trolls, though.

Probably. I'm not promising anything on that front.

This has been my first author collaboration, and I must say that it has been a joyful experience working with Martha and Michael. Creativity increases exponentially, rather than arithmetically. The story and series are both definitely the better for it.

February is always a fun month for me, as my daughter's birthday is in there. She starts celebrating with a countdown several weeks beforehand. Then it's days. Then hours. I'm sure that she'll get less entranced with it all as she gets older, but right now, birthdays are EVERYTHING. This year we got her a laser tag game. It's already been controlled chaos as we run through the main floor shooting and screaming.

It's a good counterpart to the battles I write, which are a little more violent, but hopefully still as fun to experience.

The snow is falling outside my window as I write this, and I'm struck by how many days I've spent inside, near a window, reading tales that took me out of the ordinary world and into someplace I could vividly picture in my mind. My first love was fantasy, then science fiction. I detoured through mysteries, into thrillers, and finally into the lands where magic and technology meet. I like to think that you can find pieces of most of those in the stories I tell.

Plus movie quotes and significant levels of sarcastic snark, of course.

If you're a multi-genre reader like me, there's a science fiction series out there with my name on it. I think it's pretty good, and most of those who have commented on it seem to agree. Also, you can find me in all the usual spots on social media. I love chatting about most things, especially media likes, loves, and guilty pleasures, so do feel free to reach out!

I continue my quest to get my daughter to watch Star

Wars. I'm pretty sure that at this point she's just refusing me to be mean.

Joys upon joys to you and yours – so may it be.

AUTHOR NOTES - MARTHA CARR

FEBRUARY 18, 2019

There's a new voice in the Oriceran Universe! TR Cameron has bellied up to the bar with a new Urban Fantasy series, Federal Agents of Magic that's a nice combo of Brownstone kickin' ass and Leira's magic. But you already know that because you've gotten this far.

The really cool part is that we found TR from the first anthology of Oriceran Fans Write for Fans. (Volume 2 is coming sooooon) One of the editors whispered in his ear that he should talk to Michael and myself about writing in Oriceran. Everyone could see this diamond of a writer just waiting for someone to hold open a door.

And TR stepped up and tapped me on the shoulder. The rest is recent history. He's already off somewhere busy writing book two – Agents of Mayhem.

Don't worry, he'll catch on soon enough this is a ravenous reading crowd and we love you for it!

One of my favorite things about hanging with Michael Anderle and company is the opportunity to reach back and help someone else achieve their dreams. There's always been a company ethos that there's more than enough to go around. Hell, we go one step (or ten) beyond and espouse an idea that by sharing what we have everyone will end up with more – not less.

It's worked like a charm.

But wait, there's more! Imagine watching one person after another improve their life and achieve a dream. Imagine being one of those people. I am very grateful to say I'm one of them and here comes TR stepping up to bat to take a swing. There's even a new troll!

It's like making magic out here in the real world. A community is formed that believes in the possibilities in life and cheers for everyone at all the victories.

The really cool part is that kind of mindset tends to have an affect on the rest of my life. Anything becomes possible and courage appears out of nowhere to try even bigger things that have nothing to do with books. All of life opens up.

It's kind of like that idea – whatever I focus on becomes my reality. Pretty good reality sitting here in the dream house, writing a note to all of you – while Lois the good dog tears through the house barking away. It's a good life.

Welcome to the party TR! We've been waiting for someone just like you. More adventures to follow.

BOOKS BY TR CAMERON

For a complete list of books by TR Cameron, please visit:

http://trcameron.com/

BOOKS BY MICHAEL ANDERLE

For a complete list of books by Michael Anderle, please visit

www.lmbpn.com/ma-books/

All LMBPN Audiobooks are Available at Audible.com and iTunes. For a complete list of audiobooks visit:

www.lmbpn.com/audible

CONNECT WITH THE AUTHORS

TR Cameron Social

Stay up to date on new releases and fan pricing by signing up for my newsletter. CLICK HERE TO JOIN.

Or visit: www.trcameron.com/Oriceran to sign up.

Facebook:

https://www.facebook.com/AuthorTRCameron

If you enjoyed this book, please consider leaving a review. Thanks!

Martha Carr Social

Website: http://www.marthacarr.com

Facebook: https://www.facebook.com/groups/MarthaCarrFans/

Michael Anderle Social

Michael Anderle Social

Website:
http://www.lmbpn.com

Email List:
http://lmbpn.com/email/

Facebook: https://www.
facebook.com/TheKurtherianGambitBooks/

Made in the USA
Columbia, SC
19 January 2020